Praise for *The Girl on the Roof*

"A dreamlike tale unfolding amidst the nightmare of war, The Girl on the Roof will transport you into another world—and beyond. Debra Moffitt pierces the thin veil that separates life from the afterlife, the hunted from the haunted, the ghost story from the love story. Through her eyes, we are offered a glimpse of the eternal energetic bonds that connect us throughout time and space. An evocative, transcendent, and truly unforgettable book."

—Amy Weiss,
Hay House author of *Crescendo*

"Debra Moffitt brilliantly weaves the visible and the invisible in this wartime story of love lost and found. As life and death play out against a brutal occupation Moffitt keeps her hand steadily on the human pulse. A haunting, beautiful book. I loved it!"

—Mary Alice Monroe,
New York Times bestselling author of The Beach House Series

OTHER BOOKS BY THE AUTHOR

Awake in the World:
108 Practices to Live a Divinely Inspired Life

Garden of Bliss:
Cultivating the Inner Landscape for Self-Discovery

Riviera Stories:
Just Below the Surface (Short Stories)

And many more to come!

ABOUT THE AUTHOR

Debra Moffitt is the award-winning author of *Awake in the World and Garden of Bliss*. Her book, *Riviera Stories*, explores the wealth and extremes of the French Riviera through an interconnected series of short stories. Debra leads workshops and retreats on creativity, intuition, and writing at many venues including her French Alps Writing Retreats. Her articles, essays, and stories appear in many publications worldwide and were broadcast by BBC World Services Radio. Visit her online at www.debramoffitt.com. Books are available in Spanish, French, and other languages.

First Edition
First Printing, 2020 by Divinely Inspired Books an
imprint of Divinely Inspired Living Media LLC - USA

Cover Design by Damonza
Library of Congress Cataloging-in-Publication Data
Library of Congress Control Number:2019952854
Moffitt, Debra
The Girl on the Roof/Fiction
Debra Moffitt, 1st ed.
ISBN Print Edition: 978-0-9969941-4-9
Ebook: 978-0-9969941-5-6

the
GIRL
on the
ROOF

A NOVEL

DEBRA MOFFITT

DIVINELY
INSPIRED
B**OO**KS

For Nick

...death is but the next great adventure.

—J.K. Rowling

1

THE WOMEN ARE all crying. Standing in knee deep snow, trailing out of the chapel. My sister, Claire, seems the worst off. And I tug at her elbow.

"What happened, Claire?" I say.

But she's so full of sorrow that she sees no one. Not even me. So I let her pass. Jean-Michel's over by a large oak tree, obscured by the fog. He's not supposed to be here. And Herr Schmid, the German SS officer, who employs my sister watches through the thick lake mist from the alleyway. His black leather coat absorbs the light and his blue eyes pierce the fog. There's something about him that fills me with longing and regret.

Granddad must have died. He was so old that it's no surprise. But their level of grief for an old man seems unusual. I mean we expected him to die anytime really. But it's not just Claire. Others weep too. Of course, tensions and anxiety run so high from the recent state of siege that the funeral could be an excuse for them to release pent up tears. I watch the funeral procession from the angle of the white stone church and try to put together the puzzle pieces. Father along with my brother, Alain and some neighbors carry the small figure wrapped in a white linen shroud and place it on the horse drawn wagon. Ginny, my very best friend's eyes stream with tears. Her mother pulls her away into the mist before we can talk.

Claire lovingly adjusts the shroud around the figure stretched on the cart. Dad and the others back away when Farmer Elli slaps the reins against the back of the workhorse. The priest looks grim as he watches the black horse pull away. Other people advance in a slow procession through the snow. Their boots tread forward in heavy silence. The wagon and some black cars stop at my house. I wish they would tell me what happened. But no one ever tells me anything. That's the problem with being the youngest. Everyone thinks you're a baby, even when you're almost sixteen.

"We've got to do it," Father says. He rams a shovel against the frozen ground and it clangs as if he's hitting stone. "Too hard now. We'll do what we've always done."

A ladder leans against the wall and a series of chords hang over the roof of our house. My brother and father place a flat board underneath the figure shrouded in white with rope at both ends and pull it up horizontally. I can't bear to look. They did this to Mom last year. For months, I wept in bed at night thinking of her so cold and still on the roof above. Alain climbs a ladder to the roof. Dad stands on the ladder on a lower rung and helps to tug the corpse up while the others lift the body into the air from below. They make steady, even progress until the rope knots and one uneven tug nearly sends the shrouded body tumbling back to the ground. Claire's pained voice cries out.

"Be gentle!"

"Too late to think of that," Madame Noiret mutters under her breath with a tone as sharp as a butcher's knife. A puff of steam exits her mouth and fills the arctic air. My father and brother exchange glances and steel their faces as if they want to say something, but can't. I sense their anger at Claire for something she did. But no one tells me anything. They think I'm too young to understand.

"It's cold out here. Can we go in now?" I tug at Dad's jacket and plead. I feel him tighten and steel himself. He concentrates hard to blink back tears and steady the body. Alain tugs from above and the body floats in the air like a ghost as it reaches the edge of the roof.

"Not yet," he whispers and glances up at Alain. "Not quite there yet."

My brother lifts the body over the edge onto the roof's tiles where he adjusts the linen-shrouded figure so it lies horizontally on the North side of the roof out of the sun. Poor, poor grandfather. We'll sleep under his frozen body until the ground thaws. Then he can be put to rest in the churchyard next to Mom and we'll be in peace.

"Claire," I whisper.

I want her to hold my hand and comfort me. I know I'm almost an adult now, but I've needed Claire more since Mom left. But she's always busy now. I'm the youngest in the family, the unexpected one who arrived six years after Claire and seven years after Alain. Long after Mom thought about babies. Life's not been easy since Mom died. I miss her every day. I could bear the occupation when she was around. She'd reassure me that God would take care of us. Now everything just seems bleak and lost.

"*Maudit.*" Cursed. Monsieur Noiret mutters. He's a neighbor who once lived in Paris. He hates the *Haute Savoie* winters and compares the annual freeze to an icy hell. "What land puts dead people on rooftops?!" He hisses. "Cursed place!"

"It's the way we do things," Madame Noiret says. "Just remember not to die in winter, dear. Otherwise you'll have no peace until spring thaw." Her nasal voice grates like nails on a chalkboard and Claire places her hands over her ears.

Many neighbors huddle together inside the house and the heat stifles me. Dad drinks *genepie* herb alcohol straight from the bottle then hides it under his pillow before returning to face the crowd in the kitchen. Madame Renault brought her special savory cake with bacon and Madame Noiret empties her canned green beans and beets from glass jars into Mom's porcelain dishes. We've not had green beans since Mom died and though I'm sad about granddad, it's good to see something other than chestnuts, potatoes, and cheese on the table. So few people have decent food now that I shouldn't complain. Even flour is rationed. The neighbors brought food when Mom passed too. I'm grateful for their sacrifice. My sister, Claire thanks them while I linger in a corner and wait for someone to say grace so we can eat. Hunger is my constant companion now.

"You know it's not your fault, dear," Madame Noiret says and pats Claire's hand.

"She's right Claire," Madame Renault says. "We know you do your best. But you should really spend less time with Germans."

Claire smiles tersely and escapes to the outdoor toilet where she doubles over in grief. I watch through the fog as Jean-Michel calls her over to the edge of the forest and hands her a cigarette. Claire leans into him and lights it against his.

"You shouldn't be here. They'll shoot you if they see you," Claire says, sullen and grim.

"You going to inform on me, dear one?" He wraps an arm around her waist and draws her in tighter.

"Can't tell who's an informer or not anymore." Claire huffs. She exhales a long trail of smoke, head tossed back. "I'm sick of it."

"It's better here with you than hanging out with all of the goats in the barn. Don't think I can bear another piece of goat cheese."

Like other young men, Jean-Michel hides in the mountain villages a few kilometers away on the plateau above Lake Annecy. They aim to avoid the Gestapo-imposed draft on young Frenchmen that would force them to go to work in Germany.

"Good to hear you prefer me over a goat." Claire forces a smile. "I prefer you over those old goats in there." Tears trickle down her cheeks.

"Hey, you're a big girl." Jean-Michel lifts her chin. "Besides it's too cold to cry." He wipes her cheeks with his calloused thumbs and kisses her face. "Those tears'll freeze on your pretty cheeks." She returns his kisses with passion. I watch from behind a tree, curious about what happens between men and women and wanting to know more. A chilly breeze carries their scent to me. Jean-Michel smells of wood smoke, warm skin, and fresh air and Claire...she smells of *Heure Bleue*, the expensive Parisian perfume our exotic aunt gave her.

Claire reaches into his pants.

"Now. Let's do it now," she insists.

"Crazy woman," he says and gently holds her wrists. "People would be angry if they knew. Especially today."

"I need to. Now!" She kisses him so hard that her tears stop. "I'm sick of caring about what others think."

"Go back inside," he urges. His back leans against a damp larch tree. "Please, Claire. You know how those old goats gossip." His voice is warm and tender.

"No. I want you. Now."

"You don't want me. You want to forget."

"Help me to forget then." Claire's tears begin again. "I don't think I can bear it."

He hugs her gently to his broad chest, then turns her to face the house. "Go."

Claire glances at the roof. "That'll remind me of my sins all winter long," she whispers.

2

THE STONE HOUSE feels so, so cold in January. There never seems to be enough heat even with thick wool blankets and wooden shutters closed to keep the cold out. My teeth chatter and firewood grows scarce. So I go outside at dawn and pickup sticks. Dig them out from under snow. They'll dry and we can burn them in the fireplace. I stack them on the stone step this morning. Claire will feel proud and happy that for once I'm doing my chores.

Claire steps out of the house on her way to Herr Schmid's and sees the stack of sticks on the top step. Her brow crinkles. She looks up, and covers her mouth with her hand. Tears again. But I can't tell if she's happy or mad.

"What's wrong?" I want to say. But Alain strides out of the door behind her on his way to the garage where he works. He leans over her shoulder to see what caused the disturbance. The two trade silent glances.

"Someone wants to help out. That's all," Alain says. He scoops up the sticks and turns away to carry them inside.

Claire chokes on grief. "It's her. I know it's her."

"Of course it's me. I'm sorry I didn't do it much before," I say. "I want to make up for it now." They both ignore me. I don't like it, but I'm used to it.

"These need to dry out," he says over his back.

"You're right," Claire says and escapes through the snow to work. She cooks and helps Herr Schmid and some of the other Germans. They're everywhere since the occupation. Claire negotiates with the French farmers to get eggs, bacon and fresh food for them. It's all stuff that most of us can't get any more since food is strictly rationed. Claire sometimes sneaks food from Herr Schmid's and carries it home to keep us from starving.

I prepare my twill book bag, my thick wool scarf, and brown coat, and plod off through the snow. It feels so, so cold today. A small group of us huddle together and trek toward the school in Annecy on the other side of the lake. We live between the towns of Annecy and Veyrier and the youngest kids stay close to home, but the middle and vocational school kids, like me, walk or bike a kilometer or two to the town and take classes with the nuns. Even though the Germans declared a state of siege, we try to keep life normal.

I slip into my seat next to Ginny. A fat pencil lies in the space carved into the wooden desk. The classroom feels colder than usual with less and less wood for the fireplace. I keep my mittens on and my teeth chatter. Ginny listens half-heartedly to Sister Marie. Her head hangs on her fist, shoulders slumped forward. Her golden hair curls down and hides her glistening eyes. She fingers the spine of the books in my desk then scribbles a note, folds it into a square, the way we've always folded our secret notes to each other, and slips it into my desk. I pretend to pay attention to Sister Marie, but open it and read it. "I will always be your friend, Aurelie. Love, Ginny." Her attention makes my heart soar. I nudge Ginny's elbow under the desk. Her lips pucker with grief. When I try to ask what's wrong, I lose focus and drift off.

In the afternoon when school lets out, I go to Herr Schmid's. He lives in a luxurious apartment requisitioned from a Jewish banking family. Claire forbids me to come here. But my belly aches from too much hunger again. Watery school soups with a little barley and onions and meager rations of a little dry bread for breakfast left me starving, just like the other kids. But sometimes Claire gets real food from Herr Schmid and once she brought me here when he was away to show me the place.

The first time I met Herr Schmid, hunger and cold blindly drove me to find Claire. The courtyard door stood open, and I walked unnoticed up the four flights of stone stairs to his apartment, dreaming of a warm hearth and buttery apple tarts like the ones Mom used to bake. Rain drizzled outdoors and I'd never felt so hungry, depressed, and alone since Mom died. I tapped lightly on the door to get Claire's attention. A young man, about my age opened the door instead. He wore a German soldier's uniform.

"*Bonjour,*" I said, and asked for my sister between chattering teeth. He must not have understood French because he led me straight to Herr Schmid. I stood at the threshold of his study, head down, feeling so anxious that I couldn't breathe. The young German retreated and left me alone with the imposing SS officer. I was struck by his broad shoulders and refined hands and the red arm band and swastika on his uniform. I'd imagined him with blond hair, but it was black and wavy. His skin looked pale as ivory, and his presence exuded power and authority even before he spoke a word. I stood there in fear and awe.

"Yes, *frauline,*" Herr Schmid said. His eyes remained fixed on an expensive linen paper as he wrote. My heart raced with anxiety and the stress combined with lack of food made my knees buckle and I collapsed. When I came to, I was on the floor with Herr Schmid kneeling beside me.

"What's wrong?" His indigo eyes stared down at me. The fright, hunger, and grief from my mother's absence all poured out at once. I sobbed like a little girl with my knees pulled to my chest and my head down.

"So sorry, sir. I…I didn't mean to…I tried to…to tell the solider not to bother you…I…It was Claire I was looking for. But don't blame her. Please excuse me."

I raised my eyes to the wooden beams and high ceilings and then dared to look at him. His razor smooth cheeks looked luminous and healthy; he held his slightly cracked lips apart, and his eyes looked like untouchable blue oceans filled with wild currents and storms. He helped me into the red velour seat by the fire, and I worried that I'd be in trouble. My teeth chattered uncontrollably. He picked up a wool throw that lay on the edge of the couch and draped it around my shoulders. The scent of his vetivier cologne filled my senses with comfort. It was like the one that Dad used on special occasions.

He touched my forehead. "You have a fever." His cool hand sent a warm rush of pleasure and confusion through me.

Consumed by hunger, my eyes lingered on a mound of almond cakes coated with a snow of powdered sugar on his desk. I said nothing. Girls were not supposed to speak much or ask for anything, according to the nuns. Especially not food. But my stomach growled loudly.

"I must be going," I said. But my knees wobbled when I tried to stand and I collapsed back onto the red velour seat.

"Ralph," he called. The young soldier appeared from the other room. "Is there any soup left?"

"I'll check, sir."

"Bring hot tea and more pastries. And soup if there's any." I felt light headed and weak, so I let him take control.

"You're pale. You must eat." He towered over me.

I needed to leave. I knew Claire would be upset. But this felt like an order. Ralph entered with a tea set of beautiful Limoges porcelain cups rimmed with gold, a pile of pastries on a silver plate, real sugar, and even an orange. He sat them on a low table. Such luxury and abundance was rarely seen these days.

"Sorry, no more soup, sir."

"This will do," Herr Schmid said and dismissed the young soldier.

"Here." He lifted the plate of sweets. I had overheard Claire sometimes tell Jean-Michel about how strict and harsh Herr Schmid could be, so I cautiously took one coconut macaroon and gobbled it in two quick bites. Then I stared at the dish with longing. "Have more," he insisted.

I ate four before the gnawing ache of hunger started to subside and leave me feeling stronger. He handed me a cup of steaming tea and I wrapped my numb fingers around it to warm them and closed my eyes. The chill subsided and I'd finally stopped trembling. It was the first time I'd felt cared for and properly fed for months. Since Mom's funeral, actually when the neighbors had brought food to share. When I opened my eyes, I caught him staring at me.

"You are a beauty," he said. I blushed and lowered my eyes. He poured more tea and touched my knee. "Feeling better now?" I nodded. "I was ten in the last war," he said. "We had nothing to eat. My mother and I scrounged for roots."

"So sorry, sir." The tea cup rattled on the saucer as I sat it on the table.

"My mother died. But thanks to Herr Hitler I survived," he said.

"My mother died too. Last winter." Probably also thanks to Hitler, I thought secretly. If we'd not had the hardships brought on by the occupation, she might still be alive.

He took off his officer's jacket and hung it on the back of his chair. A rust-colored house cat jumped up and purred on my lap and I dozed off until he touched my arm to awaken me. Surrounded by food and luxury, my heart sang and I wanted to stay there in the comfort and warmth.

"You saved me, sir," I whispered. My heart filled with gratitude and affection. He stood, paced away, and then returned to his chair.

"Hans," he said.

"Hans?" I looked up at him.

"Yes. My first name. Hans, from Stuttgart." An aura of charm surrounded him and I yearned to be closer and touch him. I'd heard some of the school girls snicker about an awakening of their senses and desires for physical love, but this was the first time it happened to me. In that moment, I wanted him to kiss me.

"I'm Aurelie." I lowered my eyes, embarrassed by my thoughts.

"Claire's sister," he added and smiled. "We'll keep this a secret from her."

"Thank you, sir," I said. "She would be upset."

"Yes." He stood beside me and lifted a lock of my hair. I sucked in my breath. "We'll keep this between us."

A trill of pleasure and excitement blossomed in me. All of the blackness of the outside world and the war temporarily vanished in the cozy warmth of the glowing fire between us. Claire had described him as untrustworthy. She said he kept things hidden in deep inner rooms, walled off and remote and called him fickle and moody. But to me he was a warm, kind blessing. He lifted his tea cup and his sleeve slid up to reveal angry deep burns above his wrist.

"You're hurt." I instinctively took his hand in mine. He started to pull away like an injured animal, his mouth open between a snarl and surprise. Then he relaxed. Without thinking I did what my mother had always done. I kissed his wound.

"Mother always said nothing heals better than a kiss," I said to explain.

His eyes watered, like he might cry, but he blinked back what had surfaced. I smiled a little and released his hand. He braced himself on the arm rests as if to flee. "It's okay to cry," I said. "It doesn't mean you're weak. It only means you've been hurt."

He looked at me like I'd touched his deepest fear, that somewhere inside he was weak and unmanly. My heart broke for Hans and I felt his pain as if it were mine, as if we were mystically connected. It felt we already knew each other. Hans' face turned pale and softened an instant. His pain ran so deep that not even he felt it fully, but I did. I cried. It seemed I shed the tears he couldn't. The blue of his eyes paled as he stared at me, puzzled and momentarily disarmed.

"Aurelie..."

A knock resounded at the door and startled me back to the reality that separated us.

"I need to go," I said.

"Yes, but we'll meet again. Soon. Will you promise?"

"Yes, sir."

"Hans," he said and he leaned down and kissed my forehead. He jerked his officer's jacket from the back of the fireside chair, pulled it on, and trod over the polished wooden floor to sit behind his desk, back rigid. The red swastika glared on his armband. In a blink, Herr Hans Schmid shifted from broken-open to closed up tight; from engaged to indifferent; from warm and vulnerable to cold and aloof. He looked like a different man, like Herr Schmid, the powerful SS officer now, and no longer like Hans, the sensitive young man from Stuttgart with a tender heart.

"Enter," he said in a monotone.

The door flew open and Claire walked in with a blast of cold air trailing her. She sucked in her breath when she saw me by the fire.

"Aurelie?! What are you doing here?!" I walked to her sheepishly and she shook my shoulders. "I told you not to ever bother Herr Schmid."

Her eyes raced to him and she checked me all around with narrowed eyes. My buttons. Hem. Legs. When she seemed satisfied I was fine, she shot a fiery, warning glance at Herr Schmid.

"I forgot my purse," she announced and lifted it from the fireplace mantel. "Let's go. Now!" She pushed me toward the door. I turned back and saw Herr Schmid staring after me.

"Thank you," I said.

Claire jerked me across the threshold and the door closed behind us. She marched me to a deserted side street and erupted.

"You foolish, stupid girl!"

I looked down at the ground, embarrassed and upset. An empty basket hung on Claire's arm. "Look at me," she said. I kept my head bowed and lifted my eyes. "Don't you understand?! We cannot afford…" She lifted a hand to smack me then stopped and hugged me tight to her chest. "Mom's gone now. I'm here to protect you. Don't ever go there again. It's not safe. I've warned you before. You must listen to me."

"But I was starving, Claire. I passed out. I thought I would die. But that man, Hans, he gave me food. He saved me. He's a good man," I protested.

"You call him Hans? Don't let him trick you. He's not good. Handsome, yes. Seductive and charismatic. But not good. He's the enemy, Aurelie. We can't trust him." She held both my shoulders in her hands to mark the point.

"I'm sorry."

"Please. If you need anything ask me. I will help you. Promise me you will never go there again."

"But you go," I pleaded. "Besides he helped me."

"I go because I have made choices. I'm an adult. You're not."

"But…"

"No!" She shook me hard. "You must listen to me. You cannot go back there."

I nodded agreement. But a dreamy feeling surged inside of me as I thought of his blue eyes and the way he'd wrapped the blanket around my shoulders and touched my knees and hands. As I replayed the scene over and over, I remembered every detail about him: his angular face and sensuous lips; his tapered waist and broad shoulders; his power and the sense of protection I'd felt next to him. My heart fluttered, and I fell in love with how'd he'd rescued me.

In the romance novels that Claire hides under her mattress, I read that a man can take you away and save you. I so want to escape the misery of rationing, war, and death, and feel whole and happy again. I fall asleep now and imagine Hans' arms around me and his gentle kiss on my forehead. In my dreams, we escape into a beautiful paradise. I cannot tell Claire. She would be upset.

3

MY DREAMS HAVE taken on a quality of reality and vastness that I can't explain. I see and know things that I shouldn't and it frightens me. They hold a feverish quality, like once when I got sick at age five or six and saw mice scurrying under my covers. The mice weren't really there. But these "dreams" are real. I hear the thoughts of the men fighting in the resistance and see their faces as if I'm standing beside them. In my dreams I'm free to go anywhere. Above the Parmelan Mountain's white limestone cliff, I see the ibex stand fierce and tall in the morning moon light, long horns arched high over their backs while wolves hunt rabbits in deep snow. And Jean-Michel, Claire's lover, stands on the plateau beyond the town with a group of men uncrating weapons and hiding ammunition at dawn. I am not supposed to know this. Their resistance is a secret that could put me and my family in danger. Claire knows about it too, I believe, but never shares with me. Maybe this is why she warns me not to see Hans. Even though he is generous and kind, if he knew, duty would make him arrest us and send us to the prison or to one of the city's many internment buildings. The thought brings dreadful visions and a desire to protect Claire and those I love.

⌁

Light arrives late on winter mornings and the classroom offers welcome comfort. Chatter and laughter once filled the class before the teacher arrived. Now no one has much energy for laughter or talk. Everything seems tinged in shades of gray, cold, and hunger. The ration tickets never allow us enough food. Even Ginny, who always glows with smiles, looks grim and pale today. When Sister Marie arrives, several German soldiers accompanied by French militia enter our class behind her. Their presence sends ripples of fear through the room, accompanied by the stench of metallic sweat. It starts with our teacher, Sister Marie and moves out like waves from a stone thrown into a pond until anxiety grips us all in its steely hand.

The soldiers at the front of the classroom read a list of students' names. Issac Steiner, Rudolf Hershberg, Ida Hessinger, and Abraham Anner. Sister Marie nervously threads and unthreads her hands together and announces that these children must go. Ginny blanches and I tremble. Because of war restrictions and extreme conditions, the nuns mix different age groups and sexes in class to conserve heating and have enough teachers. A young boy of eleven or twelve wets his pants from fear. It dribbles onto the floor. Two of the children, whose names are called, walk reluctantly to the front of the classroom, heads down.

"Where are the others?" one of the soldiers barks.

"I'm sorry, I do not know," Sister Marie says. Her hands tremble as she sits behind the desk and stares at the floor. The men push the boys out of the door ahead of them. One of the soldiers raises his rifle and points it at Sister Marie.

"You'd better not be hiding them," he says. "We know about you Catholic swine." Sister Marie sits frozen with terror. When the men go she collapses in tears. We're disturbed to see our teacher crying.

"Why are they taking them?" a girl beside Ginny whispers.

"They must be Jewish," Ginny says to Odile.

Ginny told me that the Jewish are considered bad by the Germans and this is why they are disappearing from Annecy. Monsieur Meier's shoe shop stands boarded up. Ginny said he was Jewish. She even says that her mom knows someone who owns a hotel in Annemasse on the French-Swiss border who helps the Jewish escape to Switzerland. Ginny met a boy at the café with her dad who was headed for the hotel to wait for papers to cross the border. He told her he'd lost his parents to the Nazis. Of course our parents don't tell us much. They want to protect us from the dark news about German patrols, barbed wire, and firing squads, but we still hear rumors.

Through the classroom window, I see Hans, standing by the canal, his back rigid against the cold. Our eyes meet through the window and I wave. Without moving a single facial muscle, his jaws tense and his cheeks pale. He's Herr Schmid now, unreachable in his black leather coat and stiff boots. The soldiers join him with my Jewish classmates and together they disappear in the falling snow.

&

I can't stop thinking about Hans and I sneak out to see him after class. It's late but Dad won't mind. He'll be at a cafe drinking and Claire will probably find Jean-Michel in their secret spot in the woods. They go to an unused animal shelter that protects them from the wind and snow while they kiss until curfew. At Hans' the door's ajar and I slip in unnoticed and choose the chair by the fire again. When he sees me a cloud of confusion traces across his face. He closes his eyes tight like he's fighting to keep something out. His hands shake and he pours himself a whisky and downs it. His eyes return to the papers spread on his desk and he clenches his pen in his right hand until his knuckles turn white, but he's unable to write. I stroke the cat and wait patiently. He lights a cigarette from the pack on the mantel, inhales deeply, and burns the back of his arm with the glowing tip. He's so numb he doesn't flinch or grimace. It's like he must prove to himself he's still alive.

"Stop! Please stop!" I beg, but he seems too far away to hear. I reach for his hand and want to kiss and heal his wounds.

"Leave me in peace." His voice breaks. When I touch his arm to soothe the pain, his skin responds with goose bumps. I want to help him the way that he helped me. But he pushes me away and drinks more. When he looks at me I'm filled with love and compassion.

"Why do you torment me?" he says. "Go away." He drops into the chair beside me. The cat nestles beside him, indifferent to his angst. I curl up with my head on his knee to calm him too. But I must not fall asleep. I've got to return home before Claire finds out I've been here. She would kill me. But as soon as I close my eyes I drift into the lucid dreams and travel out to the mountain tops to spy on Jean-Michel. I watch the resistance fighters prepare for war, and see the spirit of the wild ibex standing firm and solid on their high cliffs. What beautiful, feverish, vivid dreams. I must be sick. Is this why the sadness lingers in my parents' house? Even my brother, Alain, who always joked and found words to make people smile, does not laugh or say much anymore. I must get well. I must clear this up and get back to being myself.

4

AT SCHOOL TODAY, a new girl has taken my place next to Ginny. I find my things stacked on a back table. I sit there beside my books with a heavy heart. Why didn't Ginny save my place and tell Sister Marie that I'd been sick and that I'd be back? When I try to ask Ginny about it at recess, she ignores me.

"Please listen," I beg. But she looks right through me like I'm not there. "Ginny!" I plead. My heart breaks when she races off with the new girl and leaves me standing alone. I don't know what I've done to offend her. The tears splash out against my will. I love her so much. How could she do this to me?! A kind woman notices me and touches my shoulder.

"I'm so sorry. Come with me," she urges. "Let's talk." She speaks with a soothing voice and tries to guide me into a bright, warm room near the school, but I resist.

"No. I can't. I'm supposed to be at school."

"Your mother is here," the woman says. I wipe the tears from my cheeks.

"What? That's impossible. My mother is dead." The woman allows the words to linger like a long, drawn out note so that I can focus on them. Am I still dreaming?

"I must go," I say. "Claire will expect me home soon."

Dusk falls around four o'clock in the winter. So sometimes Claire walks me home. But tonight she's nowhere in sight, so I go to Herr Schmid's, drawn naturally to his warmth and the promise of refuge in the light, away from this dreary, dampness that surrounds the lake. I ring the doorbell and wait. It's bold to come so openly. The neighbors and anyone passing would not approve. Claire would kill me too, but he needs my help. He opens the thick, ancient wooden door and gasps when he sees me. I put a thin finger to my lips and motion for him to be silent. Then I slip inside.

He's usually tidy, but papers liter the floor now. I settle into the red velour chair by the fire with one foot under my skirt. Hans hunkers behind his desk to focus on his report. I know he's preoccupied with war and lists of names. So I slip over beside him and kiss his cheek. His eyes close tight.

"You're not real," he says.

"Don't be silly," I laugh. "You asked me to come back soon." He pushes back his chair, marches to the wall, and bangs his head against the stone until it bleeds.

"Stop," I say. "Please stop. I forgive you." Then I wonder why I said that. But he's lost in anguish, overtaken by madness.

✒

The second time we met, he was waiting at the bottom of the school steps when school let out. My eyes fell on him and the shock took my breath away.

"Come with me," he said. The other students looked at me with fear-filled eyes. Despite my anxiety, I gravitated to him like a magnet and fell into step beside him. I glanced back embarrassed and ashamed, wondering if he'd take me away like the Jewish kids. But I was curious too, and hoped that Herr Schmid would shed his armor so I could see soft, kind Hans again. Ginny stared after me, mouth open in horror.

I followed him in silence along a path that ran parallel to the lake, but out of sight behind a long row of hedges. When we were completely alone, he spoke. "I have something for you, my pretty one," he said. I felt afraid and excited, but didn't speak. When we reached a hidden, rundown garden, he stepped over the wall, took my hand and led me inside to a gazebo perched above the grounds.

"It's lovely," I said standing at the top of the steps looking out at the snow covered branches of cherry and apple trees.

He remained silent and indrawn, staring out at the barren garden. A small rabbit hopped out to gnaw at the bark on one of the fruit trees. When Herr Schmid cleared his throat, it looked up startled and ran away. Again, I felt his heart ache. He was filled with only pain and I so wanted to help him. My eyes must have revealed my heart, because he sat down on an old wooden bench and the rigid Herr Schmid melted away to leave the place to Hans. I stood near him.

"Here." He held out a small blue satin jewelry box.

"Oh." I unlatched the tiny hook on the edge and lifted the cover. The box held an exquisite parrot pendant necklace made with what looked like diamonds and tiny blue stones with emerald green eyes. "It's lovely."

"Here, let me put it on you." He turned me around, hands on my shoulders and lifted up my curls. His touch brought a stirring through my body.

"There." I turned around and he held my hands. "What do you think?" I glanced down at the brilliant gold pendant, startled by his generosity. Then I lowered my eyes.

"Thank you, sir. You shouldn't have."

"It's a beautiful object for a beautiful young woman."

"But..." When I started to protest he silenced me with a finger to my lips.

"Aurelie, I want you to know how special you are." He held his hands on both sides of my face and I looked into his eyes. My heart pounded wildly, not from fright but from excitement and possibility. Yet I felt confused, like something forbidden and hurtful lingered at the edges of the garden about to encroach upon us.

"I must go." Would he be my prince? The one who would take me away from here and make everything perfect and good?

"Not yet." His sternness halted me. "I'm not done yet. Here." He pulled a sack of pink hard candies from his pocket. Without thinking, I almost hugged him, but stopped short.

"Thank you." I pulled the pink waxed paper from a sweet and sucked on it.

"Is that all I get? That merits a kiss, don't you think?" He pointed to his cheek and I leaned in reluctantly to kiss him.

"Where did you find this?! It's impossible to get them now." I touch his wrist with my fingertips to chide him.

"Magic," he says. His mirrored blue eyes drew me in and I saw beauty sparkle in the depths of his soul.

"Very grateful, sir. I meant, Hans." I bent my head and didn't dare to look at him. It felt like there was something new between us. Something interwoven with desire and yearning like the kind I saw between Claire and Jean-Michel. I felt painfully aware of my lips and ached to be kissed. Ginny had been kissed by her cousin a few weeks earlier and I really wanted to know what it felt like too. But he remained still and distant. I reached for the clasp of the necklace. "You must take it back. I can't wear it. Claire would be angry."

"I'll talk to her."

In the meantime, I took it off and hid it away in the precious box in my pocket. It's still under my mattress in my bedroom.

⬧

I watch Jean-Michel slip down to meet Claire in the night. I sneak out and spy on them shivering together in the animal shelter. It's better than a romance novel, but I worry about curfew and that we may all get caught.

"A battle soon. Tomorrow or the next day," Jean-Michel says. "We received a drop of ammunition and artillery. Can you get information from the *kraut*? Find out their whereabouts. That map you saw. It will help. Their troops must be located on it. Can you sneak it out? Or memorize it?"

Claire shivers from more than just the cold. She digs her hand into the inner lining of her black coat and hands him a note.

"Here."

"Aahh." He smiles.

"I'm always thinking of you," she says. "It's already done."

He kisses her. His heavy steel lighter flicks open with a ping. His lips move as he reads the note lit by the lighter's flame. "500 K's arriving in Chambery. One unit of tanks. No new packages." He frowns. "It's not as bad as we thought." He kisses Claire with gratitude. "The info you get, it's for the good of us all. For our freedom." Claire looks downhearted and shifts her face to indifference.

"Freedom." She shakes her head as if she doesn't believe in it. "All I want is to get them out of here. I hate Germans and the French who collaborate with them for power and money." She sucks in smoke from a filterless cigarette and exhales. "Yesterday, Madame Noiret informed on Mademoiselle Lesseur. I think she expected favors from the Germans and collaborators. But they just despise her more."

"Ah, *cherie*, you spend lots of time with Germans. You could make good money informing on others." Jean-Michel grabs her chin with his calloused fingers and pulls her face toward him. She wraps herself tight to him and I imagine how it would feel to wrap myself around Hans.

Claire snorts a breath of air and punches his arm. "Like you?"

"Hey, you could trade me for some extra rations or a red arm band."

"Stop it," she growls and glares at him hard, hurt and silent.

"I'm sorry," he says and pulls her closer. "I'm joking."

"I wish she could hear me. I wish she knew how sorry I am."

"Maybe she does. Maybe she knows." Jean-Michel shelters Claire close to his chest.

"I have to see the blue-eyed tyrant again tomorrow. I'll see what more I can find out.

"He may get suspicious."

"With you guys sabotaging bridges and setting fire to their provision trucks, everyone is on edge now." Claire sighs and rests her head on his shoulder.

"Be careful," Jean-Michel says.

"Yes," Claire's eyes flare with anger. "I do it for her. That's the only reason. And if I have a chance to kill him, I will do that too." Jean-Michel smiles.

"Now you scare me. You're becoming a tiger. Grrrr. I like it. The war is bringing out your character." He flirts and teases and she kisses him harder. His rough hands reach under her blouse and she gasps from the chill. "It may be awhile before I can come back." He pulls away and presses a very small pistol into her hand. "A present for you. It's what you asked for. But be careful. You'll be executed if you're caught with it. Those are the orders now that we're under a state of siege. No questions asked. No one's allowed to carry weapons except for the Germans and French collaborators," he says and kisses her palms and the backs of her hands. She shivers as the bristle of his unshaven face pricks her skin. He kisses her red mouth hard and deep, one last time and steps back, his face sad and soft under the full moonlight. Claire tries to hold him back. Tears rim her eyes.

"*Je t'aime*," she whispers. The words stretch out of her mouth in a long, exhale of steam that spreads through the chill air. The steamy words kiss Jean-Michel on the mouth. He squeezes her hand and disappears. Her words and the excitement and passion between them stir up emotions of confusion and anxiety, and I am suddenly aware of the cold. I run after Claire to ask her if she's working with the resistance too. But if she knew I'd been spying on her she'd be mad. So I slip into the house ahead of her and climb into bed.

5

AT SCHOOL AGAIN, I take a seat at the back where someone has stacked my books on the table and I sit downhearted with my head on my hand. I've always been a good student, always followed the rules and been the first to raise my hand. I don't understand this punishment. Why did Sister Marie move me away from Ginny?! I want to protest and make a scene, but I sit quietly in the back listening to the history lesson. Sister Marie talks about the fall of the Roman Empire. Rene raises his hand and asks about the Germans. He wants to know what happened to the Jewish children who the soldiers took. He says he heard rumors about trains of them going to Germany and executions. I don't believe him. Sister Marie clears her throat and bravely faces his innocent question. A ripple of excitement runs through the room as if a great box of energy is opened and let out. A Pandora's box.

"Rene, times are complicated and complex. We're living through something that is unprecedented. But don't be too caught up by all of the rumors you hear. God will protect us."

"What's that mean, 'unprecedented'?" he says hungry to learn and grow.

"Unlike anything we've ever known or seen before. There's nothing preceding it that is similar." The boy nods and continues to listen intently. The whole class waits hushed and yearns to know more. "Some things we only understand in retrospect. And the things that are happening now may fall into that category." Sister Marie pauses. She looks down at the floor, embarrassed. "They were put into an internment house, I'm told. They may be sent to Germany."

"But what did they do wrong?" Justine demands.

"They were born Jewish," Sister Marie says apologetically.

Ginny raises her hand. "And what about Aurelie? She did nothing wrong. Why didn't God protect her?"

I feel excited and happy that Ginny defends me. She knows there's no reason to put me at the back of the classroom. Sister Marie looks pained and rings the bell.

"We will take a recess." The students file out in silence into the steel gray fog that wraps around the schoolyard. I move close to Ginny and hug her.

"Thank you, Ginny," I say. She huddles behind a tree, closes her eyes, and fights back tears.

"Why?" Ginny says. I feel the ache of her grief as if it's my own.

"What's wrong, Ginny? I hate the war too, but it will be alright." The more I try to comfort her, the more it seems to make things worse. She leans her head against the tree and weeps.

"Don't despair. We'll always be friends." I put my arm around her. "It's going to be okay. I don't understand all that's happening either. Everything seems so different. You seem so distant sometimes." Ginny turns away from the tree trunk, eyes open wide.

"Aurelie, listen to me. I will do what I can to make things right. I promise," she says.

The anxiety of the morning sends me into the feverish dreams again where everything sparkles with clarity and light. When the sun sets on the frozen lake, I wave goodbye to Ginny as we stand on the worn stone school steps out front. She steps over the frozen puddles. Beneath one of them, a frog, frozen solid, waits for the thaw. Ginny kneels and pokes her finger at the transparent ice.

"You'll be okay," she says. I've seen it too, how the frogs miraculously survive even the hardest winters and come back to life. That's when I see him. Herr Schmid, stands near the plantain tree and stares at Ginny. Just stares like he has seen a ghost. His blue eyes seem to hold facets, like polished diamonds. They flash with life, and seem like a hall of mirrors that I could step into deeper and deeper and not ever find the way out. "Aurelie," he whispers. Ginny's mom arrives and jerks her arm. Her mom glares at Hans, and the two hurry away leaving him alone in the drifting fog.

He walks up the smooth church steps and enters. I follow him and feel his thoughts penetrate me. I don't know how his thoughts become so transparent. He thinks of the rituals and rites the Gestapo performed in Germany to initiate him into the occult powers based on fear and will power. He's not sure he believes in any of it, but he feels the surges of powerful energy they bring.

A few women sitting in the wooden pews in front of the gilded statue of Mother Mary turn around. At the sight of him they immediately bow to the Virgin and slip out a side door.

The priest nods at Herr Schmid and motions to the confessional. But Hans shakes his head no.

"How may I be of service?" Father Ansen says, his young face even and expressionless.

"I…My mother… She was Catholic."

"Ah. The Fuehrer does not approve of Catholics I believe. But we welcome everyone."

Herr Schmid stands rigid and tall, looking out of place in the candlelit sanctuary. The priest waits patiently for him to speak.

"Yes. She…" Herr Schmid begins. But his mind crushes the impulse and he pounds his fist against the top of a pew and strides to the door, frustrated. The golden Virgin looks down at him with compassion, but he flees over the black and white marble floor out to the nearest bar without giving the priest the possibility to say, "*Ego te absolvo*. I absolve you from your sins."

Drink numbs Hans' pain. But when the French collaborator soldiers in the bar grow too loud and the women who wear dark lipstick try to talk to Herr Hans Schmid, he gets annoyed and strides home. I've been waiting for this moment. I know there's a brief time when Claire's not yet home and Dad will not notice my disappearance. Hans unlocks the door to the inner courtyard where a few plants weighted with snow struggle to hold onto their leaves. I follow him up the steps to his room and take my seat so silently that he does not notice. He settles behind his desk and pulls out the bottle of expensive scotch that someone brought him to trade for a favor. When he looks up, his eyes focus on me and I smile and wave. He's drunk now and I think of what others would say if they knew I'd come here so late.

"Are you hungry again? Is that what you came for?" he says.

"Not so much now. Are you okay?" I ask. But when I go to him, he steels himself and pulls away. I return to my red velour seat by the fire.

"Ralph, bring tea," Hans says. The teenaged boy in his German soldier's uniform carries in a tray with a porcelain pot dotted with pink roses and sets it on his desk. "No, over there." He motions to me and the young man's eyebrows crinkle with confusion.

"Here, sir?"

"Well, yes. Can't you see we have a guest?"

The boy sets the worn tray on the table next to my chair.

"Biscuits. Are you fine with biscuits? We have no almond cakes today." Hans Schmid nearly yells as if I might not hear otherwise. The young man looks at him, mouth open in shock. "What are you staring at? Don't you see? It's the only way I know to appease her." He holds up his gun and points it at me and then at his own head. The soldier nervously backs out of the room. Ralph and I trade glances of confusion about the strange behavior.

The doorbell rings and the soldier returns with a message.

"Show her in," Hans says. Claire appears with flakes of snow melting in her honey-brown curls and her green eyes flash with life. She looks more beautiful than I have ever seen her, dressed in her tan wool skirt, silk stockings, and ruby red lipstick that makes her mouth look as fresh as a ripe Savoy apple.

"You can go now," he orders the solider. Claire stands firmly inside the large room. The solider follows orders and the door closes with a small, quiet click behind him. I slip away, into a storage closet and leave the door ajar to watch.

"Here's the wine you insisted on having tonight." She slaps a small wooden crate on his desk. Her eyes narrow. "Your high commandant should be pleased if he has any taste."

Herr Schmid pulls packing straw from around the bottles and reads the label. "Nuits St. Georges, 1937." He uncorks a bottle and pours two glasses. "Where did you find it?"

"It only matters that I found it, no? I paid with the gold you gave me." Claire turns on her heel to leave.

"Wait. We must taste it."

"I can assure you it is the best." Claire says over her back.

"I'd suggest you stay and try it with me, *frauline*. For your own good." Claire hears the menace in his voice and freezes in her tracks.

"You'll be well compensated for your loyalty. Don't worry."

The thought of loyalty to him or any German makes Claire bristle. But it's to her advantage if he thinks she's on his side. She hesitates and stands at a distance, arms crossed over her chest. The pop of the cork has always been like music to her ears. So natural and easy, but mixed with the threat from Herr Schmid, it grates against her skin and she grimaces.

"Here." He extends a thin crystal glass and I think of the family who must have used the beautiful etched glasses for their parties and holidays. "To you, *frauline*," he says. Claire snorts a puff of air through her nostrils. A disdainful frown marks her face, yet I sense she's acutely aware that he could send her to prison in an instant simply because he has the power to do so. She accepts the wine and he clinks his glass against hers.

"A fine wine, dear. We shall drink to Hitler's health?" He sips and studies her over the edge of the glass.

"I must go."

"I'm sure no business is more important than the Gestapo's." A small tin container of Pervitin, lies on his desk. Doc Norbert calls the brain-numbing drug, the preferred "vitamin" of the Nazis. He pops two pills in his mouth and swallows with a gulp of wine.

"I have something for you. Over there." Hans points at a burlap sack on the floor.

She hesitates then tugs at the drawstring and peers into the bag. It's filled with tinned rations of meat, German hard crackers, split pea soup, chocolate bars, and real coffee.

"You know some children who could use it?"

Claire looks confused, nods. She lights a cigarette and ponders him, suspicious and wary.

"Good. Put it by the door so you won't forget."

"What motivates that humanitarian move?" Her tone carries a note of sarcasm. She moves casually to the fireside and places the crystal glass on the marble mantel.

"Sit," Herr Schimd says.

"I'm fine standing."

"Fine." He pours more wine and joins her by the fireside. "You're like my poor brother. You won't sell it. You'll actually give it to someone in need." Claire ignores his disdain and notices the steaming teapot.

"You're expecting a guest?"

"It was just a moment of madness. But now you're here and it's gone."

"Yes, tea at this hour is mad." Claire sips the ruby-tinted wine. Her cheeks flush from the smooth pleasure of the fine flavors that roll over her tongue, but the tension between them makes it impossible to enjoy it.

"Wine numbs the soul and makes things bearable. And this is very good wine, which makes it most bearable." His eyes light up from within when he looks at Claire. She relaxes a little.

"I can't stand war." She saunters to a shelf and pulls a photo from between the books. The Jewish family who once lived here stares back at her. "Do you think they're dead?" A ripple of discomfort crosses his face. He rips the photo from her and throws it in the fire. Claire runs a finger over the leather spines of the books. "You have a twinge of conscience?"

"No. I do my duty. It becomes as natural as breathing," Herr Schmid says and empties his glass.

"To Germans maybe. But not to us, French." Claire lifts the bottle from his desk and pours him more wine. With her back to him, she taps a small dose of morphine from Doc Norbert into the glass and hopes it will make Hans sleep.

"You French prefer to make love not war. That's your weakness."

Claire hands him the glass. "Love is not weak," she says. He towers over her as if to test her. She pushes her purse against his chest and he backs away.

"Love's worthless against guns, you know." His eyes fill with radiant desire and he settles onto the sofa. She stands behind him, out of reach, her breath shallow, the pistol nestled silently at the bottom of the purse.

"We'll see...," she says. The silence surrounds them. She waits and watches until he drains another glass, and she refills it again. "It's late. I need to get home before curfew." But he grabs her wrist.

"Stay. I'll give you a pass." A note of desperation pierces the air.

He quickly moves to his desk and writes out the pass while she hovers over his shoulder. Her eyes survey every inch of the desktop for war details to help the resistance. He seems unaware of her aims as she scans the map above his knuckles.

"This *laissez-passer* will allow you out anytime. Anywhere." He signs it and hands it to her.

"But it won't protect me from those brutes who call themselves soldiers," she scoffs.

"They know you're mine."

"Oh? Is it stamped on my forehead? I'm your employee. I don't belong to you."

"Claire." He reaches for her hand. Her body stiffens.

"I'll give you money. Whatever you need." He's drunk now and an unusual softness seeps out of him through the cracks made by the alcohol and morphine. "Stay, Claire," he begs. "Just a little longer." He reaches out to caress her cheek and stumbles on the edge of the chair. Claire tenses and steps back.

"I must find the loo. I'll be back," she says.

I want to slip out of my hiding place and help her. Maybe I could find the information she needs in his reports. But if she sees me, she'll kill me.

Claire's heels echo over the wooden floor. When she returns from the toilet, Hans is sprawled on the couch asleep. She tiptoes to his desk where the papers spread out like a fan. Worn maps, war plans, even some photos of people and places. One map with yellowed edges marks the Plateau de Glières where Jean-Michel hides with the other resistance fighters. She scans it and reads the German notes, eyebrows furrowed, before tucking everything back exactly in the same place. The floor board cracks when I sneak out. She glances up and sucks in her breath at the noise, but I slip away without her seeing me.

6

CLAIRE ARRIVES HOME and makes a drawing on a slip of paper. I watch through the keyhole of my room. She quickly writes a note to Jean-Michel. My brother, Alain puts on his snowshoes and obediently carries the note up the mountain. I had no idea they were working together for the resistance. Why didn't they tell me? It must be the fever again and the lucid dreams that allow me to follow Alain up the goat path. My brother silently passes along the note to a young man who used to work for Farmer Eli. By the time he returns, it must be very late because the fire is nearly out in the hearth. Claire curls up shivering in her bed, too cold to sleep.

I should be in my bed sleeping soundly, but it feels more like I'm hovering near the ceiling watching. From this perspective I can observe and see everything, including some of Claire's thoughts and dreams. When I look down at my bed, I see my stuffed doll, the one I loved but insisted I'd outgrown, and a teddy bear. The brown wool blanket lies tidily over the edges of my bed and the covers look unmoved. Where am I? I don't see me there. I don't see my body, but I know that I'm up here looking at everything from a high perspective. A feeling of panic races through me. Have I gotten lost? Did I not go to bed yet? Claire and Alain must have been worried. I don't understand. It must be the fever. I must be so sick.

My Mammaw told stories of being able to rise out of your body and visit the lake and lands at night when you sleep. "It's an old sorcerer's trick," she said. "You naturally know how to do it. Just like I did." When I was a child, she told me tales of the lake people who once lived in houses built on wooden stilts at the edge of the lake, and of their rites to honor nature. She believed in fairies too. She said sometimes she saw them in the forest. They would lead her to the best places to find blackberries and morel mushrooms. And sometimes they would tickle her shins and dance around her to make her laugh. I loved her stories and made fairy houses out under trees and built fairy rings of dead leaves with stones piled in the center for them to dance on. We kept this secret from my mother. She disapproved of grandma's stories. "Fantasy," Mom said. "It'll get you into trouble."

Mom's reflections filled me with sadness. I loved the fairies and sometimes sensed them dancing about too. It's so, so late now and Claire has stopped shivering and fallen asleep. Alain turns restlessly in bed. I feel really tired and cold and make an effort to go back to bed to rest under the covers.

✧

Today I awaken with excitement. It's the annual march around town to chase away winter. We bring tin cans on ropes that hang from sticks. With the help of the school's headmaster, some of the boys slapped together dripping papier-mâché over a chicken-wire frame during the past weeks to create Old Man Winter. Today the ten-meter-high effigy stands at the school entrance, dry and ready to go. We boldly parade out of the schoolhouse at noontime and onto the streets banging the tin cans behind the cart that carries Old Man Winter. The Old Man looks like a snowman with a long black beard. This year the students gave him an evil face and he looks a bit like a German with blue eyes and blonde hair, but maybe this is my imagination. He holds one arm up in a Nazi salute. We walk through the streets banging the tin cans and yelling, "Vas-t'en", behind him to chase him out of town. Shop owners and women on their way home from the market and people out on the street join us and walk in a growing procession. I walk beside Ginny and yell as loud as I can. Some of the students from the conservatory carry drums and bang them too. The noise grows louder. The drums send the thick vibrations across the town, and in their minds, people collectively replace Old Man Winter with the repressive and corrupt French collaborators in government and the abusive Germans who occupy the town who take things that don't belong to them and hurt people simply because they can.

The German soldiers and French police look uncomfortable as the crowd passes. I notice how they slip inside inner courtyards to observe us like spies. Even though we're not allowed to speak our minds, we Savoyards seethe from the oppression, rationing, and rigid rules. We're mountain people who live fiercely independent lives and hate foreign domination. The noise rises to crescendo and Old Man Winter arrives on the Paquier, the large open field by Lake Annecy that borders the town. One of the leaders of the group, a tall, gangly boy with some stray beard hairs sprouting on his chin, lights a torch and announces that Old Man Winter must go.

"He's not welcome here anymore," the teenaged boy roars. The crowd yelps and bangs the tin cans as the flames soar and engulf the Old Man.

"*Vas-t'en. Vas-t'en.*" *Get out. Get out,* people chant until a group of French militia forces and German soldiers move across the field to break up the crowd. The threatening and ominous German SS soldiers stand like a wall in the background by the school with immobile faces and shiny black boots. They wait to see if the French militia can maintain control. Their SS leather boots shine and we can see the symbols of the death skulls on their caps even from here. Panic sets in and I grab Ginny by the hand as the crowd disperses in many directions.

"No gatherings allowed," the head French collaborator announces through a megaphone. "No public gatherings. You'll be arrested!" But by the time he arrives at the feet of the burning effigy, the crowd has already dispersed into the park and off toward Veyrier on the other side of the lake. I glance back to see the police chase after the adolescent boy who lit the fire. They capture and beat him.

"Let him be an example," I hear a French officer say. The smoldering anger that the crowd released goes back underground to fester. Herr Schmid stands always in the shadows, always alone on the edge watching and observing like a spy quietly collecting names and information about who appeared during the "protest".

I follow Ginny into a bakery, but remain in a corner, head down and out of sight because I'm grounded and Claire insisted I stay at home. The bakery doubles as a café. Ginny sits beside her dad who orders her a hot chocolate. Some men join him at the table. *"Gare a elle."* *Keep an eye on her,* the man says and nods toward Ginny. "They found another one today. One of the herder's dogs found it at the edge of the forest." Ginny sits up, eyes wide, uncomprehending. I move in close to try to understand the man's talk too. Her dad shudders. His mouth tightens into a grave frown.

"A girl?" Her father says.

The man nods.

"Same?" Her dad says. The man shrugs and runs a hand over his beard.

"Yes. We think it's another murder. An evil bastard, in any case." He shakes his head, stares into his chicory coffee.

"Maudit boche. Maudit traitors," Ginny's dad mutters quietly glancing around to make sure no one else has over heard. The other men at the table nod in silent agreement.

"Brutal," one man whispers. "Not more than fifteen or sixteen years old. The priest told me."

"There are a lot of evil Germans around," Ginny's dad says. "How to protect them?" He nods over in Ginny's direction. She nibbles a butter cookie and sips the bittersweet hot chocolate in her cup, seeming not to pay attention to the men. "These are trying times," her father says. "Cherie, go get another chicory coffee for me." Ginny walks to the bar and the conversation continues behind her back, but I hear every word.

"Strangled," one of the men whispers. "Third one so far. The priest confirmed it." They all glance over at my dad who I notice sitting alone in a corner staring into his empty wine glass.

"The damned French police won't do anything. They suspect it's a German's doing too. That's what Father Ansen said. The girl was a gypsy. The Germans consider gypsies no better than dogs, so case closed."

Ginny returns smiling, her upper lip dotted with a little milk froth from the hot chocolate. She holds up the steaming espresso for her dad. He wipes the froth from Ginny's mouth and pulls her close.

"Gare a toi," one of the men says softly to her. "Be careful."

Ginny looks as innocent as an angel. We're the same age, but she always looked younger than me. Her cheeks look as pink as the summer roses and she's budding like a flower. When we walk around town lately the boys whistle and stare. She doesn't care much for boys. Inside she's still all cotton-candy and dolls. She still chases butterflies and believes that no one can hurt her.

I lift up my head and slip beside her.

"Ginny, let's go to my house and dress up in Claire's clothes. You'll come? We can try on her lipstick and bras," I say. Ginny stops eating her croissant and tears sting her eyes.

"What's wrong?" her dad says. Ginny blinks to fight back the rush of emotion.

"*On y va*, daddy?" *Let's go.* She puts on her mittens and tugs at her dad's hand. "I don't feel well." Her dad nods at the men and he walks behind Ginny who leads him out the door.

I don't know why Ginny won't speak to me. She loves playing dress-up at least as much as I do, and Claire has some pretty dresses she inherited from my aunt who danced in a cabaret. I like to make Ginny laugh when I put on one of the feathered hats, prance around like a cabaret dancer, and wiggle my butt. We have so much fun doing this. But Ginny left without speaking to me. Maybe she's catching the flu too. It's going around. Or maybe she wants to avoid getting this fever like I have. The one that gives me the ability to see so much and fly over the mountains at night. Maybe she's afraid of getting sick, like me.

7

WHEN I GO home, Clarie's there unexpectedly with Jean-Michel. I hear them whisper through Claire's locked door. Claire moans and I wonder if he is hurting her. I wish that dad were here so I could tell him. He protects us. I wait outside seated on the floor, my back against the door, and listen to the sounds. I stare at my hand that's so pale it almost seems transparent against the wooden floor. A vague memory of Herr Schmid comes back. Something dark and cold chokes my throat with fear. Then the door opens and I slip aside. Claire comes out wearing an expensive lavender silk dressing gown that belonged to my aunt. Her golden-brown hair falls loosely over her shoulders and face. The corners of her lips lift up in a tiny indication of happiness. She searches the room for the packet of *Gauloises*, lights a cigarette, and returns to her room.

"Claire," I whisper. Her eyes widen with fright, then narrow. She glances at me and then disappears into her bedroom again leaving me at the threshold.

"*Aii*, your feet are cold," Jean-Michel says as she climbs into bed next to him. He holds her feet firmly against his bare thighs. But Claire looks distracted, worried. "What's wrong?" His rough hands stroke her cheek. "You look like you saw a ghost."

"She's here," Claire whispers, throat constricted, shoulders tense.

"Don't worry. I'll stay out of your way," I say. "I just don't want to be alone."

Jean-Michel closes his eyes tight an instant as if he wants to keep something out or be very careful about what he will say.

"Why do you keep saying that?" He seems annoyed at Claire.

"Because it's true," Claire lies on her back and stares at the ceiling. Jean-Michel props himself on one elbow and looks at her. He rolls onto his back.

"God, I can't stand that thing on the roof above us all winter long. It's making you crazy and I can't come when I look up at the ceiling and think of her."

"Him," I correct. "It's granddad and he's fine. It's not like when Mom was there." I felt her restless soul wander about the house until after the burial. But granddad's different. "He's peaceful. Really," I say. His soul's not wandering about the house.

Claire remains silent and the air feels oppressive. Her cheeks look wet.

"Just stop the guilt, okay?" Jean-Michel says. "It's not your fault that your sister died."

The words jar me. I'm not dead. I'm right here. "He's gone mad, Claire," I say. But she's caught in her turmoil of emotions and ignores me.

"You're probably the only one who thinks I'm not to blame," Claire says. "You should see the look in dad's eyes. Every time he sees me he turns away. And Alain..." Her voice trails off.

"The war's driving your boyfriend crazy, Claire. I'm your sister. I'm right here." I walk to Claire's bedside and shake her arm to reassure her. "See."

Goosebumps rush up her arm where my fingers touch.

"Oh, god," Claire gasps and jerks her arm away. Jean-Michel observes her with cautious eyes.

"I'm sorry for interrupting, Claire." I don't understand. "But I really, really need you to talk to me now. But I can wait until after he leaves."

Claire stares at me, eyes wide. "Don't you see?" She says to Jean-Michel and points at me.

"You think about her way too much," he says, concerned. He sits up on the edge of the bed and I turn my eyes away as he puts on his trousers.

"That's not true! She thinks way more often about you," I say.

"You're just tired. Too much stress from being around that *boche,* Schmid," Jean-Michel says to Claire.

But Claire's frozen in the moment. "I'm sorry," she says. "I'm so, so sorry. Please forgive me, Aurelie. I love you so much. Forgive me." She sits up and pulls her knees to her chest weeping. Jean-Michel wraps his arms around her. She looks so beautiful and they've just had a wonderful moment. I could feel the joy between them like a ball of warm, glowing light. Until I barged in.

"I'm sorry," I say.

I slink to my room and leave them alone. But the covers are stripped away and my bear and doll sit in the window like I'm being moved out. My school books lie on the small table that looks out over the woods. I shiver and feel so, so cold. I wish Claire or whoever removed the blankets and sheets from my bed would put them back. I can't find them or my hair bow or grandma's earrings that I loved. I feel really weary and all I want to do is sleep. I must be very sick because I feel so weak and tired. I'm not even able to lift the teddy bear. But I'm not sure where I can go to rest now. The old cat lies by the fire in the living room and I curl up beside her for warmth and fall asleep.

In a little while, Jean-Michel peers out the bedroom door. I pretend to sleep. His madness upsets me and I don't want to see him. He looks out the windows into the dark night. When he feels confident no one waits in ambush outdoors, he slips into the woods. Claire stays inside and adds a log to the fire. Maybe she will listen now.

"Can we talk now?" I say. She walks past me, head down, like I'm not there and I follow her back into her bedroom. "Why are you mad at me, Claire?"

It's the first time we've been alone together in a long time. I feel the ache of loneliness, like when Mother passed and I really wanted Claire to take me in her arms and hold me for a moment. But Claire couldn't. She turns to me, eyes wide with fright. In a few minutes she puts on her dress and stockings and flees the house without a word.

Late February and the sound of gunfire echoes across the mountains like violent avalanches. I see and hear them in my lucid dreams as if I am there. I heard Jean-Michel say that the guns arrived and the Maquis Resistance are ready for fighting. But the explosions in the night air make me want to hide in the cellar. Why is no one around tonight? Not even Dad? I feel so afraid and alone and cold. So, so cold. When I drift into the lucid dream sleep, I see beautiful vibrant, red blood on the pure, white snow. The mixture looks regal. Human. Natural. Violently beautiful. Some injured men limp into stone grottos inhabited by the Maquis resistance fighters. Others lie peacefully on the snow.

"*Merde*. How did they know?" Jean-Michel curses and mutters. "How did they know?! There's been a traitor. Who in the ranks could have betrayed us?"

My brother, Alain, warms his hands over the fire. "There are many who could have sold us out."

"You?" Jean-Michel reaches for Alain's collar and jerks him closer to his face. Alain calmly peels Jean-Michel's fingers from his shirt without showing any sign of emotion. "No. Not me."

"You're foolish," my Dad says. His sad eyes bore into Jean-Michel. "He would have no gain from it. Unless he loves Germans and collaborators. You think he wants to trade champagne and French wine for schnapps?" Alain's eyes flash with amusement. Jean-Michel stomps into a shadow at the edge of the cave. The gun fire outside ceases.

"Germans," a scout says returning from a reconnaissance mission. "No French collaborators. Just invaders. They outnumber us. Probably five to one."

A sigh of defeat ripples around the small wood fire.

❧

After a terrible night with a restless sleep and strange dreams of resistance fighters, I go out and pick up more sticks. Dad trails in very early looking sweaty and exhausted in the early morning light. I run to embrace him, but a big, black crow on the roof lets out a loud caw of excitement.

"Get off of there," Dad yells. "Get away from that!"

The crow bounces up and down and cackles on the ochre roof tiles by the shrouded figure. An edge of the white fabric hangs open. The crow hovers over it, plucks at the fabric, and pulls back the corner.

"Go. Get out of here!" Dad sounds frantic. "Let that alone!" He yells and Farmer Elli who milks the cows steps out of his barn to see what's going on.

"Damned crows," the farmer mutters.

Dad digs out a handful of snow from a snow bank, smashes it into a ball, and throws it at the bird. But he misses and the bird seems more determined. It hops up and down, taunting and laughing. The crow returns to pluck at the fabric. I want to help dad so I climb the ladder to the roof and move in to see the face. A sense of dread warns me not to look. But I approach close to readjust the cloth. The edge of its cheek is visible. It's smooth, youthful, not wrinkled and spotted like granddad's old spotty skin. The crow's oblivious to my presence and plucks at the cloth again. It jerks the cloth away and reveals a narrow slit of face. A small, up-turned nose. Slightly pale, cracked, pinkish lips.

That's not granddad.

It has a pink bow.

My pink bow that *my* mother made for *me*. The one I've been searching for. On those ears I see *my* earrings that Mammaw gave me.

"Who is that dead person wearing my earrings?! Dad! I want my earrings and my bow." I call out frantic now. "Can't you get my things back, Dad?!"

With one final yank, the crow cackles and jerks the shroud completely from the face. My whole being quakes like I've been hit by a truck. I collapse on my knees by the figure and weep. Daddy's frantic now. He throws more rocks and snow at the crow until the bird flies off. He climbs the ladder to the top of the roof. His eyes redden and fill with moisture as he delicately cradles the rigid body in his arms and replaces the white shroud around the face.

"I miss you so much, Aurelie," he says with tenderness and longing. A sob slips out before he stifles the flood of emotion.

In that instant, I realize that I am dead and I can't stop crying.

8

THE WOMAN I'VE seen before, the one who tried to talk to me at the schoolhouse, who said she knew my mother, comes to me now. She takes me in her arms, but I push her away and bend in two crying.

"This is a terrible nightmare. That's not me. I'm not the girl on the roof."

The woman takes my face in her hands. She's so comforting and soothing that the tears stop even though I continue to feel the grief. "No. You're not," she says.

But I realize this isn't entirely true. Because I saw my face and my body. "But yes, I am. That was me. I saw my own nose and mouth. I saw daddy cry. Is this just a bad dream?"

The woman takes me by the hand. "There, there," she soothes. Her voice sounds melodious like a gentle, slow brook. "This world has different rules."

My eyes grow big. "What world? You're crazy. I don't understand."

"Would you consider your sweater is *you?*" There's a playfulness and lightness about her even though the talk is serious. A golden glow bathes her.

At first, I feel annoyed. How could she be so lighthearted and ask me about a sweater?! "Of course not! A sweater wears out or I outgrow it and leave it behind."

"It's the same with your body. You left it behind. But you move on."
She's clear. Matter-of-fact.

Now I'm speechless. This makes no sense to me, except I know that something about it seems true. I know that I'm here right now, aware, alive, and talking with this woman. And I see my mother nearby, but she can't seem to see me. I see her over there, smiling. Like I'm watching her through a thick glass window. "Mom!" I yell.

"She can't hear you either."

"Why? What happened to me? What happened to *it*, to my body?" The woman says nothing. "Why won't you tell me? Who are you anyway?!"

"I'm Naehelle, your helper."

I look back at my dad who walks, head down into the house. "Dad! Daddy!" I yell. "Why won't you respond, daddy?! I'm okay."

Naehelle sighs. "He can't hear you. Most people can't hear us on this side of the veil."

"What veil? What are you talking about?! Leave me alone. I need to go home. I'm not supposed to be here! I need to get out of this bad dream."

"I'm sorry, Aurelie, but you can't go home. Your body got hurt and now you're here." I'm paralyzed with fear.

"Where? What do you mean 'here'?"

"Beyond the veil."

When Naehelle says this, a rush of anger rips through me and I want to stamp my feet and scream. But I suddenly realize I have no physical feet to stamp. I feel grief, but I have no physical eyes to cry real tears in this dream.

"I'm trapped? Is this purgatory like Sister Marie describes?"

"If you think it is."

"I don't want to be here. I don't even know where I am."

"Some call it the 'in-between'," Naehelle says and the edges of her mouth turn up. "But don't worry. Most people don't stay here long."

My heart freezes. "No. This is just a bad dream."

"It's not a dream. You're in a transition place. You have a mission to complete. Your soul decided to stay and help those people until you finish it." She points to my dad and my house and the world down there, where I still see the shrouded figure on the roof. "You will move on to be with your mother once you finish. And then you can come back in another form later if you like." Naehelle seems compassionate and understanding. She's playful and easygoing. Her dark flowing hair ripples in waves down her back and her golden-white dress clings to her figure like on a marble statue of a Greek goddess, or some beautiful angel, or a wealthy, fairy princess. But I don't care. This is a nightmare.

"Go away. I need to get ready for school," I say.

"As you wish."

I go into my house brooding and angry as I prepare my books, put on warm mittens, and find my scarf. When I warm myself by the fire the terrifying images from this morning's dream return. Dad on the roof. The crow pecking at the shrouded figure. My lifeless face. That angel or devil woman who spoke to me. My fever must be out of control. The nightmares resemble those I had after Mom died while her body waited on the roof. I'm going to school anyway. I'll feel better once I'm there.

Outdoors I crunch through the hard snow and catch up with Ginny and the other kids who walk to school together. "Ginny," I yell. "Ginny! I'm so relieved to see you. You won't believe what happened! An angel-witch came to me in a dream and told me..." I hesitate to say the terrible words. My voice drops to a whisper. "She said I'm dead! It was horrible. A nightmare! Oh, gosh I am soooo glad to see you." A wave of relief sweeps through me as we walk together and I nudge Ginny with my elbow, but she looks uncomfortable.

"George really likes you," says Bernadette, a loud-talking redhead. Ginny blushes.

"No. I don't think so." Ginny sounds shy. Her lips seem redder and more womanly.

"He keeps bumping into you and flirting. And that chocolate he brought yesterday was a sure sign. Lucky his dad's a baker! No one gets chocolate these days."

"Ginny! Ginny! Stop talking about boys," I say. "What do you think about my terrible nightmare?" My anxiety and impatience mount, but she holds her dreamy focus on George.

"Joy says she likes him," Ginny says.

Bernadette nudges her shoulder. "Don't matter. It's you he has eyes for."

I hook my arm under her elbow. "Ginny, let's walk faster to get away from her." A look of shock flashes across Ginny's face. Her eyes grow wide.

"You okay?" Bernadette says.

"She'd be fine if you'd just go away," I say to Bernadette. "You're rude." But Bernadette ignores me.

"I'm not feeling so well. It's like…" Ginny stops. Looks around her. Her voice lowers to a whisper. "Sometimes I feel like she's here."

"Who?" Bernadette says.

"You know…" Ginny's voice lowers and she points back to the roof of my house. "Aurelie."

"Of course, I'm here! I've been sick and I had a terrible nightmare. But I'm fine now, Ginny." Ginny walks faster now.

"That's creepy," Bernadette says. "Weird."

"Leave us alone." I try to stand between Bernadette and Ginny, but Bernadette's like a cow. "Ginny would you tell Bernadette to get lost?! This is important!"

Ginny freezes up and pulls in on herself.

"Did you hear that?" she says.

"Hear what?" I say.

"What?" Bernadette says.

Ginny looks around and glances back at the roof of my house. "Nothing." She pulls her shoulders up and her head into her coat collar and keeps walking.

"Stop!" I yell and try to pull her back, but she keeps going. Bernadette continues a non-stop line of chatter. In frustration, I pick up a rock to throw at Bernadette, but I throw it at the farmer's calves instead and they scatter.

"She can't hear you. Not usually," says Naehelle, that woman from my dream. The one who looks like an angel. I plug my ears. "Ginny senses you're near. But you're frightening her."

"Go away…," I say. "I'm not asleep now. How can I see you?"

Naehelle waits a moment in silence and I'm halted by her will, blocked in place, unable to catch up with Ginny.

"You can talk, but Ginny won't pick up much of what you say. That's the way this world is made. You'll see that there are some who can and do hear you. Just not many. Kids and animals still see beyond the veil, but most people don't. As Ginny grows older, she will see and feel you less and less too."

"I don't know what you're talking about. You're crazy." My heart feels tight with fear, anxiety, and loneliness. "She's my best friend."

"I know," Naehelle says. "She misses you as much as you miss her."

"You don't know me. You don't know anything."

"I know that you love violets. You adore baby rabbits and chicks. You loved to play dress up. I know you miss your mother terribly. You broke a tooth when you fell against the front stoop. I know that you scratched, 'I love Didier' on a rock behind your house last summer. Then you replaced his name with…"

"Stop! How do you know that? Only Ginny knows that."

"I've been with you for a while now."

It's true she seems familiar and warm and kind, like the sister that Claire can't be. I feel loved in her presence and that love makes me want to cry.

"Ginny is like a sister to me." Instead of tears, this time a blind rage takes over and I can't see anything except the color red and an explosive wave of energy. "Get away from me. I don't know who you are. And I don't want to know you. I'm just sick and this is a bad fever dream. Go away," I yell.

"I know it can be upsetting. Call me when you need to talk."

"How?"

"Just call my name. Naehelle"

9

CONFUSION TAKES THE place of anger. Something's terribly wrong. I run to the schoolhouse to see Sister Marie. She'll help me understand. She talks about God, and death, and purgatory. Maybe she can explain the fever dreams, nightmares, and what's happening. The class bell rings through the crisp air and I go indoors. The room holds fewer students now. Daniel's seat stands empty. Frederick's books are gone from his desk. Walter's are gone too. During the break I go to Sister Marie.

"Sister, I need your help." I rub my index finger on the edge of her thick wooden desk and hope she'll tell me I need a doctor or some new medicine. Instead, she erases yesterday's lessons, and writes the catechism for the day while I wait beside her.

When we die, what happens to our body and soul?

We are made of a body and a soul. When we die, the soul separates from the body. The body remains behind and returns to the earth. The soul goes to purgatory, to heaven, or to hell according to its deeds and merits. In heaven, souls enjoy peace and joy. In purgatory, they wander restlessly until they are worthy of passing into heaven. In hell souls suffer from separation from God, love, and all things good until they are redeemed.

Sister Marie waits until the students assemble again. I return to my place, exiled in the back of the class.

"Who would like to read?"

Odile raises a hand and reads the words on the blackboard. "Thank you, Odile. Who can tell us what it means?" Francois raises a hand. Sister Marie nods at him.

"You're not just a body?" he says. "You're spirit too?"

"Good, Francois. When your body dies. Your spirit carries on. We know this by faith. There is much more to the world than only what our hands can touch and our eyes can see."

For once I listen. Her talk about faith and souls seems meant for me. But faith in what? In God? God was a white-haired man painted on the ceiling of the chapel, but not like anything I see now. Alain never believed. Dad didn't either. Mom did, but in a material way, like some people believe in Santa Claus. For her God could show up at your house and bring you rewards or punishment. Claire went through the motions to appease everyone. For appearances sake. But since the war, she rarely goes to church, even for appearances. I think she's stopped believing in anything. Claire only lives in the moment, she says. That's all that counts. It's all that we have.

Sister Marie asks everyone to write down the catechism and returns to sit in the rigid wooden seat. Her warmth and plumpness reassure me. I walk up the aisle and stand in front of her desk.

"Please. I think I'm sick, Sister Marie."

She glances up, but says nothing. She wonders how the convent will pay for the teachers, and get enough food for students now that so few people give alms. Some how I know her thoughts and feelings, but I shouldn't. Desperate for her guidance, I clear my throat. Her thin eyelashes flicker and squint, but don't focus on me. When she continues to ignore me, I knock the pencil cup over and it makes a racket as they scatter across her desk. I would not usually do this. I'm usually kind and well-behaved. This is how I've been brought up and taught by my mom and the nuns.

"*Mon Dieu.* Mon Dieu. I'll be," Sister Marie says, brows furrowed. She scoops the pencils back into the cup and firmly anchors them in the center of her desk.

"Sister Marie, please!" Desperation and anxiety sweep through me.

She frowns and seems too flustered now to focus on money or teaching. When she continues to ignore me, I swipe the pencils from the desk top and they go flying across the room near the door and land at the black-booted feet of Herr Hans Schmid. Sister Marie gasps in disbelief and some of the students stare.

"What was that, Sister?" Ginny says. "It wasn't natural."

The Sister clears her throat. "Uhhhmmm." She looks troubled as her eyes glance between Ginny, Herr Schmid, and the pencils at his feet. If Sister Marie would only talk to me, then I'd stop. She acknowledges Herr Schmid now as he stares at the pencils. I step away, embarrassed and slip back to my place at the rear of the class.

"I'm sorry sir. I don't know what happened," Sister Marie says.

Herr Schmid scans the room and his eyes lock on Ginny. People have often said we look alike with the same blond curls and wide brown eyes. A name forms on Herr Schmid's lips, "Aurelie." He stares a moment in shock then backs away into the shadows and continues down the hall.

Later I follow Sister Marie to the Notre Dame de Liesse church where she speaks to the priest about spirits, ghosts, possessions, and all matters of the "unnatural" as she calls it. The priest calls it "supernatural". He hands her a St. Benedict's medal and reminds her of the mystical formula held in the letters on the back: V R S N S M V - S M Q L I V B. "*Vade retro satana. Nunquam suade mihi vana! Sunt mala quae libas. Ipse venena bibas!*" he says then translates it. "Back off Satan! Never tempt me with your vanities! What you offer me is evil. Drink the poison yourself!" Sister Marie seems appeased.

"Pax," she says. "Peace." I clear my throat to get their attention.

"I'm no ghost and I'm not evil. I just want to understand, Sister. I thought you could help."

Sister Marie's eyes widen and she says a prayer. I watch them and wave at the priest. But something's wrong. He doesn't acknowledge me like he usually does. I listen to their conversation. Father Ansen tells Sister Marie that he's heard of these things before, but has no first-hand experience.

"If the haunting persists, Sister Marie, you must go talk to an elderly lady who lives in the tower near the castle. She sees the dead," the priest says. "If that's not enough I will contact Father Normand. He knows about exorcisms."

Sister Marie waddles into the snow, jerking her heavy black habit above the dirty ice on the sidewalk. I walk close beside her as she grips the medal between her index finger and thumb. I tug at her black sleeve and whisper one last time.

"Sister, please. Can you help me?"

A shudder ripples through her as she whispers "Vade retro satana." She's known me since I was a child and I don't understand her fear. But I give up and go look for Claire. When I find her, she's at a new officer's house. This one's gruff and coarse. Not refined like Hans.

"Did you bring eggs today and bacon like I asked?" The man stands about five feet tall in his boots, chest thrust forward. Claire towers over him in her high heels. "And I will need more firewood. You can get it from a local woodman, eh *mein frau*?" The colonel, recently transferred to Annecy, speaks perfect Parisian French. A photo on his shelf shows him posing proudly with a group of Nazis by the Eiffel Tower.

"Yes, colonel," she says. "But with the imposed rationing, you must write a letter ordering it."

Claire holds a woven basket filled with provisions and pulls out the eggs to show him. Because of her ability to speak some German, and because she's a beautiful, curvy woman, she never goes unnoticed. This must be why the foreigners love her. But she and the officer seem to carry a mutual disdain of each other. Claire has earned somewhat of a reputation as a woman who can be trusted by the French collaborators and the Germans occupying the town because of her association with Herr Schmid, but that trust remains tentative. The colonel grabs her chin with his pudgy fingers and pulls her face close to his.

"Good. *Bon travail*. Where is my change?"

Claire hands over a few coins and the man releases her.

"As long as you are honest with me, you risk nothing. Times will get harder for people here. They keep cutting the phone and power lines and sabotaging our work. But, if you are good to me, I may become your pro-tector." He puffs up his chest and runs his index finger over Claire's wrist. She jerks away and drops the eggs. He slaps her. "Clean it up." She finds some towels in the kitchen and wipes up the mess. "My god, you French are such a disgrace," he says. "Dogs."

Claire leaves the basket of goods on the scared, wooden kitchen table where the colonel and some of his men usually eat their meals. Her hands tremble with anxiety as she washes her face in the places he touched her. "A high price to pay," she says to herself. "Too high of a price." She thinks of Jean-Michel and the battle on the plateau and hopes her sacrifices make a difference.

"Claire," I whisper. "Something's wrong." Claire's eyes sparkle and she looks through me at the flowers on the wall. Her face pales and she shakes her head. "Can you help me? I think I have a fever." She feels her forehead and seems faint.

"I must be getting sick," she says.

"And no, you're not dreaming." I muster all of my energy to say that and I stand firmly beside her.

"I'm sorry," she says. "I tried to protect you."

"Something terrible has happened, Claire. Help me to understand." She washes the dishes and when she does, her mind is temporarily freed from the usual concerns, but she doesn't respond. "Claire!" I raise my voice and hope the colonel won't hear me. "Please don't ignore me like you usually do!"

She stops wiping the dishes. Her mouth falls open with concern and confusion. She arranges the final items in the basket and grabs her purse.

"Permission to leave, colonel."

"Granted. I'll expect the eggs to be replaced at your own expense." He stares at the page where his hand writes and doesn't bother to look up at her. "Swine," he mutters in a low voice.

"Thank you, sir. Goodbye, sir." She seems to fear this man, while Herr Schmid breeds a sense of familiarity and contempt. I know she probably doesn't want me tagging along, but I will not leave her alone until she speaks to me.

"Claire!" I beg when she's on the street. "Will you talk to me?" She stumbles and looks behind her.

"It's best to leave her alone," Naehelle says, suddenly appearing beside me. "She thinks she's being followed by spies. You're creating agitation and unrest. Besides she can't hear you. She can sense you, but she can't make out what you're saying."

"Leave me alone," I scream at Naehelle. "Are you a ghost?! You must be a demon. *Vade retro satana.*" She slips away and I follow Claire who rushes home and climbs into bed with a fever. In her feverish dreams I see an opening and talk to her. "Claire, I'm not dead. I need you to find me. I need you to listen and help me come home. I just want to get back to normal."

I sit at the threshold of her room and watch her until she wakes up crying. Distressed. Alain arrives and hears her muffled sobs. "

What's wrong, *ma puce?*" That's what Mom used to call us.

"Oh nothing. Just strain and worry, I think. I hate the Germans. I hate war. I just want this madness to end." She clings to him and weeps. Alain holds her next to his flannel shirt, takes a deep breath and speaks quickly.

"I need to tell you something. It's not good news." He hesitates. "We lost Jean-Michel."

The shock paralyzes Claire before the grief fully registers. "I can't take anymore. Mom. Aurelie. Now Jean-Michele." She bows her head and weeps. Blackness descends on me too. I'm on the list of the dead.

10

I STILL DON'T believe it. I don't believe any of their stories anymore. But I'm starting to doubt. I need to go outdoors and test my own existence in the streets. I travel to the brasserie and step right in front of the waiter at the café where Ginny's dad goes. The waiter carries a tray heavy with beers, some *vin mousseux,* and a couple of espresso coffees. He walks past me as if I'm not there. Next I go to the hat shop that Mom loved and touch the hats. The shop owner, who would never let me touch anything before, continues to look at her books and only lifts her head when the bell rings as a customer enters. But the bell didn't ring when I came in. At Monsieur Martin's stand at the market, I squeeze the apples and touch some expensive pears. He's notoriously grumpy and snaps at anyone who touches his produce, but today he goes about smoking his cigarette and staring at the dark, cloudy sky as if I'm not there.

It's growing dark now and I finally go to Ginny's house where she lights a candle at her mom's altar and says a prayer on her knees.

"Please be with my dear, sweet friend, Aurelie," she says. "Love and care for her." I hear her words and go flying straight to her. My heart nearly bursts with happiness.

"Thank you for your prayers, Ginny. I'm alive. I'm here!" I tell her. "No need to pray for me. Let's go sneak off to Hans' house for tea and biscuits. Or we could play dolls. I used to think I was too old. But just this once. Let's be little girls again." When I touch her arm, goose bumps rise up to her throat. She stares at the spot where I touch her and cries. "What's wrong, Ginny?"

"Mom. Mommy." She runs to her mom and clings to her dress like a little girl. I realize that whatever she feels or sees frightens her. The fear brings her to speak like a child again.

"What's wrong, *ma cherie*?" Her mother strokes her hair.

"Aurelie. She's here," Ginny whispers like we're somewhere sacred, maybe in a church. "I feel her. I wish she'd come back for good."

"I'm so sorry," her mom says. "I know. I do too." Her mom boils hot milk with some cinnamon and serves her a hot bun. But she doesn't serve me.

"Mom, why do people have to die?" Ginny says.

I stand close to her and feel sick to my stomach.

"I'm not dead, Ginny! I am right here." But her mom ignores me. Ginny ignores me too.

"It's the way of nature," her mom says. "It's the way of life."

A flood of despair nearly drowns me. Maybe Naehelle speaks truth. Maybe it's not just a fever. Maybe no one sees me and I'm only what? A ghost? I'm not a ghost! A sprit? A soul? Energy? Awareness? I don't know what I am. But one thing's for certain, I am not dead!

⋙

My heart aches. I go home, but the fire's out. Claire's gone. Alain's disappeared and I have no idea of where Dad went. Everyone seems to have forgotten about me. The darkness, the chill and the damp give me no incentive to stay home. I wander out alone to look for Claire. The wind whips through trees. The clouds encircling the earth whisper of more sadness and pain. I no longer understand anything about who I am, where I am, or what's happening. But I know something terrible has happened. For a long time, I walk alone and try to think clearly. I find a park bench and watch night fall in steely gray-blue tones over the lake. The ducks wander into quiet nests to sleep. Birds fly home. People disappear and no longer populate the streets. A drunken soldier sits beside me for a little while on the bench, but says nothing.

"I don't know where my father is," I say to the drunk. But I must be invisible to him too. I'm the loneliest person in the entire world. A few dead leaves blow into the lake. I seem to be losing my sense of smell and touch. The powers of my physical senses diminish and my connection to the earth seems to fade. No one sees me anymore. More loneliness than I ever imagined aches through my heart. I just want to go home and return to normal. But I don't know how. A cloud of desperation descends accompanied by a sense of helplessness. Then, mercifully, I lose consciousness.

❦

When I come to, my senses and feelings seem different. I seem to be floating, ethereal. There's a time, an in-between state where things remain unclear and murky. Where one's neither dead nor alive. Where you can't breathe, but you can't die. You can't rest. You can't sleep. You fade in and out. You see and know many things. Thoughts, feelings, ideas, and experiences of others. But you can't share any of the knowing with those you love most or anyone else. And worst of all, no matter what you do, almost no one seems to see or hear you.

I move up to the mountains tonight where the clouds roll over the plateau and bring a deep fog. The rams hide away from the guns and fighting men with their madness. The battle has temporarily stopped on the plateau. No one seems to have the energy to fight any more on either side. Jean-Michel's, injured, but not dead. I find him in a dark, wooded area, hidden by giant boulders. A bad wound to the shoulder leaks blood and makes it hard for him to breathe or to lie comfortably.

Some men search for injured resistance fighters. Perhaps, with a little light, I can draw them to him and help to save his life. He's in an in-between state, not fully alive now, but not dead yet either.

"Here," I cry out to the men. "Over here."

The men wear arm bands and look like rival resistance fighters who also seek power and control. I've overheard my brother, Alain and Dad talk about how the two resistance groups do not mix, but they fight for the same cause – to free the Savoy from German oppression. Jean-Michel moans from pain, unconscious now. The fighters stride on top of the snow with their wide snowshoes and walk in the direction of the sound. One of the fighters takes out a gun and aims.

"He's not one of ours," the man says. Another one pushes his hand away.

"He's still resistance, even if he is a Maquis. I'll carry him back and get him some help."

"If you insist. But I think it's a waste of time," the leader says.

11

"HELP ME," I cry out to the men. "Can you help me get back home?" One of the men with a beard looks at me.

"Did you hear that?" he says.

The others fall silent.

"Please help me go home. It's all I want. I'm not injured I don't think... I'm just lost." I stand close to him to see old blood stains and dried mud on his brown wool coat. Fear locks in his throat until he pushes through and breaks the silence.

"Let's get out of here. Now!" They all turn away and carry Jean-Michel to their cavern in a mountainside.

"Wait. Don't leave me! Please! Please don't leave me here by myself." I double over and weep. How could they be so heartless?! I feel so lost and alone. My family doesn't know where I am. It's a terrible, empty feeling. "Naehelle," I call out. "Please help." She's the only one who has responded to me in a long time.

In an instant she stands beside me. "Yes, Aurelie," she says. "I'm here."

"Help me."

"Yes, of course," she says. "Will you come home with me?"

She extends her hand and I accept. In an instant I'm no longer surrounded with snow and velvety night skies. Now, I'm basking in a glow of eternal warmth in that peaceful room of hers surrounded by her serene presence. A water fountain gurgles peacefully from a niche in the gold tinted wall. The lonely ache feels less acute. She remains close and soothing and the chill leaves. I feel calmer and begin to explore her space. Beautiful, ancient books and porcelain figurines decorate tall shelves that line her walls. A King Cavalier jumps up to lick my face and for a moment I forget the loneliness and I hold him close and bury my nose in his fur. "I always wanted a dog," I say.

"Get down, Roy," Naehelle says. But I hold him in my arms and won't let go.

"I want to go home."

"Yes, I know," she says.

"But I can't?"

"No."

"I don't know what to do."

"Come with me." She invites me into her parlor and sips some tea. She wears a loose flowing Japanese kimono, but she's not at all Japanese. "Would you like some tea too?" I shake my head no. I've not felt hungry or thirsty, only lonely. More than anything I long for a hug, for human touch.

"Have a seat?" She nods to a thick chair filled with some comfy pillows and I settle in with Roy on my lap. "Where shall we start?"

"Well where are we?" Then I pronounce the awful word. "I've heard them say I am dead. But I'm clearly not. I don't know what happened or what's going on now. Is this purgatory? I feel stuck in-between worlds. It's an awful, unsettled place. I want to get over this fever and go back home."

Naehelle observes me with her soft eyes over the edge of her teacup.

"You're not meant to stay here. It's just for a little while. You can leave when you complete your tasks."

"What task?"

"You'll see."

"Then I can go back home?"

"No. Then you move on. But you're not done with that world yet." She points out the window where I see Claire, Jean-Michel, Alain, and Ginny going about their lives. I want to leap through the window and be with them, but a force holds me back.

"Everything has changed," I say.

"Yes. I know it's a painful place to be. Especially when you long so much to touch them and talk to them."

For a long time I say nothing and just let the thought sink in as I stare into the flames in the fireplace. Grief replaces confusion. Gloom replaces my desire to be with friends and family.

"How can anyone find happiness here?!"

"You learn to accept it." Naehelle says softly. "But this place is only temporary." I notice there's no sadness about her. None at all.

"But don't you have people you miss? People you want to talk to and hold in your arms and dance and play with?!"

"I hardly remember what touch feels like." A pensive smile crosses her lips. "I wish you'd not reminded me. It's easier just to forget."

"How can I get back there? I want to go home."

"This is your home for now."

She leads me down a white corridor lit with amber tinted alabaster lamps and opens a door. "This is your room." All of the things I loved are here. Dried lavender sachets. My worn teddy bear that I out grew. The wooden doll dad made for me. My one little boar bristle brush. A Bakelite mirror Mom gave me. The room is spacious, cozy, light with gingham curtains and a soft bedspread with a duvet. All I want to do right now is sleep so that it all goes away. I burrow into the duvet.

"When I wake up everything will be back to normal, won't it?"

"Get some rest," she says.

"Can I visit them?"

"For a little while," she says. "Then you'll forget, like I try to do."

But I don't want to forget. I want to go home. "I need to know how I lost my body? Was it an accident? What happened?"

"You'll figure it out soon enough. And when you do, and you complete your mission, you can move on."

12

IF THIS IS death, then it's not what I'd thought. It's not black and scary with demons and skeletons. It's light and easy in an odd, ethereal way. And though I don't have a body, I'm certainly not dead. I'm just in a different state, like from solid ice to fluid water then vapor. I don't feel physical pain, but my anguish and upset are worse, like hell, because I want so much to be alive to the world and back in my body. My body linked me to touch and feelings and people. It tied me to time. It needed sleep. Food. It had a regular rhythm. Without a body, I'm separated from Ginny and Hans. From their perspective, I no longer exist. Not in a way that is "real" to them. Conditions are different. Great swathes of time open out and I experience vastness as I watch the mountain rams and the snow falling, and Jean-Michel injured, feverish, and shivering in the mountains.

Jean-Michel slips between sleep and death, and I visit him at the edge of his dreams and I encourage him to hang on, to stay alive. But when I wake up now, I'm no longer in dad's wood-frame house. Instead I wake up to Roy snuggled beside me with the thick duvet over my head. The walls vibrate with warmth and happiness, but I don't feel happy. The confusion lingers between dreams, sleep, and waking. I'm starting to believe Naehelle speaks truth. That something awful has happened to me and my body that I need to unravel and understand.

I'm learning about this new in-between place. It's like being exiled to a new country where no one I love can visit me. In this country I never feel hunger, but I have cravings. I crave porridge with cinnamon. And hot cocoa. I crave touch. I want to be held in someone's arms and comforted. Naehelle comes close to me in these moments, but I can't feel her skin, only a pleasant vibrating sensation that signals she's near me, but without any direct, physical contact. It's like our energies blend and her efforts only bring frustration, so I push her away. But I seek out Claire and sit at the foot of her bed at night. When she wakes up and sees me, she gasps and weeps. She thinks she's going crazy, so I need to leave her in peace.

"I'm so sorry. I'm so sorry." She repeats over and over. "Forgive me, Aurelie."

The dry mountain air crackles with electricity and fear. I want to take Claire flowers to soothe her. She loves the roses from Provence that sometimes arrive at the market from the southern hot houses. Sometimes I stack sticks on the porch step, but then I feel really tired and need to rest a long time before I can start again. The physical world feels more and more coarse and heavy, while I feel lighter and lighter. Almost no one can hear or see me anymore. When I focus intently, I can sometimes appear to Claire or Ginny, but then they collapse in tears or feel sick, so I've mostly stopped.

"Send love instead," Naehelle says. "It will make them feel better."

When I lie down I see them in my dreams. Ginny at school. Talking with Bernadette. Herr Schmid with the glistening, house-of-mirrors eyes. Claire yearns for Jean-Michel to return, and some part of her knows he's not dead. Alain continues to work at the garage. He says little and no longer laughs. Dad goes about building cabinets and making desks and furniture for the few people who still have money to pay. He secretly supports the resistance, but since the "loss" of Jean-Michel, he refuses to fight on the plateau.

Ginny thinks of me a lot and each thought feeds my soul and keeps me alive. She burns candles at the church and says prayers for me. I tell her I miss her too. The days seem to run together now and I begin to discover ways I can connect with her and the others. Hans Schmid sees me. I'm pretty sure. He talks to me each time I go to him. But he leans more and more toward madness and anxiety each time I show up. He drinks a lot these days and seems almost to have a death wish. But I can't help it. I long for him and trail him everywhere.

Today I follow him to a clearing in the woods. Herr Schmid stares at the ground where blood stains the snow, his fists stuffed deep into his leather coat pockets. He walls in his thoughts behind his steel blue eyes, so I can't know them.

A girl appears beside me with long dark hair and beautiful reddish-purple lips haunted by a sad frown. I jump with fright. "Oh!"

"My body died there." She's painfully shy and upset and points her long thin finger at the blood stains. Her colorful skirt and red top with lace and frills remind me of a gypsy's clothes. Suspicion invades my mind. I don't know the rules of this in-between. Maybe I shouldn't trust her.

"But you're not dead."

She glances up at me. "I'm stuck in the same place you are," she says.

"What happened?" Bruises mark her throat. She shakes her head and stares at Hans with confusion and sorrow. He bends trance-like over the mark on the snow.

"Why?" The girl whispers to him, confused and anxious. Her wide, sad eyes meet mine. "I don't understand why he hurt me."

"I'm sure he wouldn't hurt you. He saved me from starving." She gazes at me in disbelief, her mouth half open and shakes her head. "Hans," I call out. His head jerks up. His body tenses and he reaches for his pistol, but his self-control holds him fast to his place in the snow where drops of ice melt on the toes of his black boots and his gloveless fingers turn red. Recognition registers in his eyes. He jerks his head around to face me.

"Aaah," he whispers, startled. "*Mein Got*," he says. "Who are you?" He points the pistol at me.

"Don't you recognize me?" I say. He backs away until he's against a tree.

"I believe in nothing. But you...I see you everywhere, Aurelie." A momentary softness descends over his face and replaces the look of terror.

"I miss you." I move close and want to embrace him. But the girl holds me back.

"Don't go near him," she says. But I shake her off.

"You've got it wrong," I say. Then I turn to him. "A girl died there. She's right here."

"Aurelie?" he whispers. Visibly shaken, he props himself with one hand against the white and gray bark of the birch tree. I'm sure he sees me. The bruised gypsy girl pulls away, embarrassed that I've drawn attention to her.

"Why would she say you hurt her? I know you're not like that."

The girl stares sadly at the stains on the snow. At the place where she left her body behind. A faint, subtle outline of her form remains. I step forward to move close to Hans again, but something grips my arm. Naehelle stands beside me holding me back.

"*Viens, les filles,*" she says. "Come girls." She pulls me toward her. Herr Schmid waits frozen and immobile.

"Can he hear you too?" I say to Naehelle.

"No he only hears you," she says.

"*Je t'aime,* Hans Schmid." I want to kiss the aching wounds scabbing over on the back of his wrist.

"Come, Aurelie," Naehelle says. She looks troubled. But I won't follow her. It feels like an invisible chord links my destiny with his.

I follow him to Claire's. He bangs at the door, so drunk that he doesn't care if Dad or Alain see him. She opens it a crack and her face runs through many shades of emotion: shock, worry, irritation, paling into frustration, anxiety, and anger. Her lips draw tight and settle on an inexpressive straight line. He holds up a wooden crate of food – flour, chocolate, tins of pâté.

"For your sister," he says. Claire looks puzzled and upset.

Claire takes the crate and pushes the door to close him out, but he blocks it with his black boot. She holds tight to the door handle, her face hard, and again her expression reveals the minute and rapid calculations she makes about the wisdom and consequences of resisting him. She takes the crate and turns away as he follows her into the house. I slip inside behind him and watch.

"What do you want?" Claire snaps.

"To see you. You make me feel sane." He stands awkwardly in the center of the room.

"You shouldn't come here. What would the neighbors say?!" Claire sets the food on the scarred wooden table. "They would just as soon kill you and bury you as ask questions. Go in there, if you must stay." She pushes him into her room and pulls the door half closed. In a swift, automatic gesture, she fills the coffee pot from one of the ration packs and places it on the hot stove top. Without thinking, her hands reach for the lipstick in her purse. When the pot heats, she pours a cup and carries it into her bedroom. Herr Schmid sits on the edge of her bed, uncomfortable and out of place. His black officer's jacket and thick wool pants give him an air of authority that contrasts with his slumped shoulders. Claire stands straight, arms crossed over her chest, and towers over him while he sinks deeper into the mattress like a stone. "The neighbors will think I'm a prostitute." Claire snaps.

"I'm sorry." His troubled eyes stare into the coffee.

"What do you want?"

"You are the only one who is not afraid of me." His hands shake. "Everyone else hates me."

"Do you blame them?"

"It's the war. If there were no war, I'd marry you."

Claire snorts like this might be a good joke, but his words hurt. I thought he loved me.

"What makes you think I'd accept?" She lights a cigarette. "My mother's dead. My best friend is dead. And her." Claire points to the ceiling. "All because of you, Germans."

"Why do you point?" Herr Schmid glances up at her, eyes dimmed from drink.

"The roof. Didn't you see her when you came in?"

"I see her everywhere."

Claire halts, taken aback. "Me too. She'll stay up there until the ground thaws. Then, maybe she'll rest in peace. Endless winter. Endless war." Claire exhales a long white trail of smoke as if this is her one pleasure. The act looks sensual. Self-possessed as if for this moment she has no other care in the world and there is no war, no Jews disappearing, no dead lover to mourn.

I watch and ache, as I stand so painfully close to them and yet remain so far from their awareness.

Hans puts the coffee cup on the floor. He walks to her and hangs his head on her shoulder, his face buried in her curls. She stiffens and her jaw tenses. He lifts his head, eyes heavy with pain, and stares at her as if she might hold a cure for his ailment. He leans in to kiss Claire, but she turns her head away and his lips graze her cheek. She jerks her head back and pulls away.

"Don't pretend. You don't love me," she says. "You don't even love yourself."

"I'm sick. You must help me." His arms hang limp at his side. "Come tomorrow."

Claire turns her back, cigarette poised between her index and middle fingers, angry, powerful and confident, like a mighty Greek goddess.

"I'm busy. What time?" she exhales. From her stare, I know that she would crush him in an instant if she could. At the same time, she feels the pull of her duty to help the Resistance mixed with a tinge of curiosity.

"Come when you can. At six or seven. Whenever."

"I'll think about it. Tell me now what you need."

"No. Tomorrow. Whenever you can after six p.m. I'll be ready."

"If I come, it will be a favor for a favor." She stands arms crossed tightly, lips tight and determined.

"Yes. Of course. It is our pact. Our deal. I understand nothing is for free with you."

"And with you?" She snorts again and smoke puffs from her nostrils. "You'd better go now. She reaches for the door handle and he unwillingly crosses the threshold into the dark.

I walk home with him. Inside his overly warm rooms, he uncorks the scotch and drinks heavily. I sit in the red velour chair by the fire again and watch him stare at a small object in his palm.

"Aurelie," he says. When the drink disappears, he shifts his focus from his palm to the chair where I sit by the fire.

"I'm here waiting for you, Hans." I say. He throws the glass at me and it shatters against the stone of the fireplace.

"I'm sorry I frightened you. Please, don't be angry."

He slams into his bedroom. Undresses and folds his shirt into a perfect, orderly square. Germans are not religious, I know. But the mantel above the fireplace forms a sort of altar with a small collection of precious objects. A single gold earring with two love birds on a nest. A leather bracelet bearing a coin-sized silver charm engraved with an "S". He kisses a silver object in his hand and lays it carefully next to the bracelet on the marble mantel.

It's the silver and pearl brooch Dad gave me last Christmas, but one of the pearls is missing. I wonder how he got it. I don't remember giving it to him.

A leather flog, like the one Farmer Elli uses for the plow horse, lies under a maroon suitcase. He removes it from hiding and studies it. Strips of leather hang from the top to make it more painful. Hans places it lovingly on the mantel and lies down in bed, indrawn and remote. I curl up beside him and stroke his head to soothe his suffering soul and when I touch him his inner life opens to reveal his restlessness. He wanders, stuck in an in-between space similar to mine – beyond waking consciousness but before peaceful sleep. My in-between is light, quiet and safe, but his fills with terror. He seems imprisoned in it, unable to reach the room of sleep. Father Ansen, the priest, would say his conscience stalks him like a beast. In his inner place, I see dark shadowy rooms and black corridors that provoke dread. They hold black secrets. Hans flees through these somber inner halls, in a sort of fearful hell and ravenous beasts pursue him. They strip his flesh and consume it. When the flesh grows back, they want more. Beyond them is an even more monstrous form with enormous tentacles. Its tentacles seek out Hans. The terror of it makes me flee.

13

NAEHELLE SCOLDS ME when I return to her house. But I slip under the duvet and sleep to rest and forget. When I wake up light streams through the window. But light always seems to stream in here. I don't know how long I've slept. There are no clocks and time seems to have no power over me. Roy yaps and we play. Naehelle serves me tea and chocolate croissants. The girl with the bruised throat who I met in the woods sits sullenly in the salon staring out the window. I look at Naehelle and hold my questions. I decide it's best to avoid that girl. She wasn't in my class at school. Alain would call her a gypsy girl, an outsider. Her parents camped in caravans at the edge of the town and sent the girl into Annecy to beg. I saw her sometimes at the market. Some pieces of her past trail her like little films. This is how I know about her. Then she turned up in the forest. I want to know if she got lost and fell and maybe this is how she got hurt. But the place where she died feels sinister, dark, unholy. And so I really don't want to know. But some mystery seems to bind us together.

"I've lost my charm bracelet," the gypsy girl says. "Have you seen it?"

I shake my head no, and avoid her.

"It's real silver. With an "S" engraved on it. "S" for Silvie. That's my name."

I remember the mantel in Herr Schmid's bedroom with the charm, but there can't be a connection. And Claire. I think of her now. I don't want to forget. I want to know what Hans wants from her. She looks so beautiful and her cheeks are gaunt from too many cigarettes and not enough food.

"Will I grow up to look like Claire?" I ask Naehelle who weaves a beautiful silk tapestry on a loom.

"You could," she says, pensive. "Would you like to?"

"I don't know. There are many things I don't understand about being a woman."

"Yes. That's true."

I yearn to see Mom. When I think of her, she's here – and yet not. Movie-like scenes of my favorite moments pass before my eyes. A time when Mom held me close like the times when I scraped my knees and cried. The time Mom gave me cakes, fresh and hot from the top of the iron stove. A wave of pleasure rolls through me and I surf on it for a long time. Then nostalgia follows when I come back to *this*. Wherever *this* is.

"Can I see Mom?"

"No. Not yet. Not until you finish your work here."

"What work? You mean to help someone?" A trace of annoyance makes me itch.

"You'll know." The luminous silk threads dance between Naehelle's fingers as she weaves a tree of life.

"Oh." I stare out the window into their world and in an instant I'm there with Claire.

Claire dresses and prepares herself for the visit to Hans Schmid's. She scans herself in the looking glass and just before she leaves, she picks up the tiny pistol that Jean-Michel gave her from her bedside table and places it securely in a secret panel inside her purse. It must be very late now as she steps into the street. The street lamps burn. Most of the neighbors have locked their shutters to keep the warmth in and strangers out. The night seems particularly sinister and black since the Germans have ordered a total blackout to save the town from bombing by the English and Americans. The law says that all windows must be covered with black cloth or paper so that not a single pinhole of light escapes into the streets after nightfall.

Nothing stirs, not even the wind and the air remains frozen and still. I fear for Claire as she bikes through the eerie fog after curfew.

Inside the apartment, Claire and Hans Schmid face off. He hands her scotch and she touches the alcohol to her lips, but refuses to actually drink.

"There," he points to some gold coins for her to pocket. "And more food." Another burlap bag waits beneath the table on the floor below the coins. Claire's brows furrow, but she appears indifferent, surly. "I can't stand to see starving kids," he says. "Come." He opens his bedroom door and Claire watches warily from the threshold. With his back to her he unbuttons his shirt and folds it meticulously into a neat, perfect rectangle. Claire observes, arms crossed.

"I'm not a prostitute. You've got the German-run bordellos for that."

He faces her. Deep, fresh cuts mark his chest. Some round burns on his right arm trail up to his bicep.

"You're a mess. Germans not treating you well, eh?" He ignores her surliness and lifts the leather flog from the mantel. She steps back, afraid he might whip her.

"Here." He hands over the flog and kneels with his bare back facing her.

"You're joking," she says and tosses the whip on the wooden floor.

Rage rises up from one of his hidden inner rooms and frightens me. He stands and snarls, teeth grinding together. "Don't...mock me." Claire's gaunt face pales.

"You're mad. What do you want from me?"

"Only this." He picks up the flog and smashes it over his shoulder. The leather strips crash against his skin and cut into the flesh.

Claire's brows crinkle. "You want me to hurt you? So, all of that is self-inflicted." She points to the cuts on his chest and burns on his arm. "But why?"

His foreboding gaze bores deeply into her. "To find peace. You're the only one who can release me."

She tosses the whip onto the bed and steps toward the door, but he jerks her back by the arm with frightening intensity. I wonder if I have the power to protect Claire from the crazed and ill side of him, the side I did not see.

"Maybe you are like my weak brother. The one with a moral stance who could hurt no one. No matter the cost to himself. Or others." He hovers over her as menacing as a black cloud before an ugly, unpredictable storm and shakes her until her teeth knock together. "If you want the food and money. Do it. Do it for others if not for yourself."

"Stop." She jerks her arm away. "You're hurting me."

"Then do as I say." He hands her the flog again and kneels. She's painfully aware of his physical strength and his power to send her to a local internment camp or off to Germany for any reason. It's like walking a razor-thin rope where a single false step could send her reeling into the jaws of the Gestapo's gnashing teeth. If she does his will she may be punished. And if she hurts him she may get punished too. Claire takes a deep breath, aware of the danger, and slaps the leather strands lightly against his bare back.

"Harder."

She hits him again with more intensity.

"Harder," he commands through gritted teeth.

She reluctantly lifts the whip again and whacks the leather against his bare skin. Claire flinches each time as if she's hitting herself.

"Harder!" He rips it from her hand and whips himself to demonstrate. "Like this." The leather rips into his flesh. He grits his teeth from the pain and seems satisfied. She takes the whip in her hands and hits harder. "Better," he says. "You can do better."

A powerful memory of Jean-Michel in her arms invades her vision and tears fill Claire's eyes. *Germans killed you*, she thinks. *This is for you.* Revenge for her lover's death releases her fury and she hits Hans with all her force.

"Yes. Good." He grits his teeth. "Again." He commands and kneels on the bedside rug. Red welts rise up on his skin and he grits his teeth, but refuses to cry out.

"Stop!" I say. "Stop!" The madness pulls Claire lower into his energy. But the more I insist she stop, the harder she beats him. He suffers in silence and I don't know why he wants this. I try to intervene, but the beating turns to thrashing until his back bleeds. When Claire seems spent, he turns, still on his knees, and wraps his arms around my sister's thighs.

"*Meine Herrin und meine gebieterin*. My lord and my master," he says. "Thank you. You're my salvation. Thank you."

Claire trembles, stooped from adrenaline and exhaustion. She pushes him away and weeps from the emotional strain. He pulls her down to the floor, excited by his own pain and suffering. But she's emptied of her rage over Jean-Michel's death and disgusted by Hans. He takes advantage of her momentary weakness and forces her to the floor.

"No!" She struggles to push him away. "Stop." She fights him with her small fists. But he pins her arms down with one hand and lifts her skirt with the other. "Stop!" She frees one hand and claws at his face. He slaps her. Claire, visibly shaken, scratches at his eyes. Her nails and her hands are stained with blood from his injured back. She struggles away shaking, and quickly finds her coat. Herr Schmid lies immobile on his stomach, cheek against the floor.

"I'm sorry," he mutters. "It's stronger than me."

She fingers the gun in her purse. "I should shoot him now and be done with it," she says to herself between gritted teeth. She adjusts her torn stockings and skirt and even in the madness she slips over to his desk and goes through his files and reports before leaving. "A high price to pay," she thinks and pockets the coins which will be used for the resistance.

One of the gifts of being "dead" is that I can somehow feel and know someone's emotions and thoughts. At least some of them, some of the time. At other times nothing is apparent. Not a single thought or feeling. Tonight I sense Claire's state of being. She's one of the clearest, brightest people I know.

Once outside, Claire weeps with rage. I hear her thoughts, how she's worked hard to tread the tightrope to remain Herr Schmid's house help and not submit to his advances. But tonight he crossed that line. She thinks of Jean-Michel again and her heart aches. "It's not betrayal. I love only you," she whispers. But she can't afford to cry or think about the pain now. She fingers the notes in her pocket that trace the plans of the Gestapo's moves in the Savoy. Claire shudders, pulls her coat closer, and slips onto her bike wincing at the pain. Only the knowledge that her sacrifice may help others keeps her going. I surround her in a prayer of white light to protect her and see her safely home.

I return to Hans and touch the bloody wounds on his back. "Look what you've done," I whisper. I can see back into his youth, how his father and step-mother beat him. How he associates beating with love, connection, and pleasure. "It doesn't have to be that way, Hans," I whisper. "You hurt

Claire. You must stop it." I weep over him and fall into a deep sleep at the foot of his bed, feeling confused and upset.

When I see Hans the next afternoon on the streets, he's back to normal, back to being Herr Schmid. Rigid, stiff, unforgiving, and apparently unfeeling underneath the black, leather coat. He stands in a darkened alley when a young boy on a rusty bike nearly collides into him.

"Out of my way," he hisses. The boy pedals off, his eyes wide with fright and Hans' eyes narrow. His fists clench and he catches a glimpse of Claire disappearing up a set of stairs across the way. When she exits, Hans follows her at a safe distance.

She passes a crowd of boys who hover near the old well in the old town. Some of them whistle when Claire passes. She tosses her head back and walks on. George, Ginny's crush, leans against the edge of the well smoking a cigarette to impress Ginny. She waves innocently at Claire, a tiny smile on her plump lips. Herr Schmid edges close to the walls seeking to go unnoticed. At first Ginny thinks nothing of it, then she senses his connection to Claire, like he's tied to her by some invisible rope. Her curiosity pushes her out into the small crowd walking through the streets.

"I've got to go, George." She lifts a hand to wave, but he leans down and kisses her on both cheeks.

"See you tomorrow then," he says. She nods and follows Herr Schmid down the cobblestone main street at a distance so he won't notice her. My stomach knots up.

"What are you doing, Ginny?!" I say. But she hums and her bright eyes let nothing go by without notice. Claire enters into the butcher's shop and Hans lingers out of sight, eyes staring past the reflections on the windows. He's spying on Claire!

"Hi," Ginny says. She's tiny, like a doll, staring up at him. He flinches, startled. But as his eyes fall on her, his mouth clenches and his breath stops. He rubs an object between thumb and forefinger. It pricks his finger and he drops it.

"Aurelie," he whispers. Ginny says nothing, only stares up at him. She picks up my silver and pearl brooch and hands it to him, her face filled with questions.

"Here." Her pale palm lies open and his hand trembles as he takes it from her.

"But…you're dead," he says.

Ginny cocks her head and frowns. She turns and runs to Claire who exits the butcher shop. Claire greets her with a warm kiss to each cheek. Hans stares in shock and slips away unnoticed.

"You look more and more like her every day," Claire says. "You and Aurelie could have been twins." Claire swipes once at the edge of her eyes to knock away a tear.

"I miss her," Ginny says and hooks her arm under Claire's.

"I've got a package to pick up," Claire says. Ginny nods and peeks into the shadows where Hans stood, but he's nowhere to be seen. "Meet me by the bakery there later and we'll walk home together."

Ginny nods and returns to George and the gang from school who linger by the well.

14

ON ANOTHER DAY I watch Jean-Michel ease out of his coma and return to life. His blue eyes flicker open and scan the cave walls and the men around him. Others look scruffy and injured too with beard growth and a strong scent of wood smoke and sweat. He struggles to get to his feet and escape.

"Hold on, buddy. You'll need some more R&R before you can head down the mountain," one of the Frenchmen says.

"I'm going. Now."

"Well, it's up to you. But I wouldn't advise it," says a man with a beard and traces of black from cinders on his face.

"Where are the others?" Jean-Michel's eyes bore into the stranger with an intense violence. A scar marks the man's right cheek under the scruffy beard.

"Hey, I'm on your side," he says. "Don't know where your buddies are. We found you and brought you here." Jean-Michel tests his body and feels the throbbing in his shoulder. "Yep, you got good and shot," the man says light and easy.

"What the hell?!" Jean-Michel tries to reel around and head to the cave exit, but his head spins. "What happened? Did we lose everyone?"

He doesn't recognize the man and wonders whose side he's on. "I don't remember you fighting with us."

"Our guys didn't."

"Who are you?"

"We're the Secret Army. The winning resistance army." He sounds proud, cocky.

"Great, that makes three sides to battle. The Germans, the collaborators, and you guys who don't know what the hell you're doing," Jean-Michel grumbles. As a Maquis resistance fighter, he's not sure if these guys are trustworthy. "You'll just muck things up and confuse everyone."

"Now there's a real show of gratitude," says one of the guys sipping hot coffee from a tin cup. "Considerin' that we saved your life. In fact Jacques over there insisted that we keep you alive. I voted to shoot you on the spot."

Jean-Michel glares. For him, the only thing worse than being dead, is being indebted to a fellow Frenchman who saved his life. He grimaces. "How'd we do?"

"Well your guys got pretty dispersed and we can't tell much. It doesn't look good. Most have gone into hiding, like us. The Germans came on pretty strong."

"Give him the good news, Jacques," the guy by the fire spouts.

"The English finally believe we're worth something. They're sending more ammunition. Another parachute drop by the Royal Air Force. The BBC called for an insurrection."

"Lot of good that did back in January," another man mutters. "Got most of us shot. Easy for that idiot to say on the radio from the safety of his posh room in England."

Jean-Michel listens and assesses them. He's heard about the raids of the Secret Army on the mountain villages. They steal money and loot. He grumbles under his breath. "We're fighting to free our people. You have different aims. You just want power."

One of the men spits into the fire and the spittle sizzles angrily as it lands on a hot stone. "Thankless bastard," he says and points a gun in Jean-Michel's direction. "Get out." Jean-Michel struggles to his feet and stumbles into the snow. He looks at the night sky and knows where he is based on the stars and he starts walking to Claire's house. It may take him hours on the goat paths and with his injury, but he must go.

I'm worried about Ginny and head off to find her. She concentrates on the pistachio-green and pink frosted pastries behind the windows at the bakery. Claire walks toward us, caught up in her thoughts. Ginny waves and races to embrace Claire.

"Claire…" Ginny doesn't know what more to say. Claire is like an idol to her, with her beautiful red lipstick, skirts, and high heels. Ginny speaks in a rush, all out of breath. "I see her. Sometimes she comes to me… especially when I pray."

Claire tosses her cigarette butt into the gutter and gives a hard stare at the girl.

"I thought you were her," Claire says releasing a long exhale of smoke. "You two look so much alike."

"Do you see her sometimes too?" Ginny's eyes search Claire's. But Claire keeps up her nonchalant, emotionless façade, and doesn't want to admit anything. That's Claire. Cool. Indifferent on the surface. Boiling with passion, anger, energy, and unspoken thoughts beneath.

"I miss her," Ginny says.

"So do I." Ginny falls in step with Claire as she heads to the colonel's house with her basket of eggs, fresh fruit, and bacon. "Look at this stuff," she scoffs. "All of the stuff the Germans and Vichy can buy, but we can't. Such a waste. They don't even appreciate it."

"I…" Ginny almost speaks of Hans, but stops.

"Yes, what is it Ginny?" Claire seems distracted.

"Nothing." Ginny twiddles her hair around her finger and wonders what I would want her to do. Then she starts again. "Do you remember if Aurelie lost her brooch?"

Claire's sharp eyes soften. "The one with the pearls."

"She loved it," Ginny says. "Would she have given it to someone you think?"

"It was from Dad. So, no, I don't' think so." Claire says. "She always kept it pinned to her coat. We would've heard about a loss. She would've made us search the whole town. And if she gave it away, well she would have had to love the person very much. Why do you ask?"

Ginny shrugs.

"Even though we lived under the same roof, sometimes I didn't pay her enough attention. She needed more after Mom died."

"I miss her. I wish Aurelie could come back." Ginny stares down at the cobblestone street as she walks and sucks unconsciously on a lock of her blond hair.

"You need some new clothes," Claire says glancing at Ginny from the side. The buttons of her blouse gape open at her breasts and her skirts are a bit too short. But who has money for clothes these days?! And besides the tailor and his wife fled months ago. "Ask your mother if you can come by later and I'll give you some things that I've outgrown."

"Thank you. I'd like that."

"I have another errand before I can go. So you'll have to head back alone. I'll be home around eight."

"That's too late. Mom won't let me go out then. Not with the problems now. It doesn't matter that your house is just next door." Ginny refers to the curfew and people who disappear never to be heard from again. Reporting it to the French police makes no difference. They say they know nothing about the disappearances. But most people believe they do.

"Well, come right after school then."

"Ok. Thanks Claire." Ginny skips off smiling.

15

AT NIGHT TIME when stillness descends, I return to my room in Naehelle's house to try to make sense of the things I've seen and heard. I'm starting to accept living in this in-between space, even though I still ache to hug Ginny and kiss Hans. Naehelle calls me into the salon and it's so flooded with warmth and golden light that I melt into a sensation of well-being and goodness and temporarily forget the pain of separation. Tonight she's preparing chocolate-chip cookies. I smell them baking. Even in this in-between, she has the power to create certain experiences and I yearn for being back in my dad's house drinking hot chocolate next to the old cat curled by the fire. But the comfort and appeal of this beautiful place she has created makes my old home less and less appealing. Naehelle places the plate of hot cookies on the table and I sit down.

"A glass of milk too?"

"Yes, please." It's odd how the essence of milk is almost as good as drinking it and feeling it wash over my tongue. "It's not real milk," I say.

"Well, it is," Naehelle says. "Just not physical. Not in the way you were used to having it before anyway. The essence is the same. Some say it's even better."

I shrug and put my head on my hand and mope. "How did I die?"

This puts a damper on her upbeat attitude.

"First, you're not dead."

"I know. I know that's what you say. You say that I've just lost my body. But to all of those people I love the most in the entire world, I'm dead."

"Yes. That's true."

"I don't understand the point of it? Why? Why bring me here? Why did I have to lose my body?" Naehelle stares back at me with gentle eyes.

"I'm sorry," she says.

"I want my body back." Mixed emotions rise up into my throat and a pained look fills my eyes.

"I'm sorry."

A rage rushes through me. "How did I die?! I want to know." I stamp my foot. But it's not a physical foot, just a stirring of will and energy. And that energy makes the table shake. "At least you can tell me that."

Naehelle collapses into a chair by the table and I feel bad that I've brought her down. "Sweetie, there are things that I don't know…"

"And things you won't tell me! I'm not a child anymore. Tell me what you know. Now!" My anger rocks the portraits on the wall and Roy scurries under the table to hide.

"I don't know everything."

"So, what do you know?"

"I don't know *why*…"

"But you do know how." I can sense it. She knows how I died. But she won't tell me.

"Yes, but…" She sighs and Roy jumps on her lap.

"I'm sorry I yelled." I apologize but keep my arms crossed over my chest.

"I like to focus on the good and beautiful." Naehelle gazes at a glowing painting of a tree on the wall behind me.

"And how I died wasn't beautiful?"

"You need to piece that together yourself." She lowers her eyes and won't look at me.

"But how?! It's not like I have a lot of resources available right here, you know!"

"Follow your instincts. You'll be guided. Ask the right questions and expect the answers."

"Is that all you can give me?"

"Why is it important for you to know? Why can't you just accept it and move on?"

"Because I can't. I've got to know what happened. I feel like I won't be set free until I do. And as much as I like your warm and beautiful place, I don't want to stay stuck here forever."

16

"ABOUT THE GIRL, the one they found recently…," the man in the café says to Ginny's father. Ginny's dad instinctively pulls her close. "Go get a *biscuit*," he says to Ginny. He hands her a ration ticket and some coins and watches her go. But I stay close and listen to their conversation. The girl he speaks of must be the one I saw in the woods where Herr Schmid lingered and the blood stains marked the snow.

"What do the police say?" her father says. The man scoffs.

"Damned worthless police. Won't say or do anything. Especially if they think it's one of theirs or a German involved."

"Third one so far," another guy mumbles. "There's a difference between war and flat out murder. I'm keeping my girl under lock and key. Don't trust the bastards."

The young priest enters and orders a morning glass of red wine. "A constitutional," he says to explain, and downs it. He replaces the glass on the bar and the bartender refills it. The priest looks calmer now and moves slowly to the table where the preoccupied men sit. "Morning, men," he says, mouth tight with consternation.

"Morning, Father," they say.

The thirty year-old priest sits down heavily. He's younger than most of them and looks exhausted like he's been up all night. A faint growth of hair shows on his unshaven chin.

"Looks like you need a vacation, Father," one man says.

"Another glass of wine's what I need." He shakes his head with disgust, then returns to his role as the authority who intervenes between them and God. "Some deaths are too shocking and brutal." One of the men brings him another glass of wine. "Thank you, my son." He stares into the glass a moment. "The family of the girl they found. They asked me to give a burial mass today."

"But wasn't she a gypsy?" Ginny's uncle protests.

"Can't they love Jesus too?" the priest says.

"We think it's the same guy who did it. Did her death resemble the others, Father?"

The priest lowers his head and traces a cross on the table with his index finger. "I saw bruises at the throat. Marks of strangulation, probably. Not unlike the others." The priest looks into his empty wine glass and orders another. "Brutal." He looks up realizing he probably should have said less.

Ginny's dad shudders. He watches Ginny with hawk eyes as she stands close to the empty glass pastry case. "Does God have anything to say about that?" he grumbles.

"I wish I had words of wisdom for you, my son, but I don't. God works in mysterious ways." Ginny's dad smirks and glares into his empty espresso cup.

"Do you know who is doing this? Has someone confessed?" Ginny's father demands. The priest protects himself in a dark cloak of silence.

"I cannot say…many men come to confess terrible things. But none such have confessed about this."

"Well the French police may not bother to look for him, but we will. And when we find him, there'll be hell to pay," Ginny's dad says, but the threat feels empty of power. "We count on you to tell us if you know something."

The priest stands, lips clenched into a narrow line. "I must go. God bless," he says and his black soutane brushes around his ankles as he walks to the door. "Bless the youth. They're our hope for the future," the priest says and makes the sign of the cross over Ginny's head. She looks up innocently at him and smiles. "Suppose I'll see you at the burial later?" he says, and my heart sinks. I know they are talking about me.

Ginny nods.

The first crocuses push up through the snow to prove the ground has thawed some and spring's approaching. At home Claire puts on fresh lipstick and dad shaves and dresses in his one starched, white shirt. When the priest knocks at the door, they trade glances. Claire opens the door and lets him in. She automatically makes the sign of the cross from her forehead to her heart, but shows no conviction. Her thoughts on this resound loud and clear. "Why bother?!" I hear. "What good did religion ever do?" The thoughts come out so loud that I wonder if the priest hears or at least feels her attitude.

"Thank you for coming." Dad extends a gray hand, spotted with old age, and the priest shakes.

"Yes. Well…" he says scanning the small, unadorned room.

"Would you like some coffee, Father?" Dad says.

"No, thank you."

"Well, let's get on with it," Claire says.

Outdoors, Dad climbs to the roof and uses ropes and a system of pulleys to gently ease my body to the ground. The priest waits beside Farmer Elli and the two of them help to adjust the shrouded body onto the cart. Some blonde curls fall out from beneath the yellowed cloth and Claire tucks them gently back under the fabric. Chunks of snow and ice have gathered in the folds, but today the sun shines and water droplets drip from the edges. I follow their every action intently. Worried. Concerned. Heavy-hearted. Hoping they will take care of my body and knowing that it really doesn't matter. With the help of the others, Dad places my corpse in a wooden casket that he made by hand. He's carved delicate Savoy hearts in one row all around the edges and it looks beautiful. Together, they place it on Farmer Elli's horse-drawn cart. The priest climbs up and sits next to the farmer. Claire and Dad walk slowly behind.

"Father, did they find out how it happened with this one?" I pay special attention when I hear Farmer Elli address the priest from his privileged perch on the wagon. He jerks his head toward the back of the wagon. The priest clears his throat. His eyes dart away. He lights a cigarette and says nothing. The Farmer sighs and drops the subject. Claire knocks on the door at Ginny's house while the cart plods on, and Ginny joins them on their way to the cemetery. Ginny's mom respectfully nods at Claire and touches her shoulder in a sign of condolence, but stays behind.

At the graveyard, the ancient gravestones stand in the oldest part of the cemetery. But our family is in the newer part. The site of Mom's tombstone hits me in the gut and if I had physical eyes, I would cry a flood of tears. A muddy hole is dug out next to her grave. It's a sunny and clear day for the first day of April, and if it were not for this burial, I might feel happy and carefree. I might even have joked about Didier, dad's helper, with Ginny. I long to be with them, but know that I can't, not like before. The acute sense of separation fills me with an endless throbbing heartache.

My father reaches out to lift the casket from the farmer's cart. I feel the weight of his anguish and grief and hear his thoughts. "I let her down," his remorse whispers. "Why couldn't I protect her?" But Claire feels worse. She stops him, pushes the casket back onto the cart, and pulls back the lid.

"Just a moment," she says. "I want to do it properly."

She unfolds the shroud and I see my face fully now. It's frozen and beautiful, like a teenager's. So peaceful and preserved by the cold. My lips are dull and my skin looks very pale and unnaturally white. My hands lie stiff and hard, folded over my chest, one on top of the other. Claire takes out her lipstick rubs some on her finger and then spreads it tenderly over my lips. She adds a dash to my cheeks too and blends it in so that my face looks more alive, more like me, like I used to look when I was vibrant, and alive in that body.

"Thank you, Claire," I whisper grateful for her attention. "How did I die, Claire? Please tell me."

The words seem to nudge her to search for clues and she pulls back the shroud all the way down to my feet. Her heart aches to see me this way, but I feel her close it tight to numb out as she examines my corpse. I look closely at it too. My brown wool coat hides the everyday dress I love, my red and white pinafore with lace. My thick wool tights protected my cold legs, but the tights are ripped now. Something white like egg white or a cream has hardened and spotted my thighs and dark tights. My father looks away, not wanting to know. But Claire wants to see. I want her to see and discover what happened too. She touches the spots on my tights with her finger and a realization flashes across her face. A sense of rage rises up in her throat, but she swallows it back down and examines my fingernails and sees dried blood underneath.

"Oh my god," she whispers. Her eyes close tight against the pain. Her head goes limp and she almost loses the tight control over her emotions. Then she takes a deep breath and lifts her head. "Here, help me," she says to Ginny.

Together they pull the white shroud off of my rigid legs. "She won't need this anymore." Claire wraps a white wool blanket around me and it looks as if they're tucking me into bed one last time. Ginny tenderly adjusts my hair. And as she does, I see the marks. Thick, black bruises.

"Ahh," Ginny jerks her hands away and sucks in cold air. She covers her mouth with both hands.

My bruises look like the ones that Sylvie girl has. How did I get those ugly marks on my neck?! Bruises don't accompany a fever. The imprints look deep, like a thumb and finger prints maybe. Claire gently runs her index finger along the line of bruises. For a moment she turns away and a pained look crosses her face. Then she adjusts my coat.

"Look, it's torn," Ginny says. At the left breast where I once wore the silver and pearl pin I see a tear where it was ripped off. Ginny flattens the tear with her palm and feels a lump in my breast coat pocket below the rip. She reaches in to find one of the pearls from the setting. "Here," she holds it in her palm and gives it to Claire who stuffs it in her coat.

"That's where I wore the brooch, Claire. I don't remember giving it to Hans. How did he get it? Did you give it to him?" I suggest the ideas to her, but I'm not sure she receives them. Before Claire covers my face with the linen shroud one last time, she rubs some of her solid amber perfume behind my ears and on the tip of my nose. Ginny leans in and tenderly kisses my cheek. Their kindness and attention draw tears of gratitude to my eyes.

The priest performs a small ceremony and Dad latches the casket closed. The grave-diggers ease my body into the ground. Ginny cries and clings to Claire, but dad seems all out of tears since Mom passed. I want to protest and beg them to stop. But it's clear my body's not any good to anyone now.

When the first shovels of dirt and mud and snow begin to fall on the dry wood of the casket, my heart sinks. Is this all there is? A rage fills me. I had a whole life before me. And it ended. Nothing makes sense. How did my neck get hurt? My father never laid a hand on me except to carefully adjust my curls. Alain loved me and hugged me like a brother. Claire…did Claire hate me? Could she have been jealous of me and Hans? Claire must be responsible for my death. That's why she feels so guilty.

I try very hard to remember what happened. But time has become so flexible. Like time is always now, always right here. When I had a body, time expanded into mealtimes, bedtimes, days, months and years. But without one, the expansion feels infinite and unfathomable. If I can think of a place I am there. If I can remember someone or an event, I'm immediately there with them at that place and time. The question seems to be how to remember. When I had a body, smells triggered memories. A flower or visiting a place opened up a whole film of memories. But here, where everything is new and unfamiliar, I have nothing that brings up the memories. Even pain brought back memories. The pain of a bruised knee reminded me of the pleasure of not having pain. Sadness still reminds me of joy. That world of opposites keeps everything spinning forward. With no opposites or no desires or pain or joy, then everything comes to a halt and life has no meaning. There's less friction and therefore less of a chance to grow.

How I envy Herr Schmid with his strong body and his pain as he sits alone and drinks to numb out. His pain is not the kind that I knew. He suffers the anguish of a split soul trying to reunite with its better half. Until then a battle ensues where his darkness seeks to dominate and drive him. The shadow takes him over now and he tries to drown it in drink. But the alcohol only leaves more room for it to thrive as the kindness in him shrinks.

Ginny follows Claire home. Claire lays an array of clothes from her small closet on the bed.

"I can take them home and try them," Ginny says as she rubs the fabric of an angora sweater to her cheek.

"It won't take long to try them on here. It'll save you from lugging them home and back." Ginny pulls off her tan wool coat and yanks her worn grey sweater over her head.

"Here, try this one." Claire hands her the angora sweater that no longer fits her. I'd hoped to get that sweater. The pink color flatters Ginny's pale skin. But Ginny doesn't have much enthusiasm for clothes at the moment. "The color suits you. What do you think?" Claire says.

"It's nice." Ginny nods. Eyes full of sadness.

"I miss her too. But, know what?" Ginny stares at Claire.

"No."

"There's nothing you can do about it," Claire says.

"If I could bring her back, I would."

"Me too," Claire says. "Me too."

I want so much to be with them, talk with them, and laugh like we used to, but they don't consciously hear me now. I move close to Ginny and whisper in her ear.

"How did I die, Ginny? Ask Claire, how did Aurelie die?" Ginny's mouth puckers and her forehead crinkles.

"Did you see the marks?" Ginny says.

Claire flinches. Turns her back, shoulders curled forward. A hand over her mouth to stifle her emotions. When she collects her calm and the emotion passes, she folds the clothes Ginny doesn't want and returns them to her armoire.

"Dad said it was a fall," Claire whispers. "But I believe someone hurt her."

Ginny waits, attentive and silent. "Who?!" I whisper to Ginny. "Ask her! Who bruised me?"

"I wonder who would hurt her?" Ginny says. "She was so sweet and gentle."

Claire continues folding a plaid blouse and with a deep sob, the emotions flood out. She shakes her head. "I don't know," her voice cracks. I don't know. I don't know....I was supposed to stay with her. I left her for just an hour in the little café. And when I got back she was gone."

Ginny wraps her arms around Claire. "And then they found her in the field?" Ginny says. Claire nods, sits folded over on the bed. Ginny places a hand gently on her shoulder. "It's not your fault. She loved you very much." Claire squeezes Ginny's hand.

17

GINNY'S NOT HERSELF today. Usually happy and carefree, yesterday's burial leaves her pondering life and death. She walks head down and contemplates a small dead bird beside a large poplar tree near the canal, close to the Lover's Bridge. She loves birds. Once we saw a beautiful rare water bird with a yellow breast and long thin tail land on the street by the old prison. She stood transfixed as it rested and waited there, bobbing its tail up and down. The rare bird and beautiful Ginny mutually admired each other. I tried to pull her away, bored with the bird. "It's amazing," she said. "It's like I know its heart." She leaned down, held out a crumb of a *baguette*. The bird plucked it from her hands and then flew off. But the baby bird beside her foot today will not fly ever again and I know that it reminds her of me. School has let out for the day and Ginny should be walking home, but her grief keeps her anchored to the thoughts of the tiny, decaying body of the bird. Her thoughts turn her so deeply inward that she doesn't feel the woman's presence.

"Are you thinking of her?" Sister Marie says. Her cheeks sag from fatigue and age. "I heard they put her in the ground yesterday."

Ginny remains deep in the pain of contemplation and nods. "Yes, Sister. It was dreadful to see."

"I can imagine. But you will see her again, you know."

Ginny looks up, eyes pleading. "Yes, if you believe in something more."

Sister Marie holds her gaze on Ginny. But Ginny's eyes dart away.

When she turns back, I notice how she studies a shadow disappearing across the field.

"I've got to go." Ginny curtsies to the Sister and follows the shadow that walks ahead, hands jammed deep in its pockets. The figure ahead of her scans the horizon, the cloudy, gray sky, the dirty snow where a few crocuses attempt to poke their thin, pale heads into the light. Ginny slips quietly along into the shadows to trail him. I recognize Hans, head pulled down into his wool scarf and leather coat so that the bill of his officer's hat sticks out like the snout of a turtle.

"Where are you going?" Ginny says from behind. Her mouth tightens up and she frowns. He turns back slowly, pale and speechless.

"But they buried you yesterday," he says.

Ginny stares accusingly. A wild boar lingers at the side of the clearing and Herr Schmid suddenly holds a pistol in his hand. But Ginny steps between them.

"Don't be afraid of her," she says.

"Wild boars can kill you. They're dangerous." He holds his trembling arm out straight, threatening to shoot.

"Are you afraid of death?" She assesses him an instant. "She's just a mother looking for food," Ginny says in an even, kind tone. She possesses a power of courage that I'd never imagined. "She has a brood of babies. Leave her alone." Herr Schmid refuses to holster his gun. Ginny pushes his pistol to the ground. She leaves him standing alone believing he's seen me in the flesh.

⊷

Killing is such an intimate thing, probably more intimate than making love. I hear Hans' thoughts so clearly as he passes a butcher cleaning a hare in the shop. The blood splattering over the butcher's hands sends his mind reeling back. I watch his memories unfold like a film of the past. With some people it's easy to see this way. Seventeen-year-old Hans stood next to his younger brother and the commandant ordered his brother to shoot a middle-aged Jewish man.

"No different than an animal," the commandant said. "You've shot rabbits before!"

But that's not how Hans felt. His brother stood before the Jewish man, arm extended, pistol in hand. The Jewish man looked up at Hans' brother from where he cowered on bare knees. The man's eyes looked large and doe-like, full of resignation and despair. An innocent Jewish man in Stuttgart who had stolen some food for his daughter. But in the Hitler Youth, boys learned early on to follow orders or pay the consequences. Hans' brother intentionally aimed to one side to avoid hurting the man.

"Shoot it," the commandant yelled. "Shoot the animal, you coward." His brother shot again, far to the right. The commandant's face burned red with rage. But Hans' brother threw the pistol at his feet.

"His family is starving. I will not shoot him, Herr Commandant," his brother said softly.

"He's a thief and he's Jewish, you coward!" The angry commandant shot Herr Schmid's brother in the thigh. Hans flinched, then steeled his emotions as his brother collapsed in pain.

"You. You do it," the commandant ordered Hans. "Or do you have yellow coward's blood in your veins too?"

Hans stared in a state of shock and resisted running to his injured brother. The other officers laughed nervously and called him a coward, a "pussy". Herr Schmid's hand trembled. It was not in his sensitive nature to kill. He loved life too much, the scent of his mother's garden roses. The joy of cool water over his skin. The poetry of Rilke. The music of Shubert.

The Jewish man cowered on the ground with a hand over his mouth. "Do it sir," the Jewish man said. "I would rather die by your hand than his." He nodded toward the commandant.

With reluctance and revulsion, Hans looked into the soul of the man before him. He never prayed, but he thought of Mother Mary as he closed his eyes, and pulled the trigger. Spots of warm blood fell on Hans' hand. And the horror of the hole left in the man's head, made him want to fall on his knees and wretch. He locked his knees to keep from collapsing. The other men watched and any reaction of revulsion or show of emotion on his part would have meant certain punishment from the commandant. But Hans stared between his injured brother and the lifeless body at his feet. Guilt, horror, and shock of killing a fellow man ached through his being. Hans' brother looked at him with pity. His brother, Axel, died peacefully a week later in Hans' arms. But the Jewish man's soul continues to linger in Herr Schimd's mind.

I watch his thoughts whirr and feel sorry for him. Poor man. Herr Schmid had to shoot. Poor men who were shot. That day, kind and loving Hans lost ground to the cool, efficient killing machine, Herr Schmid. In his memory, I watch him later robotically execute people. The commandant orders it, and Herr Schmid mindlessly obeys out of fear. He leads groups to open holes in a forest, shuts down his feelings, and shoots. Perched on the edge of a newly dug grave, he stared at the bodies of men, women, and children, and marveled at his ability to feel nothing. A tremble of shock races through me and I turn my eyes away.

"It's horrid." I rush to Naehelle and my refuge of a room and hide beneath the duvet. "How can such horrors exist in the world?!" This is not the man I know. Roy nuzzles my arm to comfort me and Naehelle brings me hot tea. "I won't go back. I've seen too much. And it's a terrible place. I don't understand. Life or death or war."

"No one understands it," Naehelle says.

"Not even God?"

"I don't know," Naehelle says.

"Why did they have to die? He killed all of those people. But that's not who he is inside. I can feel it. Hans is sensitive. Caring. He has a beautiful light buried inside. Sometimes I catch a glimpse."

"Your Herr Schmid…he's a special man. He yearns for redemption. But he has a split soul."

I think of Ginny who would not even kill a beetle or a spider or a fly. Instead, she'd trap them and carefully put them outdoors with great love and care. But a whole world shatters around us now as war tears up lives, creates wounds, and leaves deep emotional scars that no one can see. From my bed, I think of Herr Schmid and I see him drunk. Trying to numb out or awaken to something deeper. He's so strange and unfamiliar now. He's not at all who I thought he was. I was a naïve girl. And he's a troubled man.

"But why?" I plead. "Why would this be allowed in the world? It's so terrible."

Naehelle lowers her voice to a whisper as if someone might hear. "I believe not even God knows."

18

JEAN-MICHEL TAPS AT my parent's door. It's late in the evening and Claire stiffens and listens intently, wary of late visitors. "It's me, Jean-Michel," he whispers in a low, gruff voice. She cracks open the door and pulls him in out of the cold and holds him in a deep embrace. He flinches from the pain.

"Loosen up just a little, woman," he says and she steps back.

"I'm sorry. I had to be sure you were real and not a ghost." She hugs him again. "They've just raided the town. Set up barbed wire check points everywhere. How'd you get in? Have you seen Alain and my father?" She talks fast and speaks between kisses to his cracked lips. "You're the most beautiful site I've seen."

"You're not happy to see me are you?" he says, surly as usual. She steps back and holds his face in her hands to take in his wry smile and kisses him hard. Euphoric.

"No. Not at all." She smiles hugely, eyes rimmed with tears. Her head collapses on his chest. "God, I thought you were dead."

"Me too," he says. He inches slowly into the room clutching his shoulder.

"You're wounded?" She notices his gaunt cheeks and shoulders slumped inward.

"You're a vision, Claire." His eyes fill with liquid love. She takes him into her small room and removes his dirty clothes to examine the wound.

"You still smell like a goat." He shivers and she tucks wool blankets around him. "I'm going to get the doctor."

"No," he says.

"Doc Norbert is on our side." She holds a palm to his head. "You have a fever and that ugly wound looks infected. It won't wait. I'll be back soon." Jean-Michel feels too weak to protest.

"Someone betrayed us. Trust no one."

"If I don't go now, you could die. I'm going to risk it. But believe me, he's on our side."

"If you're caught aiding a Maquis resistance fighter, *you* could die."

"And if I don't help one, you could die," she says. "I'll be back."

"Claire," he calls to her. She stops at the door and turns to face him. "I love you."

Over the days that follow, Claire nurses Jean-Michel at night. During the day she forces him to rest quietly in the apple cellar outside the house where he hides underground.

"I've got to pick up some *packages*," she tells him and he nods with understanding.

Claire slips out during the days and picks up "packages" that she delivers to Sister Marie. The "packages" are scared, scrawny, Jewish kids, anywhere from six to fifteen years old who arrive clandestinely. They're separated from their parents and accompanied by unfamiliar adults, protectors who seek to help them escape the trains that would ship them to Drancy, outside of Paris.

As I observe from this high perspective, I see that Claire acts as a tiny piece of the network and doesn't seem to know the others involved. It's the only way to keep it intact and keep the others safe. I watch Sister Marie take the "packages" to Father Ansen who drives them to safe houses or hides them in underground passages. If I were one of those kids, Claire would insist that I go to school. But not these children. They hide from the Nazis. Claire brings the frightened children food she snitches from the colonel and makes sacrifices from her own rations. I watch to see how much of the network I can understand. At certain times Father Ansen guides the orphaned kids one or two at a time, to hide in the houses of old farmers on the trail through the villages on the back roads through France to Switzerland about thirty miles away. Claire works to get some of them travel papers and the right to walk to freedom across the border. It's especially important to change the kids' names and hide their Jewish heritage. The unfortunate ones without papers slip through holes cut in the barbed wire that separates the two countries. Some are caught and returned by the Swiss authorities. I'm not sure they are all Jewish children. The Nazis declared many enemies and their decrees sow fear and anxiety. Claire speaks little and holds a firm, inexpressive face. Her heart aches for the children she smuggles, but she buries her emotions deep inside to keep them hidden, to keep her safe, and her head cool. I had no idea she lived this secret life.

Ginny's been doing odd things too. I'm only beginning to understand. I remember when her mother took her to the priest to have her baptized a few years ago. She wasn't baptized when she was born. Not like the rest of us. But in the cathedral at the age of eleven, the priest sprinkled water on her and made her learn the catechism. He gave her a baptism certificate and rosary and reminded her to repeat the "Hail Mary's". She forgets to carry the wooden beads with her most days. But Sister Marie gently reminds her of their importance.

I never understood. But now as I look into Ginny's house, I see her mother reading the Talmud, the Jewish bible. She folds it and hides it in a tear in the mattress beneath her pillow. Her parents always celebrated different feast days from ours – at least until the crackdown. They never made a public show of it, but they were different. I knew from the time Mom sent a slab of bacon home with Ginny, and Ginny's mom made her kindly return it. This difference is what makes Ginny's family less and less at ease. Ginny's mom packs Ginny's clothes and prepares to send her to Switzerland. She aims to take all of the family to America soon. But Ginny will go first to live with her aunt. I overhear Ginny's mom whispering to Claire. Something about visas and travel papers and the cost of getting them from the corrupt French government officials.

Ginny's in bed asleep already. I visit her in her dreams. I miss her so much, but at least in dreams we can talk and play. It's not like before. She usually doesn't remember our conversations when she wakes up. And the hardest part for me? I can't hug her or hold her hand or make her laugh. On those days when we want so much to connect, she wakes up sad and I leave a snail trail of sadness when I walk beside her. I want so much to be back with her, back in my body, back with my feet on the ground wearing my black leather shoes and my favorite pinafore dress. And taste the hot cocoa with whipped cream or eat shoestring licorice. These are the days when I'm filled with longing and discontent. The days when I remember how good things on earth smell and taste and feel. Even the pain of a scraped knee feels better than the numbness of this in-between where I live now. I hate it. I hate Naehelle who won't tell me much. I hate that girl with the bruises who sits and mopes around all of the time in the house. She seems to only want to read books or knit or do boring things.

Today I can't stand it. It's rainy down there by the lake. Ginny's in school. Herr Schmid's taken up with a meeting with the German Gestapo officers who have come to plan strategy and defend against increasing sabotage by the resistance fighters. Claire continues to nurse Jean-Michel. Alain, my brother is doing something on the sly at the garage where he works. He uses electrical wires and powders. Things I don't understand. It's weird being here. Seeing so much…and yet not understanding how things fit together, or how life gets on without me.

So bored by their world, today I wander restlessly around Naehelle's living room confined by my frustration and bad mood. The girl with the bruises, the one who I saw when Herr Schmid went to the forest, sits at the table playing with a wooden top. The sound of the top spinning and falling against the table when the momentum stops, annoys me. But the worst is that Roy seems to prefer her to me right now.

"Can't you just stop that?!" I growl. "That girl won't stop, Naehelle. Make her stop it."

The girl's head jerks up and Naehelle watches us from the kitchen. She's like a guardian or a protective mother. Always there and yet not. Lurking. Present. But not invasive or imposing. Tears form at the edge of the girl's eyes.

"Silvie. My name's Silvie." She pauses as she speaks and then returns to her rhythmic spinning of the top. I walk to her and snatch the top from the table. "Give it back!"

"No!" I'm angry now. "Why should I?"

"Because if you make an enemy of me you'll never find out what you need to know about Hans Schmid."

This stops me dead. "You can't know him better than me."

"I do. I know things about him that would shock you. I know things about him and you that you refuse to see."

Now I'm fuming. "Who do you think you are?!"

"A dead girl who's been sent here to the in-between to help another dead girl who doesn't want it."

I'm frozen. Trembling with fury. "You don't know anything about me!"

"I do. I know that he killed you."

"Who? Who killed me?!"

"Hans Schmid." I lunge at her already-bruised throat. Naehelle steps between us.

"Stop it, you two." Her soft, soothing energy turns my anger to tears. Sylvie cries too. Naehelle encircles an arm around both of us so that we share in her beautiful energy. My tears fade.

"Is it true?" I ask Naehelle.

"Come," she says and the three of us are lifted to a mountain-like perch where we see a scene, like a movie and yet it's real.

Sixteen-year-old Silvie dressed in her finest red skirt and a black lace shawl stares at some cash in her hand and I know Hans gave it to her. She slips out of the camp where her tribe stays, out to the edge of the forest. He waits there in the shadows, eyes hooded. Silvie's heart races from fear and excitement. She's an adventurer, a curious girl who loves mystery and thrills. She especially loves that she's caught the attention of a powerful German officer and thinks that maybe he will take her away with him to a better life. Hans, cloaked in mystery and charm, is enough to make any woman desire him. His blue eyes shimmer in the dark light of the moon and Silvie moves to him like a moth to a flame. His beguiling aura draws her in close. They don't speak the same language, but she says a few words to him in French and he leans down as if to kiss her cheek, but Silvie darts away, like a sly cat. She circles around him while humming a gypsy song, like she's casting a spell. Dancing in close and farther away. All the time eyeing him, like she's the one who will take him when she wants.

"Come," he says. "You are a beautiful woman." He touches the tips of the long black hair on her shoulders and beckons her deeper into the forest to the clearing. He sits on a flat rock shaped like a chair and Silvie slips in close until she stands shoulder to shoulder with him.

She points at the brilliant stars shining against the velvety blackness of the night sky, her head back. I feel her desire for him, her urge to kiss him. But he withholds and waits as if he wants her to make the first move and offer herself to him first. Silvie trembles with excitement like she can stand no more. A man like this has never shown interest in her before. She's drawn to him like a magnet, pulled into a kiss. When her lips, tinted red with berries, touch his, Silvie lights up like a radiant angel. Her aura brightens with pleasure and she sighs.

"I've not been loved by a man before," she says.

He slips behind her and pulls her close, sheltering her against the night chill. I stare in awe and wonder at the energy between them, lost in the scenes unfurling before me, totally lost in their movie and unaware of myself as if I'm sitting in a cinema. Silvie tosses her head back and laughs at his hungry kisses on her throat. In the throes of pleasure, his strong, agile hands close around her small neck and tighten, closing off her windpipe. Silvie's beautiful face pales against her black hair. Her eyes grow wide. She feels the pleasure turn to peril and her fingernails claw at his hands, but he's steady, powerful and determined to hold on tight until her body loses life and her soul slips away. His adrenaline spikes and he feels alive once again, enlivened by the struggle for life. When Silvie's body goes limp, he hugs her body to his chest and lays her on the hard ground and walks away. But first he yanks the silver "S" charm bracelet from her wrist and pockets it.

I'm stunned, speechless.

"No," I protest. "That's not real. Like movies aren't real!"

Tears flutter at the edges of Silvie's almond shaped eyes.

"That can't be the way it happened!" I insist. "It's not true." But a sickening feeling inside me tells me it is true. "What did you do to him? What did you do to deserve that?" I accuse Silvie.

"Why do you defend him?" Naehelle says. "She did nothing wrong. It was karma. He has drawn her in again and again over many lifetimes. Each time he has killed her.

"But not anymore," Silvie says, defiantly. "I've learned my lesson. I was able to watch and clearly understand. He only causes pain. Now that I know, I've let go of him and it can't happen to me again. He has no more power over me. I'm free."

"But that has nothing to do with me," I protest. Then I see the images. Things too difficult to remember are suddenly loosened. The film of my own demise begins. And suddenly we're back watching the last night I can remember and the memories I'd blocked are freed.

On that evening, Claire leads me into a café and orders me an expensive hot chocolate.

"Don't leave," she says. "I'll be back soon." I stare at her, defiant. I'd felt sure she was going to sneak off to meet Jean-Michel. Now I know she picked up more Jewish kids. The film of that moment unwinds. I sit with my head on my hand, twirling the spoon in my empty cup and fantasizing about Hans. When I look up, he stands beyond the window shrouded in shadows. A shiver of nerves rush through me and my fantasies win over. At first I hesitate and think of Claire, but my cup is empty. The pastry shop owner closes the thick green shutters to comply with the blackout, and Hans' eyes are the last thing I see shining as the light fades. I cross the threshold to meet him. He lures me into the darkness, his gloved hand around the back of my neck. The anxiety and excitement mount as we disappear into the broken garden.

"No!" I scream and cover my eyes. "Stop it. I don't want to see." But I already know. He murdered me too. Poor Claire. Now I understand her guilt. She left me alone for a moment, then I was gone.

Naehelle squeezes my hand and we're back in her house. I cower under the duvet. Unspeaking. Shivering. Afraid. You might ask, "How can someone who's died be afraid?" I'm no different than you. I feel just like you do. Only I can't face my fears. I don't see my way out of the pain and anguish. So I sleep. I lose consciousness and let the world go by without me for as long as I can. In the spirit world, they might say I'm a sick spirit. My spirit's filled with remorse for trusting him. For breaking Claire's heart. For losing my life and believing in a false love. I'm one aching, walking wound and I don't have any way to remedy it.

19

THAT NIGHT I get up the courage to go to him. He drinks alone in his rooms to numb out. Schubert's music plays in the background. I watch him from the doorway and wonder if he will see me. His head jerks up from the mess on his desk. His face pales.

"Aurelie," he whispers. My heart rents in two. I stare and wonder why he betrayed and murdered, and then I remember the Jewish man who he'd shot and all of the others. His own brother preferred to die rather than kill a fellow human being. But most of the Nazis became like Hans.

His uneaten meal sits on his desk along with a stack of chocolate and cakes. I remember when I was starving and he fed me. My mind struggles with the paradox. The red velour chair creeks when I settle into it and stare into the fire mulling over my loss. Stony. Silent. Heavy with grief.

He watches me with pain-filled eyes.

"I know what you did," I say. I should feel angry, but I'm flooded with a sense of despair instead. The drink releases the soft, sensitive Hans who sits there like an open, festering wound, paralyzed by pain and fear.

"Aurelie?" he says, eyes wide and uncomprehending.

"You destroyed my body. But you can't kill my spirit. If you learn nothing else, let this one thing remain."

He stares in disbelief.

"How can I ever forgive you? But why? Why did you do it?" He cowers and covers his ears with his hands, but my thoughts pierce into him and cold shivers raise the hairs on his arms. My death at his hands binds us in unimaginable ways. He takes a deep breath and works to regain solid footing.

"You're not real." He waves his hand to brush me away. "You're just my sick imagination."

"I'm as real as you are."

"Aahh." He smashes a cushion to his face to block me out, but nothing can keep me away now. "Leave me in peace."

"I loved you," I say. "You knew it." Then I realize he didn't. He can't. He doesn't even love himself. The beauty and love I'd seen in him was all mine, all my own radiance mirrored back to me.

"Stop," he begs.

He sweeps the files off of his desk onto the floor. The crystal glasses at hand fly against the stone bordering the fireplace. He grabs a sharp shard of broken glass and cuts his arm. In his room he digs out the whip from under his suitcase, rips off his shirt, and beats the bare flesh of his back. But not even this soothes him. My silver and pearl pin sits on his mantel above his bedroom fireplace. In a moment of desperation, when the emotional pain becomes too intense, he jabs the thick, shiny needle from the brooch through the flesh. It hits on open space between his sternum and ribs and he grits his teeth. The physical pain appears to bring relief, a momentary distraction from the ache in his soul.

"There. For you, Aurelie." His eyes scan the air to search for me. "Are you happy?"

"I'm glad you ache too," I say, but that's not how I feel. I feel sorry for him instead and want him to heal.

⚜

Claire arrives early the next day and finds him rigid and cold, slumped over his desk. She tries to pretend things are normal between them, but her stiffness belies her anger. "I've brought you fresh croissants and found two fresh eggs. You should be grateful. I could have given them to Herr Kaiser."

Hans focuses stonily on his cold coffee in a thin porcelain cup. He says nothing, but stares into the unknown. Once Claire places the goods in the kitchen, she returns to him. I sit on the red velour chair and he watches me. I know he sees me. He can't not see me, now that we're bound by my death and my brooch buried near his heart. I stand there, staring back at him to remind him of what he's done.

"Is something wrong?" Claire glances at the red velour seat, but I'm invisible to her now. Only he sees me. He fears me, and this brings some small satisfaction. It means that some part of him still has a conscience.

In the light of day, I watch Ginny walk to school and smell the tiny violets growing along the road. Despite the war and hunger, she smiles at the touch of the flower petals against the tips of her delicate fingers and the scent lights her up with pleasure. A tiny rabbit appears and sniffs the air. I dream of all that I will miss, I feel frustrated, angry, betrayed, hurt. All of the fear Hans created in me has no place to go, no way to be released. And so, I sit there seething and burning inside, angry that I've gone from an innocent child to a woman who knows more than anyone should about human nature in such a short life. I would have been sixteen tomorrow. But with no body, time no longer means anything. Not like it did before. And I have Herr Schmid to thank for this. Anger seethes in my heart, the anger of frustration. And the more frustrated and impotent I feel about not being able to effect change around me, the more it grows. The one change I can bring comes through appearing to him. That's at least one of my powers and I intend to use it so that he gains no peace as long as he lives. I will be there to constantly remind him of the pain he caused. So I sit there and seethe and he stares at me, while Claire sees nothing. I don't want her to see me this way. It's my choice.

"You look blanched like you've seen a ghost," Claire says and tries to make it sound surly and ironic, but it falls flat.

"Stop the chatter," he growls.

"Well, if you don't need anything, I'm going." Claire marches to the door, glances back briefly, then goes on her way.

He says nothing. No protest. Not a sound. He looks like an empty shell of a man, like those strange cicadas that leave their shells and then you never see the living part, only the shell.

"Wait," he says as she crosses the threshold. "I need some gauze. And some poultice. For a wound."

"If you'd stop hurting yourself you'd not need it." She talks back at him, flippant and edgy. "You're half mad, aren't you? You don't know what's real anymore and what isn't. You should stop taking those 'vitamins'."

"Living with demons isn't easy." He stares at me. I see the demons that eat away at him in his dreams. They rip away his flesh and it grows back to be ripped away again.

"I've got to go. Herr Kaiser awaits." Claire's curls bounce as she pivots on her high heels and crosses the threshold, heels banging angrily against the wooden floor.

"Are you screwing him too?" he says dully.

"You're a bastard, you know that?"

He grunts. "The crate's for you."

Claire lodges the wooden crate of German army rations on her hip. The door slams behind her and I continue to sit stonily in the red velour chair. He remains immobile, staring into nothingness. The clock strikes and he finally pulls on his uniform jacket and his leather coat and struts rigidly out the door.

20

MORE SS OFFICERS arrive from Germany's highest ranks. Chests puffed up and shoulders back. Big, important men. They seem not to notice the people on Annecy's streets, the way the locals spit on the ground behind them, even though spitting, just like profanity has been outlawed by the Germans. The rebellious, independent, spirit of my mountain people pushes them to fight. And though I watch some local people collaborate and take advantage of the state of affairs out of love of money, almost no one loves the Germans or money more than they love the land here. In fact, their presence tests how much we love it.

It's funny that I couldn't see this before. I was too young, too self-absorbed, too much of a child, but lots of things become clearer now. Unlike people in other parts of France where they adopted the attitude of the path of least resistance, here, in the Savoy, we take the occupation as a personal affront. The German officers may not see the twitch of the eyelid of the woman they just passed, the way she clings to her intention for liberation and revenge. But it's there. The officers may not notice the men who smoke with immobile, inexpressive faces inside of the Bergère Café and see the disdain and rebellious gleam in their eyes. But those looks promise that sooner or later the Germans will get what's due. They may not see my brother, Alain, as he slips under the bridge near where they found my body, but he's there, hooking up wires to an explosive unit that will blow the concrete to bits and disrupt the rail line.

Another convoy of German SS officers arrives from out of the town. Herr Schmid sets off to meet them at the entrance to the city. Before he arrives, a bomb explodes sending bits of SS officers and high-ranking Germans flying high into the air and splattering against the buildings on the Avenue de Genève. Herr Schmid sees the explosion from a block away. An instant sooner and he too would have been splattered against the walls and onto the street. The fear of his own death turns his blue irises stormy black from anxiety. The German survivors recuperate from the blast and rise from the ruins like scorched phoenixes. The survivors along with Herr Schmid corral local French men from the neighborhood who just happen to be walking in side streets or innocently standing by when it happened. Under Herr Schmid's orders, the Germans execute all nineteen men they round up, aged sixteen to seventy. Their bodies fill the hole left by the blast.

"Let that be a lesson to them," the commandant snaps.

In his apartment, Herr Schmid steels his hands from shaking as he serves the German officers the Burgundy wine. The commandant curses about the lowly French and disgusting Jews. From their thoughts and the energy they carry, I see little films of the atrocities going on in Germany. Their inhumanity horrifies me. I'm swept up by a protective angel who soothes me and shows me a perspective from a very high place. All of Europe is clouded over with a dark shadow of fear and oppression. The smoke from bodies burning in gas chambers haunts the whole of Germany and seeps out all over Europe, including France. But the prayers of the victims fly out like flashes of lightening to overpower the darkness. A deep nausea sweeps through me and I feel engulfed in darkness so severe that it could suck a soul into oblivion. But around the Haute Savoy, the light grows where men hide in the mountain plateaus and caves and prepare to fight. And around Claire who is linked to a whole chain of courageous men and women working together to save innocent people. The Jews, gypsies, Poles, handicapped children, and political refugees. The network leads them to freedom across the border into Switzerland. Their chain of resistance sparkles like stars at night to conquer the darkness. The battle between light and dark rages, and even though I see the light, terrible clouds of darkness roll in and it looks like the darkness will win.

❧

Ginny carries a small handmade bracelet to my house and knocks at the door. She's learned to work with thin strips of bark and bits of yarn to create a colorful and beautiful braid with a small metal hook taken from one of her mom's old dresses. Claire watches from behind the window as Ginny walks up the steps with the gift in her hand. Ginny waves at her and smiles.

"*Bonjour, ma belle*," Claire says.

"Hi Claire," Ginny says.

"Come in for some chicory coffee? It's about all we've got."

"No thanks. Here." She holds out the gift. "You know what day it is?"

"It's Saturday."

"Besides that."

"It's your birthday?"

"It's our birthday. Hers was on the same day as mine." Ginny holds out her palm with the bracelet on it. "I made this for her so she'll know I didn't forget." Claire's eyes brim with tears.

"Oh, honey." Energy rises in her throat and Claire chokes down the emotion. "That's so sweet." Claire lifts the thin, finely woven bracelet from Ginny's palm and examines it delicately. "I'll put it here. This is where I've kept her photo. Next to Mom's." She lays the bracelet in front of my photo like an offering and brushes back the tears. Claire can't afford to be weak and vulnerable right now, she thinks. She hugs Ginny abruptly and pushes her away to regain composure.

"I think of her all the time," Ginny says. "I can't help it. I wish I could help her in some way."

Claire shrugs, her throat constricted.

"Mom says to light a candle for her, to keep her memory alive. So that's what I do almost every day."

"Thank you, Ginny." Claire touches Ginny's shoulders and turns her toward the door. "I need to go soon. Herr Schmid's Germans expect supper." She sighs. "Pigs," she mutters.

"Bye." Ginny waves and smiles as she skips down the stairs. Claire lights a candle and places it in front of my photo and pockets the bracelet.

"Time to go," Claire says to herself. With a tense sigh and a last look in the mirror, she wraps her scarf tighter around her throat and walks out to the shed. The old bike that Jean-Michel gave her leans against the weathered wood. She thinks of him recuperating in the cellar as she pedals carefully over the melting snow and stops at the cemetery. The ground continues to thaw and my grave looks like an unhealed rusty gash in the earth. Claire kneels and places the bracelet on my gravestone. "Happy Birthday, Aurelie. If you can hear me. I'm so sorry."

"I can hear you. I can. Thank you! Thank you. I love you, Claire. Please don't be sorry. It's not your fault." I reach out and brush her cheek gently and shivers rush through her. She runs a hand through her curls as if to brush it away and stands. Kicks the kickstand of her bike up and pedals into town to do her errands for Herr Kaiser and Herr Schmid.

Sometimes, and I don't know how, I'm able to effect changes and move things in the material world. Out of sheer will, I pick up the bracelet. It's light like wind and filled with Ginny's beautiful energy. I return the bracelet to Ginny's home and lay it next to the candle she lit for me and whisper, "Thank you." I want her to know I've received the energy of her gift and I really appreciate it.

21

SOLDIERS BLOCK THE entrance to the building where Herr Schmid gathers with the officers. Since the bombing, they've cracked down on security. Claire says some words in German to them and shows them her baskets of food. One of them searches the baskets while the other runs up the steep steps and returns. He jerks his head for Claire to enter. She's admitted into the apartment and goes straight to the kitchen where she overhears the men's voices coming from behind closed doors.

"Bloody swine terrorists." One man's voice sends chills up her spine and makes the hairs stand on the back of her neck. His voice resounds sharp and harried, like a tightly strung instrument that will break at any instant causing unpredictable havoc. "You're in charge of clandestine services and surveillance, Schmid. How should I report this serious failure to the Reich?" A steely silence follows where no one dares to speak.

From where Claire works in the kitchen, she strains to hear the men. She feels the threat intended to Herr Schmid in the man's voice. A needle of dread shoots through her as she realizes they don't even protect and safeguard their own. She wants to flee, but that's not an option.

"Sir," Herr Schmid says. "The French terrorists here sabotage roads and cut electrical and phone lines. We're understaffed. We need more men to keep order."

I watch the commandant with the bluish stubble growing out of his sallow skin. His beady eyes seem limited in their capacity for humanity. In his mind I see structure. Pigeon holes. Things fit into slots in his mind or else. He is not nuanced or filled with a vast palette of emotion like Hans Schmid. The commandant studies Hans with displeasure.

"Ahh. More men is it? Is that the excuse for your lack of control and information?"

"Sir, they are hard to break, these mountain people. Tough like rams," Herr Schmid says. The commandant listens as he continues. "It's not like the rest of France where people just go on with life and accept occupation. Here they fight us. Every day."

"Well said, Herr Schmid," the local commandant confers. "We must inflict greater strain on the population," he says. "Another round up of undesirables and terrorists will teach them. You have compiled a list, Herr Schmid?"

He nods.

"Yes, another raid is in order," the high commandant says. "We must strike at the heart of their economic life and strangle them." He holds a dried chicken neck in his fist and cracks the bones apart for a chilling effect.

Claire silently arranges the rich array of cabbage, apples, chestnuts, and a goose from the butcher and listens intently to the conversation. I hear her thoughts. *More hard times coming.* Then she thinks of the food. Whatever rationing the Savoyards undergo, it's not applied to the German officers who will feast on a splendid supper.

"And do it right," Herr Schmid had hissed at Claire. "Or else... "Fear of reprisal weighed on him if he failed to provide what the high ranking German SS visitors expected.

"Anything for the Reich," she had muttered sarcastically. She thinks of it as she splits open the chestnuts and chops the cabbage, and temporarily forgets about the officers and the madness in the other room. For a moment she starts to hum, then stops.

"All of the prisons and internment centers are full," Herr Schmid says. "We'll need a temporary holding place."

"Well, then they'll be deported," she hears the man with the bow-string voice say. Herr Schmid mentions a boat.

"It sits empty on the quay in this season."

"The pleasure boat, *La France*," Claire says to herself.

"*Bootsflüchtlinge*," one man says and laughs without joy. *Boat people.*

"They're going to imprison people on that frigid boat?" Claire translates in her mind. "He just called them 'boat people.'" The men's laughter erupts from the other room. They laugh without mirth.

"So we will use the boat. Ah yes, a brilliant idea." The man with the strained voice says. "The most undesirable will be deported to work for the Motherland. It's for the good of society. The camps continue to exterminate vermin and protect our purity. Of course we will continue to use our procedures to extract information first. Eh, Herr Schmid?"

A chilling darkness descends around them and Claire feels more frightened as she realizes they are speaking not only about the Jews they capture, but also about political dissidents or "terrorists" as they call them, and "undesirables". Undesirables could be anyone for any reason. Her heart trembles for Alain and Dad. Her thoughts race. *They plan to use La France, the glass-walled tour boat associated with lazy Sundays on the lake as a prison.* Her heart beats wildly and she wants to flee at the stupid irony of it.

I slip into the room, into my red velour chair. Herr Schmid has given up his desk to a man with medals on his chest and more badges than his own. That medaled-man carries an aura of steel, and feels impenetrable like concrete. I can't see his thoughts. The whole group of them scheme over maps and lists of names. The air around them sends chills through me. Inhuman. Inhumane.

When their lunch is ready, Claire writes a note on a slip of paper that one of the guards carries to Herr Schmid.

From the kitchen, Claire hears a burst of footsteps echo lightly up the staircase and the door squeaks open.

"Ginny?" Claire gasps. "What are you doing here? I can't believe they let you in."

Ginny shrugs and giggles lightly. Herr Schmid slams into the room, boots banging hard against the wooden floors.

"*Schiesse!*" His steel-blue eyes bore into Claire and his hands tremble. He aims to unleash his fury on her until he spies Ginny. His pale eyes widen with terror. He thinks Ginny is me. Claire notices the shift and appears momentarily puzzled.

"*Guten tag*," Ginny says softly stepping out from behind Claire, her hands clasped nervously in front of her. She wears one of Claire's second hand skirts which makes her look more mature. Her cheeks flush from embarrassment. Hans Schmid reaches for Ginny's face and holds her chin.

"You're not a ghost."

"Your supper is ready," Claire says stepping between them. "Sir." She adds with a touch of surliness. "If you wait too long, the *tartiflette* will be overdone. Herr Commandant seems in a bad enough mood already."

Hans stares down at Claire as she struggles to reconcile the man who gives her food for starving children with the person who begged her for a flogging on bended knees.

He turns his back on them. "Supper is served gentlemen," he announces.

Claire turns to Ginny and shakes her. She hisses between clenched teeth. "Why have you come? I can't believe they let you in. It's dangerous now. They've barricaded the roads into town since the explosion, and everyone must be careful. Especially you!"

Ginny says nothing. She simply opens her palm and shows Claire the bracelet. "Look. It's a sign. She's with us. She knows we love her and still think about her." Ginny's innocence makes Claire's heart melt with love and affection.

"Oh darling." She takes Ginny in her arms. "I left it on her grave on my way here," Claire says.

"But that's not where I found it. It was beside the candle I lit at home." Ginny's eyes sparkle with excitement. And she really wants Claire to understand. "Can't you see? She brought it back to me. She wanted me to know she got her present."

"I'm sure there's some other explanation. Maybe your mother found it and brought it back home," Claire says to humor her.

"No!" I say.

"No!" Ginny insists along with me. She knows. They both know, but Claire's afraid to admit it, afraid of what that might mean and how it would shift her world to know about the in-between and life beyond death. A brief recollection of the kindling sticks I collected on the stoop comes back, but Claire pushes it away.

"I've got to serve them," Claire says. "But no more risks like today. Okay? Go to Father Ansen and he will help you return safely home."

Ginny nods obediently.

"Here. Wear this for good luck. She would want you to." Claire hooks the bracelet around Ginny's wrist before Ginny slips quietly out the door.

22

THE SUPPER ENDS and Claire's ears burn from the knowledge of the Germans' plans. She overhears names and details. They aim to destroy the town by destroying those who control its shops and businesses. She takes mental notes of every single detail so she can write them down later. The Germans stay on late and drink cognac looted during their latest sweep of the town. In Claire's moments of cleaning and clearing plates and wiping down the crystal glasses, she sees Herr Schmid open a slat in his desk and hide some papers.

When the men move into another room to smoke, Claire watches carefully for opportunities to steal spare moments when they'll be occupied so she can get the list. The door remains open a crack and Claire continues to clear the table. Herr Schmid serves them the finest desert wine, the best French cognacs, and aged Armagnac that dates into the last century. With the aid of alcohol and good food, the Gestapo officers shed their foul moods. Even the sallow commandant slaps Herr Schmid on the back in an unusual show of affection and camaraderie. Claire takes advantage of the good humor to move to the desk and retrieve the paper. She sneaks it temporarily into the bathroom. When she spreads it open, a list of familiar names appear. Her hands shake as she runs her index finger down the page.

She quickly copies what she can. She memorizes the rest of the names written in Herr Schmid's handwriting.

"Ellie Marie Nardin, the school teacher. Abbey Finderol from the Saint Mary of the Fins Chruch. Dr. Vincent Norbert." Claire's head spins as she memorizes. "I've got to warn them. Especially Sister Marie and Doc Norbert," she thinks. "He saved my Jean-Michel. I've got to get out of here and let them know so they can escape." Claire sneaks her list into her garter and returns to replace the list in Herr Schmid's desk. She brushes the largest crumbs from the table and each time glances at the room where Herr Schmid sits with the Gestapo who, now with a little drink, begin to look like demons. When the way appears clear, she removes the table cloth and carries it to the desk at the corner of the room, not far from the dining table. Her hands shake from the strain. I remain silent and let her concentrate. If she's caught, she knows she may not survive. As she leans into the desk to slide the secret list back into place, Herr Schmid emerges and his eyes see her behind the wine-stained linen tablecloth. Her heart stops. Too late. She stands still. Paralyzed like a doe in the lights of an oncoming car.

"Just uhh," she says. "Removing this." She holds up the table cloth.

But strangely, the wine has brought a glimmer of softness to Hans' eyes. I even see the affection there and if the General were not in the other room, I know Hans would sweep her into his arms and kiss her. He loves her in his own way. I don't understand it, but he does. Claire lowers her eyes and makes as if to move to the window where she might shake out the cloth and remove the last crumbs, if she could still open windows and let light out and fresh air in. "Oh, I keep forgetting we can't open the windows," Claire says. "God forbid any light should be seen."

"Herr Schmid." The commandant calls him back to the smoking room. Hans reluctantly turns away. Heart pounding, Claire quickly replaces the list and disappears into the kitchen. She downs a glass of cognac leftover by one of the Germans to soothe her nerves. Her task feels complete, and she can take no more of the strain of possibly being caught. Her mind fills with shadows of the rumors of those who are caught and deported to Buchenwald, heads shaven, starved, often to death.

Claire's dying for some fresh air. What she wouldn't give to open the window and be done with the oppression of it all. They all live in dark houses

- day and night now. When the blackout ordinance arrived, it required that all windows of the houses in town and the surrounding villages hide their light behind black cloth or black paper. If the German guards pass a house at night and a single pin prick of light escapes, the inhabitants inside are fined or worse. Imprisoned or treated as traitors. The blackout, the authorities say, protects the town's citizens from passing British or American planes that drop bombs at night. The bombers aim to dampen the German war effort by taking out the ball-bearing factory in town. But more often the bombs land on residential houses instead.

In the smoking room, the electric lights dim and the commandant lights candles that give off a reddish glow. The officers hover around the man with the tense voice. I watch him cut his own finger and draw a swastika on the table in blood. In his mind, he follows the rituals the SS taught them to do before any battle or raid. He calls out to the dark spirits to come and be with them and guide their mission to successful completion. An astounding rush of dark forces hurl in. I see that terrible Monstrous Force with tentacles hovering above the commandant. A tentacle of the Monstrous Force is latched into his back. While the tentacled monster saps the commandant's life energy, the commandant, through the monster, is linked to the power of the monster's accumulated darkness. A shiver runs through me and my hair stands on end. I fear for Claire and hide to avoid attracting the attention of these powerful forms of darkness. I also surround Claire and myself with light and love to protect us. Claire feels the oppressive shift in the energy too.

"I can't breathe," she thinks. "I've got to get out of here." She straightens the last dish towel, picks up her purse, and leaves. "Tell him I've gone," she says to the men guarding the door.

"I'm glad to be out of there. Too much German air," she mutters to herself as she descends the stairs. In the courtyard below she unlocks her bike, but a man grabs her wrist from the darkness and holds a hand over her mouth. She struggles and kicks to free herself. A second man helps to restrain her. One man whispers in her ear, "Come with us quietly and you won't be harmed."

Claire glances at her bike leaning against the wall and decides not to protest. They lead her through dark alleys and passages into the inky night.

Thick fog has rolled in from over the lake and engulfed the city. Claire cannot see the arches of the building at the end of the block and the gas lamps shed eerie auras of gray light. Claire walks between the two men, trembling and uncertain.

I can't help her, but I want to. I wish I knew more about where they are taking her, but tonight my vision of their world is like the fog. Obscured and murky. The streets stand deserted. Since the German occupation and the deaths, no one feels safe. There are other deaths too. Deaths of young men and women ferried away into the prisons, tortured, and executed, then buried in the forests. They're taken because someone has pointed a finger of suspicion, or simply because they looked at a German and that German decided to take them away and use his power. Death hangs over the city like a shroud.

The men bind Claire's eyes with a black handkerchief and lead her on.

"Where are you taking me?" she says.

"Best be quiet, woman," one voice whispers, his hot breath close to her ear. His breath smells of cigarette smoke and alcohol. After some time, she hears voices and the sound of scuffling feet as a door opens and some light and warmth seep in around the edges of the blindfold. I'm wondering what can I do? How can I help and protect her? My helplessness brings anxiety, but I try to not communicate it to her and I see how limited my abilities can be to help.

23

THE MEN LEAD her through a narrow stone entrance and down a stair-well into a well-lit, underground room. For the moment I'm condemned to watching without being able to help.

"Welcome to the headquarters of the Secret Army," a man says. Some-one removes the blindfold and Claire adjusts her hair and scowls.

"Not a nice way to greet a lady," she says angrily.

"A lady," he scoffs. "…does not hang out with dirty Krauts."

Claire and the man stare each other down.

"So, whose side are you on?" He says casually and taps a filter-less cigarette against the scarred wooden table top. The man who sits on the other side of the wooden table wears a beret. His dark hair waves around the edges of the cap and over his forehead. Despite his age of maybe thirty, he looks much older. He casually rolls the cigarette between his index finger and thumb.

"Who are you?" Claire says. She's heard of the many different resistance groups in the area. Some of their reputations reveal their frequent impa-tience and occasional inhumanity. Not to mention a penchant for looting and theft when they can get away with it.

"I'm Thomas Matin. We know you're working for Herr Schmid."

"I bring him provisions and cook," Claire says coolly. "That's it."

"Oh? You're not a traitor giving him precious resistance secrets skimmed from Jean-Michel and others?"

"Absolutely not." Claire glares.

"We've got your father."

"Where?" She jerks her head around to scan the dark room.

"He's been helping us," Thomas says casually.

"That's not true."

"Proves how little you know about what's going on, my dear. Even in your own family."

Thomas nods at the two men who abducted Claire. He sits behind his desk, hands behind his head, and looks at the ceiling contemplating. He stands, slaps Claire, then grabs her chin between his thumb and index finger.

"I don't know who you're working for. But if you don't help us out, we have other ways of extracting information," he says to Claire. She grits her teeth and refuses to move or speak. "Search her," he orders the men. The men move in and empty her purse.

"Here, boss." The gun falls on the table. They search her pockets, pull open her bra, and lift her skirt. Thomas takes great pleasure in running his hand along the inside of her thighs to search her stockings. He feels the piece of paper under her garter.

"Oh, so there's where she hides the goods." She struggles to keep the hard-won list. Thomas jerks it away and smiles as he unfolds the paper. "So what's this?"

"I want to see my father," Claire snaps. The men loosen their grip on her and she rebuttons her blouse and pulls down her skirt.

"All in good time," Thomas says. "Let's have a little chat about your shopping list."

Claire flinches. This strange war counts many sides to the resistance. It's more like a river with lots of tributaries than a straight line with good on one side and bad on the other. The Communist stretch along one line. Traditionalist who want things to go back to the way they were, occupy another line. The Fascists sit on one side. The brigands who simply want to profit from the spoils of war makeup another line of the many rivers. Clarie notices the initials, "S.A." scratched into the wooden table. She has heard both Jean-Michel and Herr Schmid talk about the Secret Army in unkind terms. No one can be trusted it seems.

"Bring him in," Thomas says. He runs his finger down the list. "Oh there we are. The Krauts are planning another good haul, eh?"

Claire rushes to Father and I'm happy to see he's safe too. "They're okay Claire. They're not enemies." Clarie stares back doubtfully and hugs him. "They're not allies either," he whispers close to her ear then steps away.

"How do I know I can trust you?" Claire says to Thomas.

"You don't," Thomas says with a charming smile. He looks like a mischievous school boy with a grin now. His charisma shows through. Maybe that's why people follow him. "But you don't have much of a choice as I see it."

Claire's not one to talk much. She observes and knows that it's best to keep your mouth shut. "I'm only a housekeeper for the Germans. Just so I can get some extra money and food. Not so much different than you all. I don't give a hoot about politics or resistance or war. I hate war."

"Oh, really. That's not what Jean-Michel says."

Her eyes narrow at the mention of his name.

"We met in the mountains during that battle in March. I thought you'd be more grateful. I kept these crazy men from shooting him." He motions to the men standing on either side of her.

Claire eyes Dad. I remind her to look for the scar on the man's cheek. Jean-Michel told her about the man with a scar who helped him in the cave when he woke from his injury. Right cheek. On the bone. There it is. See Claire. There it is. He is who he says he is. I remember him, only then he looked black from soot from the cave fire and several days beard growth. Now he's clean, his mouth curled up at the corner smiling as he tries to charm Claire into liking him. The tough approach will not work with her. He sees her strong will and ability to resist, even against great violence.

He softens his tactics and pours her a whiskey. "Sit down."

She does.

"So, how's the German Gestapo?"

"Unhappy with the bomb on Avenue de Genève." She glares at Thomas. "You have anything to do with it?"

"Better ask your brother."

"I cook and clean for the Germans. I don't get involved in their machinations. I don't want to know the rest."

"Tell me about your shopping list." He nods at the list of names and offers Claire a cigarette. She reluctantly accepts, but says nothing. "We know you're helping people to hide and escape. If we were working with the Germans, you'd be on the train to Auschwitz already." He leans in and lights her cigarette and casually lights his too. "You're working with the Maquis resistance, right?"

Claire sits, back straight. Dad stands behind her.

"Who are you working with?" Claire exhales smoke.

"We're working with the Allies to destroy the bloody Germans. We need to know their next move so we can prepare. The BBC has given us a message from de Gaulle to resist. And to wait," Thomas says.

Claire scans her mind for all of the information and rumors she's heard about the Secret Army. Jean-Michel says they're another group of resistance fighters, not as trustworthy as his Maquis resistance group. She knows of at least four other resistance groups in the area now and debates the merits of helping Thomas' Secret Army.

"They're planning another sweep of the city. We'll be under lockdown again soon, so you must work fast to help those people on the list or they will be caught," Claire says. She narrows her eyes and stares at his reaction. Thomas meets her gaze.

"So that's what the list is about." Thomas taps his finger on it. Claire makes no sign of yes or no. "The prisons are full. Will they shoot everyone? They've already executed hundreds of people." Thomas stares thoughtfully at the list.

"They're going to put people on the boat, *La France* until they're sent away to German camps or tortured or tried for treason.

"*La France*, huh? Now that's a hoot. From holiday boat to wartime prison."

Claire pulls back her shoulders out of pride and fearlessness. "Those on the list will not have such a sense of humor," she scoffs. "You must work fast to save them. They plan to act tomorrow."

"We can save the ones who count," Thomas says.

Claire reaches out to nab the list, but he grabs it first and the paper tears in two. She knows that if Jean-Michel and his group get the names they will warn everyone tonight. But this man, she does not trust.

"You must save all of them." But she somehow feels they won't. *Minable*, despicable, she thinks so loudly that I wonder how they can't hear her. Claire's used to memorizing names to give to Jean-Michel. Many of the names remain in her mind. She aims to recreate the list as soon as they free her. "**A.** Monsieur et Madame Aaron. **B.** No one. **C.** Monsieur Caron. **D.** Monsieur Donato..." She glances over at her father who nods okay. Something in her tells her that these men do not have the same integrity as Jean-Michel and his men.

Thomas reads some of the list aloud and Claire reinforces her memory. "Monseiur Valerio of Garage Valerio, on Avenue de Geneve where Alain works. Monsieur Nardin. Monsieur and Madame Lens, the school teacher and schoolmaster. Madame Grillon, the owner of the tobacco and cigarette shop. Madame Heritier, the seamstress. Monsieur Levier, the lawyer." The names trip off of his tongue. She remembers them in alphabetical order and recites them in her mind. This is the way she trained herself to remember.

"They're shop owners, lawyers, and school teachers. Why they aim to destroy the fabric of the economy. Soon this will be a ghost town." Thomas says as he runs a finger down the list of names. "Alain, your brother, where is he?"

"Why do you want to know?" Claire stares at him. Then she shrugs. "I've not seen him in months." I know she lies. And they suspect it too.

"Well, he's good with explosives," Thomas says. "We know he's the one who did a good job on that train bridge. If you see him, tell him we have some work for him." Thomas seems satisfied. "Get them out of here," he tells the men.

"You've made me lose precious time. They'll start the round up early," Claire hisses. "You need to warn the men and women now. If you don't pull them out of their beds, the Germans will. You will warn them, won't you?" Clarie stares down at him. He smiles up and exhales a long and casual puff of smoke.

"All things in good time, my dear," he says. "Oh, and don't forget this." He pushes the small pistol across the table to her. She pockets it. "Of course, you know they'll shoot you if they find it on you."

Claire's face refuses to gift him with a single emotion as she pockets the gun.

"Let's go, papa." She hooks her arm under Father's. Her voice sounds tender, concerned. The men blindfold Claire and Dad to lead them out so they can't find this hiding place.

"Their blood will be on your hands," she hisses at Thomas. One of the men puts a gag around her mouth.

"I like having the last word," Thomas says. "Au revoir."

The two men who abducted Claire lead them out, and after what seems like a long walk, they release Claire and Dad and disappear into the shadows.

"I'll have to come back for the bike later. It's way on the other side of town. Now we must hurry," Claire says. I watch them rush back home. They take a hidden path to avoid the German patrols. "How did you get involved with those men? Did you tell them anything?" Claire says. Father looks up at her wearily.

"It's okay, *ma chérie*. Everything's going to be okay," he says. Jean-Michel intercepts them just before they make it into the house and kisses Claire on the mouth.

"It's past two a.m. Where the hell have you been?" He glares at them.

"Your friends at the Secret Army abducted us. Remember Thomas Matin? Says he met you in the mountains," Claire growls. "They've made me lose way too much time. Here. Quickly now." She gives him the names as she remembers them. Jean-Michel quickly writes them down.

"You'll be okay?" Claire touches his healing wound.

"Almost as good as new," he says with a boyish smile and sets off with Dad to warn those in danger before it's too late.

"Thank you," she says relieved and kisses him again. "Especially think of Doc Norbert. He's on the list too. Save him. Go!"

24

I GO TO Hans' tonight. The Gestapo men have gone and left him alone, tense, and sleepless, so he sits behind his desk drinking and staring into the fire. The warmth he felt for Claire has disappeared. Instead, the spine-chilling dark forces stirred up by the Gestapo still fill the corners of his apartment. The bloody swastika anchored a column of darkness in Herr Schimd's space and the tentacles of dark energy latch into Hans even deeper than before.

I take my place in the red velour seat and watch him. If I could I would make him see the suffering he caused. I might even hurt him in return for what he did. But right now, I feel helpless and sit there seething. As he glances at the fire, I watch his thoughts begin to form as he reviews the day. The men. His fear of the general and of death. His need to make a good impression on the officers from Berlin. The plan to raid the town tomorrow. The bloody explosion from the past days. The unsatisfactory behavior of Claire who let the girl in. The ghost of me. Who was not a ghost, but a real girl. The softness. The guilelessness. The tenderness of her lips and the smooth porcelain skin. The soft bounce of her sandy, blonde curls. The innocent sparkle in her brown eyes. The legs. Her arms. Her breasts. The flush of her cheeks when he looked at her too closely. *So much like Aurelie,* he thinks. *What's her name?*

Something sickly takes root in him. The images of her churn around inside and possess him. Then one goal forms. He wants to possess her. To touch her. My stomach stops, churns. There's a sensation of sickness and nausea as I watch the details and the plan take shape in his mind. An obsession invades him and Ginny's innocent beauty becomes the thing he wants most. He's sure she wants him too. This will help him to feel real again. Right now, he's numb, empty, sick, powerless. But that connection with her will make him a man. He knows he's less significant than a shadow. Empty. Without substance and if the German Gestapo discover this secret behind his mask, that he's a nobody, they will kill him too. He must do something to become a real man again. He must. The thought of her fills his mind over and over and over. He sees only her. No matter how much I try to shatter his resolve and get his attention, I'm no longer present to him. He's annihilated me from his memory and replaced me with Ginny. Her face, so like mine, anchors in his mind and he wants to recall her name. His brain is on fire with desire and determination. A renewed sense of purpose buds in him. He's alive now. He knows what's coming next.

As his thoughts form, I recognize that this is how he thought of me and fear fills my gut. The future reveals itself. Poor Ginny lying dead. Bruises on her throat. The plan. To lure her in. Make her believe he's her friend because he cared for me. It may take time and patience. But he's like an animal, a vicious cat playing with an innocent baby bird and enjoying the execution.

I'm aghast about what he plans to do. My disgust for him increases and the dark forces hover in close until I feel them tighten around me and I see black tentacles reach out. It feels like they'll invade me if they can. I've got to get out of here. Before something bad happens to me.

⋙

I rush back to Naehelle in a panic. "Help. You've got to help. I've got to know." I'm trembling and anxious, crying astral tears that sparkle like diamonds. She wraps a blanket around my shoulders and places her hand gently on my arm as I stand by her hearth where the fire burns. I cower there, feeling so, so cold despite the soothing warmth. "He's going to kill her. What can I do? I've got to stop him."

Naehelle's silence speaks. Her eyes fill with sadness and resignation.

"Don't tell me that I'm able to see, but I can do nothing about it! I know his plan and I've got to stop him. He'll hurt Ginny."

"Dear," Naehelle says softly. "Take a breath. Warm up and calm down."

Silvie stands by the doorway listening. "Go away," I say. She hovers there, undeserving and shy. "What do you want?"

Silvie shrugs.

"Naehelle! What can we do? You've got to help me."

Panic ripples through the air of her house and Roy cowers under the chair by the fire. "We're not accustomed to such an uproar here," she says. "Please be calm. We like calm and serenity here."

But her insistence on calm irks me. "I AM NOT GOING TO BE CALM!" I yell. The waves of agitation shake the walls and even knock some books off of her tidy book shelves.

"My dear, please." She sighs like I'm some spoiled child. "You don't understand."

"No, I don't. So please tell me right now! I've got to stop that murderer."

"You can't," she says.

"What do you mean, I can't?" I'm livid. So angry that I could burn a hole in the table with my index finger if I wanted to, I believe. That's the power of anger. I touch my finger to her table to test. The hot rage leaves a scorch mark and some smoke rises from the contact.

"Stop that. You behave."

"No! Not until you tell me how I can help. You said that's why I'm here, so you'd better give me some answers fast, or else I will burst. Maybe into flames." Naehelle sucks in her breath and settles into a chair by the fire. She tries to remain calm and unfettered. But her silence makes me want to roar.

"It's like this, Aurelie. In the in-between, we cannot *do* anything. We're not supposed to have any power over their world. We can see and know, but we can't *do* anything. You've broken all of the rules by appearing to your sister and Ginny and Herr Schmid. You're not even supposed to be able to do that. But somehow you do."

"I was able to move the bracelet." I stare hard at her.

"You shouldn't be able to. It's against the rules."

"I'm not going to follow rules that make no sense when I may be able to save her life!"

"You're not supposed to interfere." Naehelle stands and drifts out of the room past Silvie. "I'm going to bed. You deal with it," she says to Silvie.

I sit on the couch by the fire, my head in my hands. Silvie hovers quietly by the fire. "Do you believe her? That we have no power? That I can see this and do absolutely nothing?"

Silvie shakes her head no. "I think I can help," she says.

25

HERR SCHMID'S DISTRACTED as Ralph, his helper, lays out his clothes and helps him put on his uniform. I hear his thoughts so clearly. A strategy forms in Herr Schmid's head. He's so fixated on Ginny that it relieves him of his own physical and emotional pain. He settles behind his desk drinking coffee and the images in his mind horrify me.

"Stop," I say. "You must stop. What you want to do is wrong." But he only sees my precious Ginny, and her sweet innocence. He's determined to possess her.

How can someone get this way? "I loved you!" I say. "But I didn't see all of you." I pace around him in a state of anxiety that stirs the paper on his desk. If I can just shift his thoughts and change his mind. Make him think about something else. But when I look at Ginny's future, it seems the die is cast. I see the scenes so clearly. Ginny smiling up at him guilelessly. How he leans in to brush her cheek, and then she's dead.

"God," I cry out. "I don't know who or what you are. But if you are here, please hear my prayer. Protect my friend, Ginny. Show me how I can help her. Please." I beg. "Please show me. There must be some way."

I try to focus and push the pistol off of his desk, but this time I seem powerless and it doesn't budge. He holsters it before he goes to find Ginny. It's like Naehelle has cursed me with disbelief and broken my power with the spell of knowledge about what I'm supposed to be able to do from this in-between world. Herr Schmid sighs and exits stiffly down the steps. The guards no longer stand at the door since the Gestapo's high-ranking officers left some days ago. He loves being alone to scheme and drift into the shadows. He walks to the pastry shop that still sells some chocolates and sweets. "I'll take that," he says in German and points to a chocolate heart decorated with white flowers inside the glass case.

"It's expensive you know, sir," the bakery owner says. "Handmade." She must be a collaborator to still be in business. Herr Schmid stares back with his impenetrable blue eyes and waits. "But we'll make an exception for you, sir. Fifty francs for you."

He nods and she carefully wraps the weighty chocolate heart in one thin golden sheet of waxed paper. The paper alone would make people envious if they saw it. "No ribbons sir. We have none now. Not like other times, you know. No luxuries now." The woman holds out her hand for the money.

He says nothing, but waits stonily for his change while patrons in the café glance warily at Herr Schmid. It seems everyone in the shop holds their breath, waiting for him to go.

"*Dankeshen,*" he says.

"*Bitteshen,*" the woman says begrudgingly. Some of the customers' heads jerk up. Like me, they feel angry at her for using the language of betrayal, but it may be her way of staying in business. So many others have been eliminated or deported or wait on the boat shivering in the humid chill, while the Germans decide their fate.

The school bell chimes and Herr Schmid waits at the angle of the school and watches Ginny step into the courtyard by the lake, under the leafless plane trees. When he spies her direction, he circles around ahead of her. She walks with Bernadette, and when Bernadette skips away with a boy, Ginny continues on alone, head down, staring at the dirty, melting slush and mud under her feet. She seems numbed out and indrawn. I want to shake her and say, "Wake up! Wake up, Ginny! You're in danger," but she's in another world where I can't reach her right now. Her thoughts weigh heavy and dark like thunder clouds. Herr Schmid stalks her stealthily like an old cat after a baby bird. With careful, calculated movements he maneuvers across a short cut and arrives from the other direction. He approaches so that she bumps into him, like it's her fault, her inattention, but he made it happen deliberately.

Ginny frowns, startled out of her reverie.

"You ran into me," Herr Schmid says.

She stares back at him silently with narrowed, angry eyes, aware of his deception.

"Oh, I'm sorry," she says, but she stands firm and defiant.

"I'm sure it was nothing."

"I was thinking of a friend."

"What was her name?"

"Aurelie." Her face softens as she speaks my name.

"Mmm. Yes. The girl who they buried recently. Condolences," he says and drops his head. "What a terrible thing." His voice sounds sincere, like he really feels this way. But I want to scream when I see he feels nothing. Absolutely nothing about me. He's manipulating Ginny!

"Yes, sir," she says and continues to walk along the lakeside toward home, staring out at the water.

"Here, I want you to have this. It won't replace her, but it's something." He hands her the gilded present. She shakes her head no and walks on. "But you must," he says and opens the paper to reveal the chocolate heart.

"Oh my," she gasps. I feel her hunger and the scent of the chocolate warmed by his hand makes it impossible to resist.

"Ahh, you would like some, I think."

Ginny hesitates. Her anger disappears into deep sadness and she feels empty and forlorn.

"Don't Ginny," I yell. "Keep walking. Walk away. Don't stop. Don't eat it. It's filled with his energy. It's like poison."

But she's mesmerized by her desire for the sweetness. Just like I was. Just like he did with me! Only I didn't see it. I must warn her! How can I stop him?!

"Here. Take the whole thing. Just for you." Ginny's eyes widen.

"Really?!"

"Yes," the demon says.

"But I don't think I should. It's not right."

"Go on. You must be hungry. No one will care. There's no reason not to. It will be our secret." He places it in her open hands and thrills at the touch of her palms against his fingertips. Ginny breaks the heart in two and pops a piece into her mouth.

"Mmmm." When she looks around, Herr Schmid has already set off in another direction. "Wait. Thank you. I forgot to say thank you."

He glances over his shoulder at her and walks away.

Ginny waves at his back. *Maybe that's why Aurelie loved him,* she thinks as she savors the chocolate.

"No Ginny, he's not a good man," I say. But she seems not to hear.

26

IN THE QUIET night hours when the world outside is dark, the in-between remains always vibrant and animated. I haven't been able to rest since I discovered Herr Schmid's intentions. I watch over Ginny to protect her. But it's true, what Naehelle said. Ginny feels my presence less and less with each passing day. Some days go by when she forgets to light a candle for me. This hurts. But *c'est la vie*. People in that world forget us when we pass.

Tonight, Naehelle went to bed early. She's fed up with what she calls my teenage phase of rebellion. I keep insisting the world, even the in-between must change, and we must be able to do more to save and help our loved ones. But she swears that we can't. Her insistence sends me into rages and I can't stand her, or being here, or anything right now. So she avoids me, and I walk around seething with anger and frustration.

Tonight I sit by the fire and watch the flames flicker. Silvie comes in and sits on the couch. "Can't sleep either?" she says.

I shake my head no.

"Sometimes I miss my mom so much that I think I'll die. Then I remember I'm already dead. How frustrating is that?!" she says.

"I'm sorry," I say and I truly am. Silvie is a kind girl and like me, she didn't deserve to die. Especially not in such a brutal way. Our death at the hands of the same man binds us together. "I'm sorry I was rude to you."

"It's okay," she says. "I'm used to it. It was the same in that life too." She points out the window where we see that world unfold.

"But I am truly sorry."

She shrugs.

"How did he find you?" A chill runs through her and she crosses her arms over her heart. "You don't have to talk about it."

"He saw me with my mother. We were at the carnival and came into town. She's a palm reader and I sold flowers. Roses from the South of France. I pedaled them on the streets with my brothers. Men out strolling with their women liked to buy them."

"Was he with someone?"

"No. He stood back watching. Always watching everything happen. He beckoned to me. With those eyes. So full of light and temptation. Such a blue. Like the Mediterranean at Les Saintes Maries de la Mer." Her voice speaks in sighs, filled with longing for romantic love. I felt the delight of being recognized and suspended in his sparkling, magnetic eyes.

"Did you love him too?"

"Oh, no I wasn't a gullible, young girl like you."

"You're only a year older than me." I insist. She shrugs it off.

"I'd seen other men look at me like that. He bought the rest of my flowers and asked to meet me later, at the edge of the forest. I said my sister could, that I wasn't old enough. He gave me a little money and said it had to be me. I thought I knew what he wanted. I said yes, because some part of me wanted to be wanted by him. 'You'll be my first. That has a high price.' I told him. He nodded. My older brother usually came when I'd give a *rendezvous* to a man. He'd knock them out and steal from them, and we'd slip away giggling and rich. But that time I didn't tell my brother. My heart leapt with desire and I felt excitement like butterflies in my belly. I could feel how hot and cunning his kiss would be. I wanted him to take me away from that life. I thought that with the help of my grandmother, I could cast a spell and make him fall in love with me forever. Stupid girl," Silvie says about herself. "And you? How did he get you?"

"I was missing Mom and everyone at home ignored me. But he made me feel special. First, he showed me I could come to his house and trust him to keep our secret. He gave me attention I was missing. He touched my hair so gently, that I thought he loved me. He took time. Now I see he calculated every step. He was a liar with one goal. I hate myself that I believed him. Why couldn't I see through it? All I saw was his handsomeness."

"Yes. It's like he puts a spell on girls. Grandma says the Nazis learn to use secret powers to seize another's will. The SS officers are initiated into this. They use some of the same spells we gypsies do."

"Oh," I'm stunned. I know nothing about spells and charms. It sounded like something from a fairytale, but I knew she spoke truth. I could feel it.

"In wartime he knows he can get away with murder. He's a powerful man. Who will investigate?" Silvie stares into the fire. I shudder again at the thought of Ginny. "Are you serious about wanting to help your friend?"

I nod.

"I can introduce you to someone who knows secrets about the in-between. She can help you, I believe."

"Oh?" I'm almost out of hope and sound unconvinced.

"Really. She can. I was in contact with her before I lost my body. She taught me about it."

"Oh?" Now I'm really curious.

"Yes. It's my grandmother. I loved her so, so much. And before she died, she said she'd stay in touch with me. And she has."

"And do you see her now? I see my mom, but Naehelle says I can't communicate with her yet because she's in another world."

"Sometimes I sneak off and see Gran." A mischievous smile breaks across Silvie's face. "Naehelle says I'm not supposed to."

"Oh I love your rebellious spirit! Let's do it. Let's go see her."

27

SILVIE EXPLAINS THAT there are challenges. We have to stick strictly to the path. And follow the exact same path back. We must each keep our candle lit to avoid the demons along the trail. And we must not tell Naehelle. She's like a gatekeeper and if we tell her, our plans to help others from the in-between will be ruined. She could send us away to some other place for punishment where we could not help or see anything of Ginny's world any longer.

"What about the risks?" I say.

"Well, we can't see that other world once we leave the garden. We could also get stuck there for a really long time if we lose focus and allow the demons to pull us off course."

"Wait." I turn to her before we leave Naehelle's warm fireside. "Have you done this before?"

She smiles slyly. "How do you think I endure this awful, boring place?!" We both giggle and step across the threshold, out of Naehelle's protected sanctuary.

Just before I disappear into the darkness, I watch Claire slip into the court-yard of Herr Schmid's quarters and feel her relief to see her bike still waiting against the wall. A little smile edges up at the corners of her mouth as she pushes it and runs smack into Herr Schmid's chest.

"Coming to see me?" he says.

She can't say no. So she simply stares at him in silence.

"Come. We have some business to take care of."

"I can't. I've got to help my father."

"Your father can wait for the wellbeing of the Reich, no?" He motions for her to pass into the entrance and up the stairs. She replaces the bike against the wall and walks heavily up the marble steps. "Who was it you brought in. The girl?"

"I brought no one. Only a goose to feed a bunch of thankless faces."

"The blonde girl. Who is she?"

"A school friend of my sister's. She was sorry and apologized. It won't happen again." Claire holds her breath even though the stairway is long and steep and usually brings those who ascend it to pant helplessly.

"Yes," he says. "I hope so. What's her name?"

Claire's eyebrows furrow. She hesitates. "Ginny."

"I want to make sure she's protected."

Claire flinches. "Oh." Claire thinks of Ginny's secret, of her Jewish heritage hidden by a false baptism record. Herr Schmid opens the thick wooden door to the wide apartments and motions for Claire to enter in front of him. Ralph, the young soldier who sometimes helps out is nowhere in sight.

"So what do you want from me today?" Claire stands insolently in front of Herr Schmid's desk. He's testy and irritable.

"Take my shirts to the laundry. I need them cleaned." He scratches at the center of his chest and grimaces.

Claire scoops the shirts from the pile in his bedroom and stuffs them in a cotton laundry bag. "That's it?"

"That's all," he says.

She escapes quickly.

At the laundry, she hands over the shirts. The laundress pulls them out of the bag to count the items before Claire's eyes. "They want to be extra sure they'll get what they sent," Claire says.

"Wouldn't want to get shot for a missing shirt," the laundress smirks as she examines them. The two women trade an understanding smile. They both see the stains. Blood and puss in the center of his white shirts and undershirts from a wound at the level of his heart. They trade glances, but say nothing.

❦

As I make my way down the path beyond Naehelle's door, we slip outside of the realm of the peaceful secret garden we inhabit. Just beyond the gate, all light is absorbed by an inky, black veil. I grip Silvie's shoulder and suck in my breath.

"I'm not so sure, this is a good idea," I say. In fact, now that I think of it I'm not sure I can trust her. Fear and excitement fill my belly with nausea.

"Come on. I know the way," she urges.

I look back at the gate where a light burns in a lamp on the old stone wall and then turn to look at Silvie's shadowed face in the lamp light from my candle. The candle flame's protected in a glass jar and I hold it by a wire wrapped around the mouth of the jar.

"Wait." I pull her back. "Have you told me everything?"

She halts. "Listen. I want to save her too. I don't want Ginny to die like we did."

This brings tears to my eyes and courage grows inside my heart. A fierceness that I never knew existed roars up inside. "I would do most anything for Ginny."

We step onto the path and the chill clings like a damp coat. Bad smells of rotting flesh and wild animals try to distract me. The chill feels similar to the dark forces the German general invited into Herr Schmid's house through his blood ritual. I keep looking back and that window through which I see the world of Claire and Ginny begins to fade. Silvie turns and faces me.

"You will have to let your loved ones down there go for a little while. You won't be able to see them from this dark place and you'll need to put all of your concentration on the path or you could end up in hell."

I frown at her. I don't want to let them go even for an instant, but this may be my only hope for saving Ginny. "Hell? You mean like burning in fire?" I say.

"No. I mean like your beloved Herr Schmid with the flesh-eating demons who tear at him each time he tries to sleep. They're here, in this in-between and so is he when he wants to be. They'd love nothing more than to distract you and eat your flesh too. They thrive on your fear." Silvie seems unusually tense. "This is no joke."

A shiver runs down my spine and I consider going back to the safe, familiar confines of Naehelle's garden and house. I've seen that awful in-between where Herr Schmid spends his nights when he can't sleep and I've seen the treacherousness of those demons.

"Are they the same as the dark forces that I saw descend on his house when the Nazis did their rituals? I saw these black tentacles, like a monster, attached to the commandant and many of the men." All I have to do is imagine them and Silvie sees and feels what I saw.

"Dreadful," Silvie says. "Yes. It will not be easy and you mustn't fall into that low, dark vibration or it will latch into you too. And if they discover you're trying to interfere with their power over someone like Herr Schmid, those flesh eating demons will seek you out and try to destroy you. They use him and he uses them. You must remain focused. They will do all they can to make you lose your way. Just keep one hand on my shoulder and stay focused on the path and on your candle. Don't let your candle flame go out. And remember this. If we get separated, if anything happens, don't let fear take over. They'll swoop in and try to possess you and make you their prisoner if you do."

"Is it possible to die here?"

"Not the physical death like in that world. But yes, you can lose touch with the light and that feels worse than death."

"So what's the alternative?"

"Well, you can stay home by the fire."

"That's not an option. Not if I want to help Ginny."

"Then Love. Love them and everything with all of your might. Repeat 'thank you' even when it hurts."

"That's stupid and crazy. How do you love a demon?!"

Silvie shrugs. "You'll just have to try. That's what Gran says."

I swallow, and look back at the light on the wall toward the warm fire flickering behind the windows at Naehelle's house. We could go back now. But this is the only chance to save Ginny. "Let's go."

"Good. We won't have much time outside the wall. Only an hour at most."

"But time means nothing here," I protest.

"That's not true." She pulls out an hour glass and turns it over. The sands pour quickly down to the bottom. "The garden black bird will tell Naehelle about our absence if we're gone more than an hour. She'll search for us and expel us if she finds out where we've been. Then we can't do anything to help Ginny."

We walk and walk in silence. I see nothing and only feel eyes staring from out of the darkness. I start to speak, and Silvie "ssshhhh's" me with a finger to her lips. Silence seems important. Keeping a low profile in the darkness when you're carrying the light is not an easy task. Even. Steady. One foot in front of the other. One at a time. "Stay focused," I repeat to myself over and over. "Light. Light. Light. Love. Remember Love."

The creatures, the flesh-eating demons like I see around Herr Schmid in his in-between, breathe their hot breath upon us and make the hairs stand up on the back of my neck. "I feel so cold, Silvie," I whisper.

"Shhh! Focus. Love. Remember?"

"Yes. All right." In my mind I repeat "love, love, love," But that's not what I feel. The stench reeks so much of death and rotting animals that I fear I'll be sick. "Thank you. Thank you. Thank you." I'm not sure what for, but I say it over and over. It keeps them at bay. And I see their snarling, salivating mouths turn away in agitation.

28

IN THE DARKNESS I do not know if we go up or down or left or right. Every footstep seems the same. I feel the heavy, clammy presence of the demons as their energy curls in and brushes my arms and shoulders. Some have claws to tear. Others have tentacles to suck out life.

"Go away," I nearly scream at the oppression as they try to steal my life force. Then I stop myself. "Thank you. Thank you. Thank you," I say in my mind and focus on the candle flame in the jar.

The air feels so heavy and the demons so close and oppressive now that it feels like we're walking through a dank, very narrow tunnel in a swamp.

"Silvie," I whisper, my hand claps tightly to her shoulder. But I can't see her. I can barely see my hand. "Silvie!"

When I see her face, distorted by the candle light she looks ghoulish too. I nearly let go of her, but I feel a force stronger than fear. A force of love holds my hand in place. "It's in your imagination," Silvie whispers. "Just stay steady. Remember. Love. Love. Love. It destroys the fear."

I hold fast. The darkness lifts into gray tones now, and a forest of trees appear. On the edge of the forest a black lake shimmers. A gypsy caravan on wheels sits on the lakeshore. The light from the window of the caravan illuminates the darkness and acts like a beacon in the night. Silvie leads me skillfully up the steps of the blue caravan with green shutters, to the door.

A beautiful, black-haired woman opens the door even before Silvie knocks. "Welcome child." Her eyes sparkle with light like she can look across worlds. "I've been expecting you."

"Is that your Gran?" I whisper. Silvie nods.

"Isn't she beautiful?" The woman's olive skin glows with radiant beauty.

"She looks like she could be your older sister."

My hair stands on the back of my neck and I shiver and crouch close to Silvie. "I don't know how you stand it with the stench of the swamp," I say to her gran. When I look down, I see my hands and knees tremble.

"Come in young women. You're very courageous," Silvie's grandma says and wraps a gentle arm around my shoulders. "Sometimes the best places are far away and hidden. No one bothers me here," Silvie's gran says to answer my question. "They don't like my kind of intervention in the world out there. But no one bothers me here."

I can't stop my teeth from chattering. "Here. This shawl will chase away the chill," her gran says. "My name is Simza," she says to me.

"Naehelle would be very unhappy to know we're here," Silvie says.

"She's not what she seems," Simza says.

The caravan vibrates with magic inside. An animated statue of the Black Sara of the Camargue stands on an altar dressed in blue, next to a carved hand with a palm that reveals a blinking eye, as if the hand can see. If I'd come here as a child, this place would have tantalized my imagination and made me dream of crystal balls, seeing the future, and wild stallions ridden by gallant heroes who protect and save women from distress. Crystals sit on the windowsills and hang from the ceiling by red, green, and turquoise silk chords. The rich dark mahogany wood-lined walls smell of beeswax. And golden beeswax candles burn and fill the air with sweet, rich and potent scents of warm honey in summer sun. Incense and myrrh waft up from a metal burner.

"I can see the smells," I whisper to Silvie, excited. "Look! They look like gold and silver intertwining in a beautiful, magical tapestry around us!"

She smiles. "Yes. The scents protect us."

"How did you ever find it the first time?" I whisper. Simza sits by the fire and chants over the tea. She prepares a special potion to welcome and protect us.

"Before Gran died, she gave me instructions."

I scratch my head. "My mom doesn't even know I'm here," I say.

"Don't feel bad. It's a gypsy tradition to know about the in-between. We use it in dreams and all of the time to change outcomes and sometimes to do our own will," Silvie says.

"Oh. Does it always work?"

"No." Her Gran hands me a ceramic blue bowl that looks like lapis lazuli and responds for her. "Manipulating things from the in-between always brings consequences if we do it for our own bidding and not to help others." Her voice trails off. "And even sometimes when we try to help others too."

I sulk a bit as I think of my mother and wonder why she's not come to see me. Simza must hear my thoughts.

"Most people are confined to our world or that one," Simza says pointing into her crystal ball. In the ball I can see the physical world where Herr Schmid sits at his desk and schemes. "Or to the next one." Now I see my mother, sewing happily, dressed in a flower-print dress and smiling like I never saw her smile on earth.

I reach out and touch the crystal ball with my index finger and the image disappears. "So Mom is one of those who has to stay put?" I say. Simza nods.

"But some are not confined to just one world. They have big spirits and fly out across worlds at night when they sleep. People like you," she points her elegant finger at me. "You have power to do many things. A strong-willed one you."

I have no idea what she means, but I'm determined to save Ginny. I feel shy in front of this wise, timeless woman. Her eyes, black as obsidian, bore into my spirit. It seems she sees and knows everything about me already.

"I saw my friend. In the future. Dead. At the hands of an evil man. Can I save her?"

The gypsy lifts her tea and turns it slowly and deliberately in her hands. "Give me your cup, she says. She turns the cup upside down on the saucer. The tea leaves form a jumble on the plate. "Some things are written in stone. These are destiny," she says. "Some things we can alter and influence by our own will and attitudes." She stares into my cup. I've heard of the gypsy gift for this. I hold my breath and close my eyes.

"Don't worry," Simza says. "All's well for you. You will have trials to come, but you're already dead so they can't be that bad," she laughs and my heart flinches.

"Oh," I say, shocked by the thought. A moment of fear strikes through my heart. Simza's laugh haunts me. The beautiful, dark-haired woman now appears huge and scary. I lose my composure and run to the door. "Let me out!"

"Love!" Silvie reminds me and pulls me back. "Love! Not fear. Breathe in," she says. "Come back here and sit down. That demon image you saw is all in your mind. She won't hurt you. It's just your own fear getting in the way."

My eyes must be bulging as I stare back at Silvie. Simza looks demonic.

"Breathe," Silvie says. As I attune to the love pouring from her, my heart calms and her Gran suddenly looks normal, kind, and nourishing. Like when we first arrived. "Gran!" Silvie scolds when she sees my discomfort. "Stop joking with her."

"I didn't mean to upset you," says the exotic woman with the hennaed hands. Her red, ruffled petticoat peeks out from under her gray skirt and hangs over her black leather boots. "It's an important lesson to learn," Gran says. "Your fearful mind plays tricks on you."

"Oh." Silvie reaches for my hand to reassure me.

"Love gives you courage. It conquers all," Simza says.

"Even death?" I say, breathless and wide-eyed.

"Yes. Even death," she says. "But it will not do our will. Love has its own wishes and ways."

She looks into the tea leaves and I watch the images unfurl like a movie before her. Like me, she sees Ginny. On the ground. An injured neck. Dead. I beg her to help me change the things to come.

"It has been done," Simza says. "You can influence people. But they will, in the end, have to decide finally if they will act in accordance with your urging or not. Even Ginny must decide if she wants to die by his hand or not."

This sends me into a rage. "You mean she may want to die? It's her choice?!"

"Shhh." Silvie calms me with a squeeze to my forearm. "Anger invites in the demons."

"Maybe not her choice on the conscious level. But ultimately, yes."

"Then you're saying I consented to my own murder? And so did Silvie?"

"Yes. You agreed to be a part of this." Simza glances at Silvie. "So you could help her. And to learn…"

"No." I'm emphatic. "I would not ever have done that."

Simza stares back at me and leaves the silence open for reflection.

"You must get back, girls," she points to the hourglass with sand sliding through it which keeps time in this world. "Your time is almost up. Naehelle will report you and you may not be allowed to stay in the in-between much longer if they find out you want to change events on the other side," she says.

My heart aches and this conversation has brought no peace and few answers. "You must tell me one thing I can do. One practical thing that could save Ginny from that violence."

Simza sighs and tosses back her mane of hair. "You're an insistent one." She looks into my eyes. "You can affect electricity. Some people have the power to physically move things in their world. You can do this when you believe. Sometimes. This may help." With that she lights the candles in our jars and sends us out the door. On the path I feel the demons again and their desire to pull me off course. Silvie walks ahead, my hand on her shoulder.

"I hope it helped," she says.

"Shhh," I say and focus on my footsteps and on the path and the tiny light. "Why are the demons more powerful now?"

"They're drawn to your desire for good. It makes you glow with brilliant light and it's the total opposite of their darkness. They cannot help but be attracted to you and what you're doing."

The candle in my jar snuffs out and my hand falls from her shoulder. Fear constricts my lungs so tightly that I cannot breathe. "Silvie," I whisper. The darkness engulfs me and I see nothing. All I can do is work to focus on another type of light. By drawing my focus inward I begin to see an inner light in my heart. That inner light shows me the path, but it's not my physical eyes that see. I see with my inner senses. The oppressive forces of darkness encroach and hang close to me. The hair stands on my arms and a chill makes my teeth chatter. Fear wants to take control.

"Love." I hear Silvie and her Simza's voices whisper in unison. "They're testing your Love." And that light inside of me grows stronger and brighter. I can still see nothing around me, but my feet know where to lead me. When suddenly out of the darkness, a demon so black with glowing red eyes steps in front of me.

His tentacles reach for my throat, and all of the adrenaline that pumped through me when Herr Schmid took my life, comes rushing back. I remember the sense of helplessness. My inability to scream and say, "Stop!" The shock and how I froze, unable to push him off of me and run away. All of those terrible memories come rushing in like waves and the demon grows stronger and more powerful. His eyes glow more intensely and he will consume my spirit unless I forgive and let go. I stand still. So still. I stop. Everything stops. The whole world. Until there's nothing more. Nothing. Only me and the demon and the fear and the small light in my heart.

I close my eyes and go deep inside to focus on that light. It's not easy because the fear and panic nearly consume me. My memories of pain from the murder bring the desire for revenge rushing in and I think of all the opportunities I've lost. But I stay with the light. It's only a tiny glow in the darkness, but I love it. When I hold that focus, the light radiates and love flows out of me. I cannot explain it. I've never had this kind of experience before, but the beast feels it too. I look fiercely into its eyes and know that no matter what happens next, nothing will ever extinguish this light inside of me. With that one, courageous thought, the light explodes and my heart opens. This path of darkness is illuminated and I see Silvie up ahead waiting for me. The beast backs away into the shadows, but I sense that it's frustrated with not having taken my soul. It will return to test me again. But for now, I race ahead and catch up with Silvie.

"I thought I'd lost you there for a moment," Silvie says.

"I just want to go home, Silvie."

A low, little chuckle ripples through her throat. "Whatever on earth does that mean?!" I feel annoyed at her. But when the light at Naehelle's place illuminates our way, a sense of relief engulfs me and the oppressive dark energy that felt suffocating and heavy subsides as we step across the threshold and back behind the walls of the secret, protected garden.

29

SINCE I VENTURED into that dark place where the physical world was only visible through a small crystal ball, many things have happened. The Germans and French militia raided the town and rounded up many people on the list. Thomas' people warned and protected a select few. The prisoners wait on the boat to discover their destiny. It's cold and they shiver even though they're packed together so that there's barely room to sit or move. They're not treated like humans, but rather like cattle on their way to slaughter. The boat, *The France*, docks at the quay. People used that boat for lake tours, dances, dinners. But now family and friends of the prisoners bring food and blankets to the dock because the guards give them nothing.

Rumor says that Thomas and his men swooped in shortly after the shopkeepers, doctors, and lawyers were led away from their homes and stole jewels and any money that the Germans hadn't taken. Claire hates both the Germans and the Secret Army who profess to liberate people, when their true aim is to make money from war.

Herr Schmid's obsession with Ginny eats at his heart. He follows her in the shadows. He's adept at surveillance and Ginny travels home from school with a sense of unease, but doesn't see him. At the same time Herr Schmid keeps more lists of those the Reich should eliminate. Anyone who glances at him the wrong way. Anyone who he spies in the streets who might dare to laugh gaily. They should die for being frivolous and happy when the whole world is nothing but pain, Herr Schmid thinks. This is how his mind works, now that he has pinned my brooch to his chest and the wound festers bringing more infection and illness into his life. Claire avoids him when she can, but she feels obligated to continue work as usual.

In the dark hours Herr Schmid coerces her to stay with him under threat of being handed over to the Gestapo if she resists. This evening he grabs Claire by the back of the neck and drags her into the bedroom where he takes off his shirt, and hands her the flog. He stands, hands stretched against the barren wall. A gauze bandage wraps around his chest over and over, just under his arms.

"What's that bandage around your chest? The Nazis do open heart surgery on you?" Claire says sarcastically. But she feels less confident of her own safety. He turns to her, eyes filled with emptiness.

"Shut up," he hisses. "Do your duty."

The leather flicks lightly against his back and he flinches. She hates inflicting pain, and she aches at every blow of the whip against his tender skin. She grimaces with anxiety, too uncertain about how much longer he will tolerate her.

"It's not enough!" he roars.

Inflicting pain strangely activates Claire's pity and binds them together. He insists that she flog him until his bare back bleeds. As much as she steels her heart, Claire simply wants to cry. It's not in her nature to harm. But in the exchange of energy, the pain relieves Hans Schmid of his numbness and brings him alive, while Claire empties of vitality. He thinks of me, briefly as the horror of his crime surfaces into consciousness, and he hates himself so thoroughly that life holds little value. He also hates his obsession with Ginny and his desire to kill her. His mind whirrs and the beating gives him enough exhaustion to fall sleep.

When she's certain he's unconscious, Claire sneaks out of the bedroom and searches for anything that will help Jean-Michel and her neighbors continue to survive. Nothing tonight. She wonders if he suspects her. He hid the most secretive information in a secret panel in the wall. I show the image to Claire and put it in her mind. She moves the portrait that covers it and noiselessly opens the panel to find some rubies and jewels, a few gold coins, and some papers. She opens the documents and reads them.

"Dr. Carlisle, the dentist. Francine Terrine, the owner of the bakery."

Her heart splits in two. A part of her despises Herr Schmid, while another side of her makes excuses for him, not wanting to believe that anyone is truly evil. *It's the war. If it weren't for the war... I hear her thoughts. I can forewarn them. The resistance network will help. The targeted people can escape into the mountains or into Switzerland and find their way to safety before they're deported, or set before firing squads.*

She checks her watch. Curfew requires everyone be off the streets by eight p.m. She must slip out and make it home fast. Herr Schmid has given her a permanent *laissez-passer* so that she's free to go even when others are supposed to be locked inside their homes. But the soldiers on the streets would like nothing more than to violate a beautiful young woman. Her liaison with Herr Schmid keeps her safe to a degree, probably because the others fear him and his authority. The Secret Army considers her a traitor for frequenting the Germans. They might use the opportunity of finding her alone out after curfew to rape her too. No one ever speaks of it. Not the history books or the papers, but it's always the women who suffer the most during war, Claire thinks.

Claire needs to think of herself and save her own skin. Herr Schmid keeps a secret list of the most notorious and suspect criminals hidden inside his bedroom. Claire is on it. Along with Alain. They are not safe. No one is. I whisper to her in the night in her dreams, *"Gare a toi!" Please be careful.* I send my protective energy to surround her, but Herr Schmid becomes ever more powerful and demonic. I watch her tolerate him because she aims to help Jean-Michel and to save others. But be careful, Claire, he's beguiling. I fell for him once and look how it ended.

My own emotions were clouded by love. But from here I see Hans' heart is like a diamond at the bottom of a deep sewer. He's more and more absent and seems to stand aside and watch life through the empty eyes of a robot. In rare moments, he said the words, "Dear one." But when I compare his love with Jean Michel's love for Claire, I see the truth. Jean-Michel values Claire more than his own life. He would die for her. Hans' fear means he would rather kill than make a sacrifice for anyone. I wish I could have seen that sooner.

Claire leans over Herr Schmid's desk and writes down the names quickly. There are so many she can't trust them to memory. Some will be helped via her friend who works at the town hall, the one who can create fake resident cards and travel papers. The woman gives these people new names and changes some of their destinies. But not all of them. The lists have become too long and the means of maneuver too tight and treacherous since the German occupation. Herr Schmid stirs and I arrive from behind and touch Claire on the shoulder to warn her she must leave. She jumps with fright when she feels my energy, and a chill runs through her.

"Go, Claire," I whisper. "He's stirring in the other room. You must go now or he will catch you and you'll be deported or shot. Make no mistake. He loves no one, not even himself."

Before she slips out, she turns back to the bedroom, the list tucked deep inside the inner lining of her purse next to the small pistol. She glances beyond the door to his bedroom and wonders about his sick heart. As she swivels toward the door, she sees a small trinket on the mantel above the fireplace. It's the bracelet with the silver "S" charm and the single gold earring of lovebirds on a nest. Seeing them makes her feel uncomfortable. But she shakes her head and pushes the impression of discomfort away. He seeks her out and needs her now, but she wonders if he would spare her life in darker times. Like me, her heart wants to make a difference and can't bear to feel the suffering of others. But sometimes that desire to help is misplaced and only weakens and blinds us.

"Pay attention, Claire," I say. But her kind heart and her desire to help put her own life in peril. She slips out the door that locks softly behind her.

30

CLAIRE KICKS UP the kickstand on her bike and steps out onto the silent street. The white stone women carved into the high façade of the building across the way seem to stare down at her with cool indifference. She glances at them and mounts her bike. Some soldiers farther down in the direction of the lake watch her, but say nothing. As she rides the lake path back toward our house she yearns for Jean-Michel. After Doc Norbert's visit, Jean-Michel moved up to a mountain village, where some women with an Alpine farm and livestock feed him. The farm women shelter half a dozen men and refugees. Most of them are young men who want to avoid the German forced labor draft and listen to the secret messages broadcast on BBC Radio for instructions on when to fight. Claire admires the silent resistance of those solid women who wear flower print dresses and milk cows. She's heard that these women help hundreds of men and Jews hiding in the villages and mountain caves. A stone falls on the path in front of Claire and catches her attention. Her adrenaline pumps with vigilance as she scans the area for movement. Another rock lands closer. A sharp whistle follows. Their signal.

"Jean-Michel?"

He responds from the darkness with a light laugh. "You were expecting

Archangel Michael, maybe?" I see a pink light shoot from his heart in an energy of pure, selfless love at the sight of her.

"You scared me. We could use some miracles," she says. She stands back and studies him. He opens his arms.

"Hey, I could use some love," he says playfully. "I'm getting tired of sharing a bed with goats." His face shows days of beard growth, and he smells like he's been sleeping in a barn. Claire stands back, hesitates. The scent of Herr Schmid's French cologne stains her skin and the imprint of his energy touches deep into her soul. She doesn't want Jean-Michel to see the impression Herr Schmid has left on her, so she glances at her feet. She leans the bike against a tree and steps closer. He takes her in his arms. "What's up? Don't you miss me?"

"Yes," she whispers. The contact with his heart, with her hand against his chest, reminds her of sane, solid love that supports and transcends terrible times like these. Her fear of losing him dissipates.

"Hey, you okay?" he says and lifts her face by the chin so he can look into her eyes. She glances away, then meets his regard. His face, though dirty and scarred, reveals a fierce love so passionate and real and accepting, that tears edge her eyes. She nods and hugs him close. But the scent of Herr Schmid's flesh and blood clings to her and she feels guilty and ashamed.

Claire feels tainted by Herr Schmid and undeserving in the face of Jean-Michel's pure love. Her shame makes her question her own heart. Jean-Michel is strong-willed and will survive. But Herr Schmid's like a deadly octopus with tentacles leaching Claire's good energy to keep himself alive. I see his sickness seeping into her, creeping into her being, and she's no longer safe like she was.

"You must go, Claire. Go away. Escape, before he tears you apart," I say.

Jean-Michel's intention to liberate his country and make sacrifices gives him a shining purity and innocence. His injury and closeness to death from the shooting, means he can now sometimes perceive me and hear me. "Please protect her Jean-Michel," I beg. "Tell her to stay away from Herr Schmid."

"I don't want you near that man anymore, Claire. Don't go back there," Jean-Michel says. He sees the wavering in her heart and feels the shift in her emotions. "We have other ways of getting information. You're not the only one."

She lowers her eyes. "You're jealous," she accuses.

"Yeah," he says. "But mostly, I'm worried about you."

She pulls the list of names from her purse. "Here. More names. Please tell Alain he must go and hide now. My brother won't listen to me, but he will listen to you. I fear for his life. And Dad's too. Will you take them up to the mountains with you? Of course, they'll both put up a fight." Jean-Michel accepts the list folded into a small square and slides it down the inside of his boot. He holds her close. Some sense of reality comes back to her. "Herr Schmid says he's protecting my family. But I'm not sure that's true."

"He's following you, Claire," I say. He slipped out behind her after she left. But Claire can't hear me.

"You always said he was a questionable character," Jean-Michel says.

"Sometimes I believe he's possessed by evil. And sometimes he's just a weak human. I wish I could help him..."

"You would help the whole world if you could. But some people don't deserve it, Claire. Don't trust him. The war will be over soon. Then I'll marry you." Jean-Michel pulls a stick from a tree, rips off a sliver of bark and makes a ring to put on her finger. "Here. We're engaged."

Tears fill her eyes. She looks around at the trees bearing tiny buds, the mud under her feet, the melting snow. "This has been the longest winter yet. Will it never end? I'm starting to feel like Father. Like I don't care if I live or die. Like it doesn't matter. Like life means absolutely nothing. I'm sick of it all."

Jean-Michel hugs her tightly. "Hey, don't talk like that," he whispers soothingly. "You've saved a lot of people. Every list of names you smuggle out of that hateful office, every detail you give us..." He holds both her arms intently. "Everything you do makes a difference."

She looks up at him, swallows. "But how do you stay pure when you're surrounded by evil? You keep me sane." She pauses, stares out at the fog. "I don't want to go back there anymore. I don't want to see that Kraut ever again."

"Then don't," Jean-Michel says. "Come away with me."

"Where?" she scoffs. "Maybe we'll go to the French Riviera on holiday. Spend time on the beaches under the shade of German bunkers." She shakes her head. "Where can we go where there's no war?"

"Maybe we can get papers to escape to Switzerland together, and then onto America. Let's go to America, Claire. We'll thrive there." He stands in front of her, a hand on each of her arms. "You've got that contact at the government office, the one who makes false papers for the Jewish kids. Ask her. I can get the money. Get the papers for you. Then I'll join you once the war's over."

She bows her head and doesn't dare to hope. Right now, she can't see any future. "Yes, I'd like that. Now I've got to go." She turns and makes her way heavily back to the bike path. With a brief glance she looks back at Jean-Michel through the shrubs into darkness and I feel her heart yearn to be married to him and to live in peace.

31

THE THERMOMETER DROPS below freezing for several days, but the detainees on the boat at the quay sound like they're on holiday. They play cards. Laugh. Drink wine that family and friends bring them. Even though the Germans give them no provisions, family and friends hand them blankets and baskets of food through the open windows. The prisoners cordially workout ways to feel less crowded by moving up to the top deck when the sun shines, and they take turns lying down on the benches to sleep. A constant stream of people line the quay and bring pots of soup, biscuits, hot chicory coffee for their family members. On the boat the prisoners share the provisions in a spirit of cooperation and camaraderie. The Germans provide nothing. They only stand guard to make sure no one escapes.

Claire's in a panic. Alain's missing. While other men fled to the mountains to prepare for war, Alain has continued to show up at the garage where he repairs cars and fiddles with engines every day. He's a top rate mechanic and much sought after, even by the Germans. But his gifts are double-edged, because as often as he makes repairs, he's also capable of putting water and sand in gas tanks so that a German car will run, but not make it very far. The mischievous sprite in him revels in the treachery. Since he's so much older than me, we weren't very close, but I still watch him in a corner at the back of the boat telling jokes to make people laugh.

Sometimes he sings to lift the prisoners' spirits too. I move in close to listen and feel his feelings. I never understood his playfulness beneath his silent demeanor. Or his preference for aloneness to being with a girl. But he's shy. That's what I see now. Women scare him and this makes me smile to see how embarrassed he is to be scrunched up against a beautiful young woman on a bench next to him.

Clarie observes the boat from a distance. She doesn't dare get too close, because the soldiers and guards might associate her with the detainees and imprison her too. So she sends Ginny with a basket of fresh bread and some blankets. Ginny's too young to be a suspect. The guards search Ginny's basket, then allow her onto the plank that leads to the boat deck. Ginny hands out bread and blankets and quietly asks people if they've seen Alain. But everyone seems clueless about him or what fate awaits them. Most don't even know why they're detained.

"Thank you, honey," says a balding man with wire-rimmed spectacles. Ginny recognizes the doctor.

"You're welcome, Doc Norbert. Are you okay?"

"I'm not injured, if that's what you mean. Another doctor was taken off to help with an emergency. Maybe I'll be released too."

"Have you seen Alain, Claire's brother?"

"No, I'm afraid I haven't. But there are lots of people on this boat. Too many for hygiene," Doctor Norbert answers.

"Claire's worried about him."

"Yes, there's good reason to be. With all of the deaths and imprisonments at this rate, the whole of Annecy will be locked away or dead by May." The doctor looks out at the cliffs across the bay. Ginny frowns. "I'll have a look around to see if I can find him. And please ask Claire to tell Mrs. Norbert that I'm fine. Will you do that?"

"Of course, sir."

"Thank you. Here's some bread for Alain if you see him." The French guard pushes Ginny with the butt of his rifle.

"Enough. Get off now or you'll end up like them," the French guard says gruffly. Ginny nearly slips as she steps down the plank onto land. She turns back and looks up. "Alain," she cries out in one last attempt to find him. "Alain." But to no avail. Then a dark curly head pokes out of one of the windows. "You're Alain. Aurelie's brother?" He holds a hand of play-ing cards and waves at her with a slight smile. With his beard growth, she hardly recognizes him.

"Alain who?" he says.

"Claire and Aurelie's brother."

"Yeah. S'it's me."

"Claire. Sent some things. She's worried sick about you. Doc Norbert has a basket with food. He's over here." She points to the space near the entrance to the boat on the deck below him.

He waves at her. "I'm fine, you see. Thanks, little one. Good day."

Ginny waves back and heads straight for Claire who tries to appear indifferent as she sits on a green wooden park bench deep in the garden. Claire pretends to stare out at the gulls swooping over the lake, but she eyes every move Ginny makes to protect her. Claire's eyes question the girl.

"Well, it was kind of like a big party," Ginny says. "Except they can't get off of the boat. And there's no food from the Germans."

"That's why they need our rations," Claire says.

"And Alain?"

"I saw him and Doc Norbert too."

"Not Alain too." Her spirits plunge. She thinks of all of her efforts to save Doc Norbert and the others on the list. "You're sure you saw the doctor?"

"Mmm," Ginny nods.

Claire wonders if her efforts matter at all. "He should have escaped. Thomas' men were supposed to warn them."

"He didn't escape. But, maybe you can," Ginny says.

Claire looks up at the adolescent girl. "Yes. Maybe we can go together." Claire's brown eyes study the cotton button-up blouse with pearl buttons and the gray skirt that peek out from Ginny's worn wool coat with too-short sleeves. "My clothes look nice on you," Claire says.

Ginny steps back shyly. "Think so?"

Claire nods.

"I like them. Thank you."

"They make you look all grown up."

"Like you," Ginny says.

"Here, want a touch of lipstick?"

Ginny nods and Claire dabs a small amount on Ginny's already red lips until they turn unnaturally scarlet.

A commotion on the port attracts their attention. Soldiers chase away the family and friends lined up with care packages to hand through the windows of The France. The guards uncoil barbed wire near the boat and along the quay and push visitors away with rifle butts. Herr Schmid lurks by the canal bridge observing. He barely notices the activity on the quay. Instead, he studies Ginny. I'm the only one who seems to notice him. I taunt a crow and send it to swoop down at him.

"I've got to go," Claire says.

"Ok." Ginny seems sad about this.

"Here's a ration ticket and some change for some hot chocolate," Claire says. "After you drink it, go straight home, okay?"

Ginny makes a playful Nazi salute and Claire pulls her arm down. "Don't ever do that unless you have to."

"Sorry," Ginny says.

"The Nazis are not our friends. Remember that. Now go." Claire sets off on her bike and in less than a minute is out of sight. I watch Herr Schmid tell two French guards to stop Ginny and ask for her papers. This is how the Germans and French who sympathize with them, control and harass the local population. Ginny clenches the ration ticket in her hand and begins to cry.

"I forgot them at home." She shudders. Her face turns pale with fright. She looks around for Claire.

"Leave that girl alone," Herr Schmid says to intimidate them. "What do you think you're doing?"

"Checking papers, sir," one soldier says confused. The soldiers step away astonished by the contradictory order. Herr Schimd leans close to Ginny.

"What are these mean men up to? Are you okay, my dear?"

"I forgot my papers."

Herr Schmid stares at the unnatural scarlet tint of Ginny's lips. His superficial warmth hides the demon burning inside him and Ginny's fear keeps her from seeing into his dark heart. He aches to have her throat in his hands soon.

"Thank you," she says and looks at him as if he's her protector.

"Where are you going?"

"To get some hot chocolate."

"I'll accompany you for your safety."

"No! Don't go. Get away, Ginny," I protest.

Ginny feels so relieved at the departure of the soldiers, and Herr Schmid seems almost like a friend in this hostile environment. "It doesn't seem right," she says. "With all of the people starving on the boat over there."

"Don't worry," he says. "I'll take care of them."

"No, he won't, Ginny," I say. I hover close to her ear. "He's lying."

"Doc Norbert has always been kind to me. Please help him especially. He repaired my broken arm when I was twelve."

"I will see what I can do. Come." He motions for her to fall into step with him as they edge along the canal away from the lake and the quay. Ginny still trembles even after the soldiers have disappeared.

"I think I'd better go home instead."

"Don't worry. You'll be safe with me now."

Ginny glances over her shoulder at the boat. "No. Thank you."

I watch the frustration rip lightning-fast through his eyes. But he buries it. "Fine," he says. "Go safely."

She treks off in the direction of Veyrier, head down, heart filled with fright of more soldiers who might stop her. An idea strikes.

"Wait." She turns to him. "Will you walk with me some of the way?" Her voice pleads. Compared to the soldiers, he seems like a safe way to get home.

"Yes. Of course." His heart thrills and he imagines where he might pull her into a deserted area. Now it's just a cat and mouse game and the pleasure comes from the anticipation. The machinations in his mind fill me with nausea and disgust.

"How could you?" I yell at him. But I know how he can and all too easily will.

"Where do you live?" he asks Ginny.

"Not far from the old cemetery. Near Claire's house."

"I see," he says. But he wants to avoid Claire. "We must stay off of the main road. We'll go the back way to be safe and avoid problems."

"Yes, sir."

"I will protect you," he says. Herr Schmid leads her through a wooded undergrowth of trees and shrubs where an abandoned villa once kept the most exquisite gardens. The stone walls crumble. Crocus poke their colorful heads above the snow and mud into the sunlight.

"The narcissus are up." Ginny bends to smell the flowers. The remains of an old Greek style temple with columns stands overgrown with vines. Her anxiety dissipates in the marvelous garden. Her golden hair flies out behind her as she runs to the statue of a Greek goddess draped in ripples of stone cloth baring one breast. Herr Schmid follows up the marble steps and stops below her. His long lashes outline his indigo eyes. Ginny recognizes the energy going out of him as desire. It makes her blood rush and her cheeks flush. Shock mixes with embarrassment at the feeling aroused in her and she stands paralyzed by her own desire as it meets his. Suddenly she realizes she's no longer a girl and this is a whole new game.

"Run away, Ginny," I whisper. But the pull between them feels too strong. It's the same power I felt when he drew me to him. I wanted to see and know more about him and understand the attraction and where it would lead me. That desire to know killed me.

The currents of energy run between them now and Ginny recognizes that this is what I'd tried to describe to her when I told her how I felt around him. Herr Schmid stands below her looking up, his eyes lit, hypnotizing her with his will and charm. She falls under his spell, and he brushes her bare knee just above her wool sock. Ginny's breath is taken away and for a moment she cannot move. I'm spellbound too, hoping I can comprehend this magical power between two people. I know that this is the kind of spell that he wove around me to create a blinding veil.

Ginny spins away like a ballerina and when she stops, Herr Schmid remains transfixed. His breath speeds up and becomes shallow with excitement, but he waits. Her coat opens and he recognizes Claire's button-up blouse. The blouse hides Ginny's small breasts, and he lowers his eyes to conceal his thoughts. He could do it now, take her now. But the evil cat inside him prefers to keep the game going. Let the anticipation build. Shy, tender Ginny with the laughing eyes leans in close like she may kiss him on the mouth, then flits away. He turns away so that Ginny will not see his scheming eyes, and this leaves Ginny frustrated and confused. Oh, what an evil game you play, I want to say to life. The way it makes us want for that which will destroy us.

Herr Schmid controls his breath as he descends the white stone stairs and retraces his steps back out of the walled garden. Ginny walks behind, watching him go. "From here follow the path straight on. It leads back around to the lake." He points.

"But…" Ginny protests. But Herr Schmid has already set off with long strides back toward the town to look for Claire.

Ginny makes her way along the unfamiliar path, filled with frustration and anxiety. I can't see into her, but I imagine the feelings he stirred up as her senses awaken. It's new, leaving Ginny moody and restless. Instead of going home, she turns back to town even at the risk of being stopped, and enters the Bergère Tea Room. But the hot cocoa seems tasteless and dull after seeing Herr Schmid.

"Ginny," I whisper. She doodles on a piece of paper and mopes. As she doodles, I use her absent-mindedness to write words. "Ginny, I love you." But she thinks of Herr Schmid. She meets his obsession by an equally powerful obsession with him and she thinks of me. I can't see all of her thoughts clearly. But I know this will not end well.

"No, Ginny," I beg. "Stop. He's not who or what you imagine."

"Oh, Aurelie," she whispers. "I wish I could talk to you."

I will for her to keep doodling so I can tell her more. But she stops and puts down the pen. It's resolved inside of her, though it's not fully conscious. "I will do what I must," she says. "For you Aurelie."

My heart trembles for her.

32

CLAIRE STANDS IN front of Herr Schmid's desk, a determined look on her face. "Alain's on the boat. With the doctor who delivered me into this world," she says. "I've never asked for anything." He sits back in his chair and stares at her coolly.

"So, don't ask now."

She stiffens. She's never needed his help before. But he stares indifferent and walled off. I hear him thinking of her with the resistance traitor, Jean-Michel, who he spied her with in the dark. If I could I would tell Claire that he's been following her, and about the many people Herr Schmid has killed. She might understand how a few more lives don't matter to him. Not Alain's. Not the doctor's. Not her own. Not mine. But worry for Alain, makes her bold.

"My brother's imprisoned."

"And you want me to do something about it. Nothing is for free." He eases up from the wooden chair and towers over Claire. She stands firmly anchored, aware of his moodiness and frustration. With an immediate and demanding push, he forces Claire into his bedroom and shoves her against the wall with frightening violence.

"Stop," she says. "You're mad." She struggles. "What about my brother?"

"Give me what I need first."

She tries to push him away, but he tears at her skirts and thrusts and groans like one of the bulls I've seen in the field and with as much violence.

"Ow," Claire protests. "Stop it." But he holds her in place as she struggles to smash his toes with her heels. If only I could throw one of the marble vases from the mantel at his head. That would stop him. I focus, concentrate really hard. I want to protect Claire. But the vase doesn't budge.

"Stop." She screams, but he holds his hand over her mouth to silence her. Her eyes bulge with fright. He grunts and groans, all of the time thinking of Ginny and murder, and with one last giant heave into Claire's body, she feels his release. He leans against her back now, spent. Claire pushes him off and slaps him hard across the face. Any chance of freeing Alain or Doc Norbert dies there.

"I am not your whore," she says. Full of determination to never return, she adjusts her torn blouse and takes her things. The door slams. He leans on one hand against the wall. His dead brother stands close by and touches his shoulder to give him love. Hans feels it and his hot tears hit the floor as he collapses to his knees. I stand next to him filled with a mix of frustration and love. He brushes his brother and me away and turns his focus to Ginny.

⚞

Claire bikes home, assailed by a wave of deep despair and emptiness. I stay near to console her, but she's broken by Herr Schmid, the war, and the dullness of the gray sky and the dark mirror of a lake beside the path. Nothing seems right. At home, she stops at the outdoor toilet behind the house and a bout of nausea strikes. She clenches her stomach and retches. A terrible dawning realization assaults her.

"I'm pregnant."

The thought of a new life coming into this world of pain fills her with deep depression. She leans her head against her arm and tries to fight back the despair. "And it could be his," she says. Disgusted. Ginny arrives with a knock on the outhouse door.

"Claire," she says softly. "I need to talk to you."

Claire regains her composure, wipes her tear-stained face, and opens the door.

"What's wrong?" Ginny says.

"Oh, just feeling a little dismal like the weather today. It'll pass," she says dismissively. Then she notices Ginny's face and the light shining from her eyes. "What's gotten into you?"

"I saw someone today."

"You did?"

Ginny nods. "It was a test."

"A guy it sounds like. Do I know him?"

Ginny shrugs.

"Did he pass the test?" Together they walk to the house and Ginny hooks her arm under Claire's. Claire seems so far away and it's an attempt to get her to be present.

"He…well…I'm not sure," Ginny says. "Can I ask you about someone?"

"Sure," Claire says thinking of what it would mean to have a baby during wartime.

"That German, Monsieur Schmid , he knew Aurelie, didn't he?"

"They met once." Claire's thoughts fill with dread of being pregnant and she seems not to notice Ginny. I want to shake her right now and say, "Pay attention. This is important. You can change the course of events if you'll just listen. You could save her life."

Claire sighs deeply. "Let's go have tea. I have some tea leaves that I took from his stock." Claire unlocks the door and Ginny sits in a chair that she pulls close to the fire. Claire adds more wood and puts the kettle on the black stove.

"Why do you look so sad?" Ginny studies the way Claire's shoulders slump forward. It seems the fighting spirit has gone out of her.

Claire's mind races back through the events of the afternoon with the blue-eyed German. How she couldn't save Alain or Doc Norbert. How Jean-Michel will feel about a child. She just wants to sleep and rest and burrow somewhere quiet. She believes Jean-Michel's right. It's time to escape to America.

"Ginny, you will be careful, won't you? You can't trust hardly anyone these days."

"Yes. I know." Ginny timidly lowers her head and lifts her shoulders. "Claire?"

"Yeah."

"Oh, nothing."

"Go on. What is it?"

"Is it wrong if a man is much older? Is it possible to marry him anyway?"

"Well, I suppose so. But you'd have to be over sixteen. That's the law."

"Aurelie wanted to get married you know?"

"Oh? To who?" Claire says, staring into her cup of tea.

"Hans Schmid."

Claire's head jerks up.

"She loved him."

"That's not possible. She was too young!"

"She was going to wait for him. He'd made her some promises, I think. Then she died."

Claire's thoughts take her back to the day she examined my body at the cemetery. Back to the flakes of white on my inner thighs and the bruises on my neck. She glances at a speck of dried white sperm on her knee and shudders. She pushes away the recognition of a truth, a reality that she does not want to see, because she could not bear it.

I feel her thoughts directed at me and see an opening. "I'm here, Claire," I whisper to her. "He killed me, Claire. Hans Schmid. He's my murderer." I know she hears me. I see the information register in her mind and I watch how she pushes it beneath the surface of her awareness so it will not trouble her. But it takes so much energy to hold it down. "Listen to me, Claire. He murders girls. He murdered me. He'll murder Ginny too."

She stands and holds her head as dizziness consumes her.

"I'd better go," Ginny says. "You need some rest."

"Yes. You be good and stay out of trouble. Okay?" But Claire's mind works frantically now with the new energy and ideas I've planted there. "Wait, Ginny." Ginny's still buttoning her wool coat. "Another girl died a few weeks ago. About a month after Aurelie. Did you hear anything about what happened?"

Ginny lowers her eyes to the wooden floor. "I overheard the priest at the café. He said that she'd been strangled and raped. But I don't know what raped means. Do you?"

Claire's eyes fill with shock and pain. "Thanks, Ginny. Please be careful." Claire sends her away and watches her until she disappears into the house next door. For once I hear Claire pray. "Dear God, wherever you are, if You exist, please protect Ginny. And please, let me not be pregnant. Anything but that."

33

IT'S ABOUT 3 a.m. now in Ginny's world, the time when the veils between all our worlds thin the most. I slip into her room, but as I enter, the dark spirit of a man moves furtively away and I'm puzzled. There's so much more going on in these subtle levels than I ever imagined. I sit at the foot of Ginny's bed, watching her dreams. A man chases her. He threatens her with a knife. She awakens in a panic. Her heart pounds frantically and I send soothing energy to her. Naehelle says I'm not supposed to interfere. That Ginny's physical world is separate from the in-between and I must respect the distance and simply watch and learn. But I can't. If I do nothing, Ginny will die.

"Ginny," I whisper. I reach out and touch her foot gently. "Ginny, pay attention to your dreams. You're in danger." She stirs. And it's very strange because my mother draws near to lure me to her tonight. In that instant my heart longs for her and I recall the sweet wonder of being a child held in her arms.

"Come away, dear," my mother whispers. "Leave her alone."

Tears fill my eyes. "But Mother." She holds out her hand to me. I've wanted to run into her arms for so long, but she's been so, so distant. "Mother…" She smiles. I wonder if someone has sent her to deter me? Or maybe she's just an illusion.

"Come," she insists.

"I must talk to Ginny. It means life or death."

"Things will be as they are destined," my mother says.

"No, she's in danger. Wouldn't you have tried to changed my fate to protect me?"

She smiles indulgently, like I'm a stupid girl. "I missed you so, so much, Mom. Why didn't you come sooner?" I feel torn between pleasing her and helping Ginny.

"I couldn't until now, Aurelie. But now we can be together. If you ask now, you'll be allowed to move out of the in-between and stay with me, here. You'll have total peace and treasures. It's like a kingdom here. All you have to do is let her go." She opens her arms. "Come."

I look down at Ginny and then at Mom. My heart feels torn. "Mom…I love you…" She reaches out her hand for me. I look back at Ginny. "But you're wrong. If I leave now, I will never have peace."

"You must obey me. We cannot intervene from here," Mother says. "There will be consequences."

"I cannot let what happened to me happen to Ginny, Mother. You've got to understand."

"So you chose her over me?"

"I chose to make a difference if I can."

"As you wish," she says and fades away into the dark night. I'm left alone, wondering if she was real or just a test.

I feel dismal and empty. "I love you, Mom," I whisper, but I no longer feel her presence. Then as if to fill my emptiness, Hans Schmid appears in the room above Ginny. He seems to love me like I yearn to be loved, with tender caresses to my hair. My heart melts, but when I look into his eyes, he transforms into that red-eyed demon from the path of darkness and clenches my throat.

"Do not interfere," he commands. He knows I aim to protect Ginny. I break free of the demon's grasp and rush to Ginny's armoire to hide, but the faster I flee, the bigger he becomes. Huddled in the darkness, I feel I will die a second death, only this time I will lose the light in my soul too. Then Silvie arrives holding a silver sword.

"Go. Now." She speaks softly and firmly to the demon, Herr Schmid.

At first, he threatens and roars, but she stands firm. "You got me once," she says. "But I'll slay you for good this time unless you back away." Her firmness and courage protect us, and he slinks away into the darkness. She turns to me. "Are you alright?"

I nod and stand shakily. "How can he do that? Hans Schmid's not dead. But his spirit was definitely here in the in-between trying to kill us."

"It's an occult power that some people possess. Before he killed me, Gran said his sick soul sought me out and slipped into my bed at night, and he seduced me in the in-between, where our souls meet on the astral plane. Then when we met in the physical, waking world, he seemed familiar because we'd met in my dreams."

"I thought I would die again."

"He knows what you're up to and he wanted to scare you," Silvie says. She sheathes the sword.

"Did he come in the night like that to me too? Before the murder, I mean."

"I don't know for sure," Silvie says. "Probably. He draws on dark forces from our subtle world to take unnatural power in the physical one. I'll leave you to get back to Ginny. You'll have to learn to face him on your own soon," she says and disappears. I'm left alone with Ginny and tug at her quilt to gently awaken her.

"Ginny," I shake her insistently. "Wake up."

She awakens again, bleary-eyed. "Mom?" She rubs her eyes and lifts up onto one elbow.

"I need to talk to you."

She pulls the quilt closer to her chest, rubbing sleep from her eyes.

"Aurelie?"

"Don't be afraid, Ginny."

"Are you a dream?" she says. Her voice trails off and she wants to drift back to sleep.

"Stop. Please, don't go to sleep."

She sits up. "Aurelie?"

"Yes, it's me." Her eyes wide open.

"Look at you, shimmering like light. Oh, such a beautiful dream," she sighs.

"Ginny, please listen. Herr Schmid. He's not who you think. He has an evil side. Don't fall for him." I stand in front of her and wait for her to respond.

"You loved him, Aurelie." I wonder if he's seduced her at night and put the hypnotic spell on her too.

"I made a mistake," I say pleading for her to listen and understand. "Please stay away from him. He will hurt you."

"He's suffering, Aurelie. I feel his pain." I imagine the images I've seen of my death and hers at his hands and send them to her mind. "I know, Aurelie. I've seen it too. But I'm not afraid."

"Listen to me, Ginny. You must leave. Go as far away as you can. Ask Claire to help you. You must. You're in danger."

She smiles at me like I'm an overly protective sister. "No, Aurelie. I'll be fine. You'll see," she says and rolls over and falls back into a deep sleep. "You'll see."

❦

"Father Ansen, do you have a moment?" Claire catches the priest fleeing from the confessional as if he's running from bad odors. He tilts forward as he walks, the black hassock hanging limp around his ankles. He exhales with exasperation, as if he can stand no more claims on his energy, but he gives her his attention all the same.

"Yes, my child," he eyes Claire's breasts evident even under her thick wool coat and glances away with embarrassment.

"Father, about the girl, the young one who died. I heard you performed mass for her family."

"There are so many dying now. Remind me."

"Rumor says she was strangled...and worse."

His face flushes. "Yes."

"Did you see her? The body, I mean?"

"Yes."

"And did she uhhh..." Claire hesitates and almost loses her nerve. "Did she have marks on her throat?" I know she speaks of my friend, Silvie.

He flinches and glances away. "I don't recall."

"It's important, Father. It will help for justice to be done."

"Revenge is God's. Let Him take care of justice."

Claire's eyes flare and she would shake him if she could. "I must know, Father. I looked at Aurelie's body before the burial. Her throat showed marks of violence. And…" Claire lowers her eyes. "On her legs I saw what looked like dried sperm." She whispers the last word to keep from being offensive.

Father Ansen's eyes dart away.

"Pardon me, Father. But I have to know. Rumors say that the other girl was also strangled and raped. Is it true?"

He sighs deeply and rubs his head. His body continues to lean forward as if he will race off any instant. "I am not a police officer. But I believe it could be true. Her mother examined the body and the brothers and father threatened to kill the one who brought her harm if they can find him. The mother said she was a virgin and she'd been raped." His voice trails off.

"Oh, *mon dieu.*"

"My housekeeper will be furious if I arrive late for the meal. I must go now." He turns to exit the cold stone edifice, then he pauses and turns back. "You know they hate the gypsies too, don't you?"

"What?"

"German hatred isn't just reserved for Jews. They murder gypsies too. And the handicapped."

"You believe it was a German who committed the crime?"

"Only God knows," the priest says. "But I suspect, yes."

Claire winces. Her whole being senses beyond a doubt that the death was criminal.

"The mother swears she saw a German in uniform. But leave it to God, Claire. God judges and punishes."

Claire sucks in her breath as he exits the door. "Wait. Do you know who?'

"No, my child. No one has confessed to me, though even if they had my position prevents me from saying. It's not my place to judge."

34

THE FRENCH COLLABORATORS and German Gestapo plan to move the detainees off of the boat. Herr Schimd makes a special request for Alain. He moves my brother from the boat to the old prison. But the dungeon in that ancient fortified prison offers no rest. Alain tries to sleep on straw while screams of the tortured echo up from the dank, thick-walled rooms below. Unlike most of the men and women around him, Alain feels no fear. Silvie calls him an "old soul." He looks upon all of the events as a sort of cosmic joke. It gives him a superhero serenity that fellow prisoners admire. He sings resistance songs and songs of the rural peasants and dairy farmers to keep up morale and occupy his mind. His songs lift the spirits of those who hear him as he sings day in and day out. I try to draw Claire here so she can hear him from the edge of the canal. She'd recognize his songs from anywhere.

I've realized that Madame Elli, the farmer's wife can hear me, and I urge her to go to the prison. She senses it's important and I guide her to the old town. When she walks along the canal, she hears Alain singing and later tells Claire.

"Your brother's in the old fortified prison."

Claire's in a foul mood. "How do you know?"

"The way we always know when Alain's around. Heard him singing with that lousy voice of his. Maybe you can get your German friend to intervene and release him."

"He's not my friend. I despise him and it's mutual."

"Doesn't hurt to try."

"That's not true," Claire snaps. She pushes her bike toward the town as Madame Elli walks beside her. "Are you sure it's Alain?"

"He was singing, 'Without the milk maids their udders will swell and burst…'"

"Sounds like him." Claire smiles sadly, her mind racing. I hear her thoughts as she wonders if she might find money to bribe the guards to free Alain.

⚘

Herr Schmid stands rigidly beside two other officers before the commandant at Gestapo headquarters. The new commandant sits in profile and taps his cigar languidly against the edge of a crystal ashtray. He looks out of the windows of the lakeside villa headquarters as army trucks and troops prepare for deployment. Herr Schmid's stomach clenches with fear. This is the same man who brutally shot his brother years ago.

"Tomorrow, gentlemen," the commandant says exhaling a long trail of white smoke. "We move to the plateau to annihilate the resistance in the mountains." He crosses to the window and watches thick wheels of army trucks digging ruts in the field. "Dismissed." The men relax. "Not you." He points to Hans. "They tell me you're in charge of the secret services here. What's your name?"

"Schmid, sir." A shimmer of sweat coats Hans' upper lip and he hopes the commandant won't recognize him. I couldn't see this before. But the one who murders lives in constant fear of death and torture. Hans' face pales.

"You're in charge of surveillance."

"Yes, sir."

"If you're worth anything, give me some valuable news. Something that will excite me, Schmid."

"The resistance is gathering on the plateau. We have reports of foreign munitions drops and BBC English Radio incites them with speeches and secret messages we're decoding, sir."

"Tell me something I don't know," the commandant growls. "Is the local population subdued, Schmid? I want them on their knees."

"The latest arrests have paralyzed the economy. Tight controls on all food supplies. We have them on their knees, sir."

"Is that so? You let them sabotage our German officers with that explosion only a short time ago. The Fuehrer was not pleased. He ordered harsh punishment. But I'm giving you a second chance, Schmid."

Herr Schmid's hands hang at his side as he stands there rigid, his knuckles clenched until his hands turn white. He knows the commandant can inflict terrible humiliation and pain. "Sir, it was a spontaneous plan. They're terrorists with no strategy. They'd not planned it until hours before. This is why we couldn't stop their guerilla warfare."

The commandant stands in front of Hans and grabs hold of his right ear. He twists the cartilage. "You think I don't remember you, Schmid. You, and your snot-nosed brother from Stuttgart." Herr Schmid knows he must not react with any show of pain, fear, or emotion. His face remains impassive, unmoved even as the commandant twists his ear and pain rips through his head. "Rumor has it that your French whore alerted them, Schmid." The commandant releases his grip.

"French woman, sir?" Hans stares straight ahead.

"I said, 'whore', Schmid. Don't play ignorant. We know all about you. We know about that whore housekeeper who comes."

Hans flinches. "No one could have accessed the files or any secret information, sir."

"Why's that, Schimd? Do you keep her…what's her name?" He sucks on his cigar and waits.

Pearls of sweat dampen Hans' forehead and soak his underarms. "Cccc…Claire," he stammers.

"Ccc…Claire," the commandant mocks. "So you keep it all locked away when you bang her?" Herr Schmid's face flushes with heat.

"Everything is secure, sir."

"You know you'll have to take care of that *problem*." He says the word "problem" so that Herr Schmid understands he means, Claire.

"Deportation, sir?" Herr Schmid does not flinch or reveal any emotion.

"I've been following you long enough to know what you're capable of Schmid. I'd suggest you do what's most appropriate to eliminate the situation."

Claire's in imminent danger. I must warn her.

Herr Commandant turns to another officer who enters the room. "Ahh, Herr Jager, you will accompany the troops up into the mountains tomorrow. I want to know precisely what happens at every step. Eliminate every bit of resistance you find. Burn and destroy the villages and chase out the farmers. How many men are hiding up there?" He turns to Herr Schmid.

"Two thousand men estimated, Herr Commandant."

"They'll be no match for us. Exterminate them all. Deport any prisoners to Germany to work in the war factories. Kill anyone who resists."

"Yes, sir."

"Dismissed, Herr Schmid."

Hans feels sickened by the stress, but when he turns to exit through the high arched doorway a red glimmer of hope catches his eye. A silver bowl of strawberries sits on the buffet. Their brightness contrasts with the dim space and soiled curtains. He's on high alert with his senses activated, like a wary animal. He smells the strawberries from across the room, and the scent whirls him back to boyhood when he played with his brother and ate wild strawberries before the wars. He yearns to pocket them as an act of defiance. But the Commandant's in the office behind him. Hans glances back and furtively grabs a handful as he slips past the buffet. With one final salute to a fellow officer guarding the exit, he disappears outdoors where he can finally breathe again. He protects the delicate fruit cupped in his large fist. In front of the commandant all of the pain, humiliation, and death of his childhood resurfaced and weakened him. But the strawberries changed everything. Their color brings a promise for something better. He knows exactly who to share them with, and his feet lead him to the school.

Ginny exits the stone edifice and her gray, knee-length dress gives her an air of serious maturity. When she sees him, she frowns and walks on alone. He strides up behind her, hands clasped behind his back.

"I knew you'd be here," she says, still frowning. "I could feel it."

"Mmm. I have something for you."

He moves ahead and casually guides her away from the frequented streets onto the back path that leads to the secret, ruined temple inside the deserted garden. They walk in silence, Ginny staring straight ahead. He steps over the broken wall of the garden, and offers her his hand again to help her over the unsteady stones. She accepts. When he releases her hand, she hurries up the gazebo steps and around the half-naked Greek goddess. Sun rays pierce the clouds and flood past the white columns.

"What is it?" Ginny says, breaking the silence. She stares down at him on the steps below.

"You must come and find it."

"You gave gifts to Aurelie too." She narrows her eyes.

He shrugs, takes a step back and looks at the path out of the garden. Ginny stands above him, arms crossed. A feeling of inner strength fills her as he backs away. "You will miss something special," he says.

She assesses him warily.

"It's here." He pats his pocket. "But you have to make the effort to come and get it or you'll never know."

Herr Schmid stands on the steps below her so they are face to face at the same level. She warily reaches for his jacket pocket and he clasps her wrist in one hand. "Not like that." Ginny's breath stops. "Gently," he orders.

She looks startled, afraid, and obeys.

"No. Wait. Close your eyes," he says.

Ginny glares now, carefully balancing anger with fear and a self-preserving sense of composure. She's aware of a very delicate balance of power that could shift in an instant. She closes her eyes. Herr Schmid climbs the steps until he's standing on the platform beside her, towering above. "Eyes closed," he warns. She reluctantly obeys. He holds one of the giant red strawberries near her nose.

"Oh! What is that?" Her mouth waters from the sweet smell and the fear mixes with desire. He touches the berry to her lips and she opens her eyes.

"A strawberry!" she says, expressing sheer delight against her will.

He pulls it away and for an instant she stands there with her mouth slightly open. "You didn't follow orders," he says. The vision of her mouth detonates the ill desire in his heart, and as much as he wanted to be that boy who played the hero in the forest and protected girls, his impulses drive him back to the present, to Herr Schmid, the killer. *Restraint.* I hear the demon in him whisper. *It's almost time.*

Ginny reaches for the strawberry, but he won't let go. "Just one bite," he says, and touches the berry to her lips. Her hunger seems overpowering now.

She takes another bite of the berry gripped between his fingers and watches his every move, prepared to dart away in an instant. But I sense a hidden motive behind her action. She remains still. "It must be from Provence." She regains her sternness. He stares at her in that transfixed way, and she slips behind the Greek statue.

"*Kome*," he says in German. The demon side of Herr Schmid aches at the view of her throat, as her chin pokes into the air, and she looks up at him from behind the statue. *Do it now*, the demon whispers. *Don't hesitate.*

My heart beats wildly. How can I stop his madness and drive Ginny away? I want to call out to Silvie or her grandmother. All I recall is "will" and how it's possible to influence some people if I focus intently enough. Claire. I must warn her. She can intervene.

Claire bikes home on her usual route, but I nudge her to take another direction. "Claire!" I whisper. "Try this path." With my energy, I urge her toward the garden. She doesn't understand why, but she follows this muddy, hidden path with a feeling that it will guide her to an important discovery.

"Oh, what's this?" she says curiously. She leans her bike against the wall and steps into the deserted space, enchanted by its broken beauty. She spies Ginny in the garden and lifts a hand to call out. But confusion sets in when she sees Herr Schmid. Claire prowls in undercover of the thick shrubs to watch.

"Another?" Herr Schmid holds another strawberry in his palm.

Ginny nods, her belly aching from hunger. But when she reaches out to take it, he shakes his head no. He holds the stem and puts the red berry to her lips again. When she bites into it, red juice dribbles down her chin.

"What are you doing!" Claire says, stunned by the intimacy surrounding them.

Ginny and Herr Schmid jerk their heads in her direction. Claire gazes up at them, and a sort of realization hits her as she attempts to read Herr Schmid's eyes. All that she's denied returns in a rush. Claire feels his connection to me. And to the dead gypsy girl the priest mentioned.

"You should be home, Ginny." Clarie's fear for Ginny brings her to speak with harsh authority. Ginny moves guiltily down the steps and out of the garden without looking back. She saunters toward Herr Schmid. "You come all the way out here to pluck young flowers?" Claire says in a mildly sarcastic tone, hoping to mask her anger.

A rage comes over him, but he holds it inside. In an effort to hide his frustration at not getting his prey, he opens his arms to Clare. Something inside of her warns her of danger. She casually steps back and slaps his chest to push him away. Her hand hits the wound where he pinned my brooch to his skin, and he doubles over, wincing with pain.

"Are you alright?" Claire says, keeping her distance.

Once the sharpness passes, he remembers the commandant's orders and knows what must be done. "Come tonight," he says in an attempt to hide his anger and hatred at being thwarted. It's time to take care of Claire, he thinks.

"I can't. Father's expecting me." She twists away and her skirt flips up as she steps lightly over the broken garden wall and glances back at him.

"It was an order, not an invitation," he growls behind her, but she's already gone.

35

THE FOG SETTLES in and obscures the path. Claire bikes home in slow, careful increments. A crow cries and Claire remembers me. Some jonquils grow along the road. She plucks two; one for my grave and the other for our mother's. A deep sadness descends and reminds me of how truly separated we are. Oh how I love Claire, with her fiery spirit and courage.

"Thank you, Claire," I say.

She raises her head, startled. "Aurelie?" Somehow my love for her gives me the ability to use the fog to create an illusion of substance and form. She sees me now.

"I miss you, Claire." I want to take her in my arms, but these arms are no longer physical. They're energy. I move closer, but she steps back.

"No. This is not real. I must be feverish," she says.

"It's not a fever, Claire. I'm here."

Her eyes stare back at me in disbelief. To her, death means there's nothing more. I can't explain to her that this isn't true. All I can do is warn her about the impending peril.

"Claire. Listen. You must go away. You're in danger. So is Ginny. Please go to Switzerland if you can."

"Switzerland?"

"Take Ginny. Go."

We hear a twig crack and Claire turns. Jean-Michel appears from behind some shrubs. She rushes to him in a desperate embrace. "Are you real? Kiss me," she says. He kisses her passionately. Claire's eyes brim with tears. "Do you love me?"

He lifts her off the ground and laughs, a low, gurgling, sexy laugh. "Do I!"

"Come," she says and leads him back to my grave. "Do you see anything?" she asks Jean-Michel. He scans the cemetery.

"In this fog? I was lucky to find you. But I followed your scent." He inhales deeply like a wolf and smiles.

She hits him playfully. "I'm serious." She stares straight at me, into my eyes, but in his presence, she no longer sees me.

"You put the flower there?" Jean-Michel says. She continues to stare at me an instant, but he grabs her by the hand and pulls her away. "Come on, you. We've got some catching up to do." Claire glances over her shoulder through the fog. I wave and she frowns as she tries to decipher what's real and what's not.

Jean-Michel pulls her into a thicket behind the cemetery and kisses her passionately. "Hey," he says. "It's D-day. No more fooling around."

"I heard the German trucks rumbling up the mountain," Claire says. "Do you have to go back up there?"

"Don't talk. Just for a moment. Just kiss me."

But Claire feels angry and depressed. "Don't go. I know you're going. Please don't go." Fear and panic grip her gut. She feels certain that he'll not return this time. A few tears involuntarily edge her worried eyes.

"Hey, what's wrong? You know it's my duty. You know this is what I've been living for."

"To die? Well, I'm against it."

"Shhh. I'm not going to die. You're my lucky charm. And I've already survived one wound. Thinking about you all of the time saved me."

"That's enough. You've done enough then. I'll hide you in the cellar until they leave. Things will calm down soon. They must. Things can't go on like this forever." Her breathing speeds up, desperate and painful. "Please don't go." Her tears turn to weeping.

"Hey, babe, what's wrong? You're always so level-headed and untouched by it all." He caresses her face and looks at her with his softness. She knows that a fierce warrior lives inside of him and thrives side by side with his gentleness.

"You can't go. Please." She wraps her arms tightly about his neck, desperate to make him stay.

"I'm not going anywhere with you like that."

Claire's body shakes as she weeps. "I'm pregnant," she confesses.

"Oh, geeze." Jean-Michel's face turns pale. He loosens her arms. "Is it mine?"

"God, how can you even ask that?"

"Is it?"

"I don't know." She weeps more now. "I think so. But he raped me. He forced me."

"The kraut, Schmid?"

Claire nods.

"I'll kill him." He turns away from her and a chill descends. When he faces her again, his jaws clinch with determination. "I've got to go back to the mountains now. I've got to carry some information. When I come back…" He braces her shoulders and forces her to look at him. "And I will come back, Claire. You understand?"

She nods. "*Oui.*"

"I will take him out. He's a dead man." He backs away from her. "You've sacrificed way too much, Claire. I'm sorry."

Terrible guilt invades Claire and she turns and vomits in the bushes. "Oh god, please forgive me." She wipes the bile from her mouth and Jean-Michel helps her to stand upright.

"You okay?"

"I'll be fine."

"I've got to go. Au revoir," he says and kisses her on the forehead before disappearing into the fog.

I watch Claire's mind work insanely fast to find answers. She thinks of the woman at the town hall who may help for the right amount of money. She can get the papers they need.

"Don't wait, Claire," I say. "You must do it tomorrow." I draw the fog around me to take form and appear in front of her again as she leans against a birch tree. "Don't delay."

"God, I'm hallucinating."

"No, you're not It's me. You must escape. Leave now, while you can." I've seen a few steps into the future and I know that very soon any movement out of the *Savoie* will be impossible. Since it shares a border with Switzerland and one with Italy, the Germans aim to put us on total lock down to cut off the movement of any "undesirables." Only those with travel papers will be allowed to journey between towns just a few miles away.

Claire's eyes glisten. "I'm going mad." She shakes her head.

"You're very sane, Claire," I whisper softly. "But you must pack. Get your travel papers and go." I send images to her mind of Mom's worn suitcase and hope she understands. "Hang on, Claire. Please," I beg. But she's no longer listening, and Naehelle pulls me away.

"I've told you not to intervene," Naehelle says, arms crossed.

"No!" I protest. "She needs my help."

"Come with me," Naehelle insists and I follow to avoid more reprimands. "You have these stupid delusions of grandeur, like you think you're some kind of superhero who can save them," Naehelle says. Her words sound light and frivolous until she turns on me. "But know what? You won't. That's not how our world is made. So get over it now. Or I'll send you on. I'll send you so far away that you'll never see any of your family ever again. That's the price to pay for trying to change fate when you're not supposed to."

Her rant anchors me in my tracks, but I feel more determined than ever. When she releases me, I retreat to my room in her house where all I can do is look out the window and watch the war unfold.

36

REGARDLESS OF NAEHELLE'S warnings, I return to the top of the roof of my parents' house, to the place where my body rested before they buried it. I hug my knees and sit in the chill fog on the rust-colored tiles and reflect. When I was a child, living on the earth, I saw so little, and I never really understood anything. Not really. Now that I'm in this other world, I see people's motives, and I'm stunned by the evil on earth. How can people like Hans Schmid exist?! Naehelle says that his pain creates pain in others. And in the material world opposites exist to make us grow.

"If there's no pain, how would you know the pleasure of well-being? If there were no sadness or grief, how would you know happiness and joy?" she said. This puzzles me. Where's the heaven Sister Marie described? In that heaven, there is no pain or death or anxiety or war. Naehelle says the earth is heaven exactly because it contains all of these things; when we see it all as Divine we're blessed. But I didn't live there long enough to find out.

My vision takes me to Jean-Michel, who puts on his cross-country skis; he treads up a hidden goat path to the plateau. The Germans blocked off the main mountain road and convoys of arms and soldiers crowd the area. British planes roared in and destroyed the ball-bearing factory in Annecy earlier and they search regularly for more targets to disrupt the Germans.

Driven by determination for what he calls freedom and justice,

Jean-Michel maintains a tight focus on passing the secret information he carries. His courage shines out like a light in the night. I'm starting to understand his sacrifices and ideals. Before my body died, I thought mostly about boys and kisses and the fantasies found in romance novels. I never saw the impact of the war because Mom, and Dad, Alain, and Claire all maneuvered to protect me from it. I'm not so sure that was a good thing. If I would have seen the possibility of evil, would I have allowed Herr Schmid to seduce and kill me?

I don't know. But I can't help but imagine I would have been less innocent and more wary. I think back to the way Herr Schmid so adeptly lured me into trusting him. Like with Ginny, he calculated every move and seemed to anticipate my reactions and feelings. He held back and withheld and promised – like he knew my every adolescent fantasy about boys and a knight who would protect and save me. He seduced me with sweets, gifts, and hot tea, and made me feel special. In Mom's absence he seemed to be the only one who really cared. So I trusted him, and then he took my life. I think of my beautiful, healthy body. He took the most precious thing I possessed. And he did it so casually. I meant nothing to him. All I feel now is deep, deep grief about the things that I'll miss out on. True kisses. Someone who would touch me with real love and tenderness. Laughter and dancing and making love with a man who really cares for me. Having a family. Growing old with Ginny as my best friend, and being able to hug her again.

Emotion swells in my throat and my eyes water. I'm not feeling sorry for myself. But I would not wish this on anyone. Ever. I don't understand God – if there is one. Or why he or she or would allow such terrible things to happen. As I gaze out across the rooftops now, I see many souls leaving the earth across the whole of Europe. They choose to move on, to go and do whatever souls do once they leave their bodies, and most of them bypass the in-between. But I sit here filled with grief and remorse unable to ascend. My heart breaking. I've never felt so alone in my life. All I yearn to do is touch Ginny. To be held by a kind man. To love and be loved. Tears form, and in the in-between, they resemble droplets of light that trickle down my nose onto the rooftop and splatter on the ground like beautiful diamonds. The vision makes me smile a little. A tiny bit of beauty in the dark night.

"Hey," I hear and turn to see Silvie sitting beside me. I turn my face away so she can't see the tears. She wraps an arm around her knees. "I know," she says. "That's how I feel too." She reaches for my hand.

I turn and look at her with reproach like no one can ever understand. But I see that she does. She wraps her arm around my shoulder and I lean into her and weep. "I'll never get married," I say. "I can never hug Ginny or hear my babies laugh or wipe away their tears. Or play in the water again." She hugs me with her warm energy. And I know that she knows how I feel.

"I know. I'm so, so sorry."

I wipe away my tears and look out through the clouds up into the skies. "If I could do it all again. It would be so different," I confess. "I wouldn't go near that man."

"You can do it again."

"You mean I can go back and repeat everything, and make the decision to avoid Hans Schmid?"

"No, not like that," she says. Silvie's eyes shimmer with ethereal light. "But you can go back again, into a new life?"

My tears stop. "What do you mean?"

"Claire, your sister."

"Yes."

"She's pregnant."

"So?"

"You can be her new baby."

This idea seems so utterly unbelievable, even more unbelievable than the existence of a world in-between. I'm stunned to silence. Silvie smiles. "Don't your pale-faced mums teach you anything?"

"Guess not. Did your Gran tell you that?"

"Of course. It's a part of our wisdom. Passed on from generation to generation. That's how we preserve our lineage." Silvie scoots away now that I'm calmer.

"You mean I can become Claire's daughter?"

"Yeah."

I'm speechless.

"You're good at focus and you have strong will. If you'd rather go back there…" She points down at my parents' house, down into their world.

"Then you focus and go into her womb. There's no soul there yet. But you'll have to decide soon. Other souls will want to come in if you decide not to go."

I laugh. "You mean people are actually lining up to get back into that world of pain and suffering?!"

"To possess a human body is the most precious experience in the whole universe."

"Wow!" The thought I might be able to return excites me and fills me with dread.

"But it would take another seven or eight months before I'd be born. That's too far away to stop Hans Schmid from hurting Ginny and Claire. And as a baby I couldn't do much anyway."

"So do what you can from here…and if you really miss that world, then go back. It's an opportunity." Silvie takes me by the hand. "Come on, now. Let's go get some rest."

In an instant, at the speed of thought, we're back at Naehelle's and I slip under the duvet. I meet Claire in her dreams and tell her about Herr Schmid and his plans for Ginny and that her own life is in danger. I don't know if she'll remember. I don't know if it will make a difference. But it's a try.

37

CLAIRE DRESSES AT dawn and bikes into town to catch the woman at the prefecture before she enters the building. Whatever happens to Jean-Michel, she's determined to leave and bring Ginny too.

"A gift," Claire says, handing her an envelope. It contains a bribe of money, some silk stockings, and the promise for more, should the young woman acknowledge what she needs.

"I suppose you want something in return?"

"I need help for two people."

"I don't know what you think I can do," the woman says, hiding the thick envelope under her coat. "It's getting harder and harder."

"I'd heard..." Claire sighs heavily and makes to get on her bike again to leave.

"Wait," the woman says warily.

"It's for you?"

Claire nods and bows her head. "I'm pregnant. I've got to get out of here."

"What's the name of the other person?"

"Virginie Jacquet. J. A. C. Q. U. E. T. She's sixteen."

"Meet me tomorrow. After work. Five p.m. By the big tree near the lake, in the park." The woman who must be no older than Claire – say twenty-two or twenty-three, glances into the envelope and eyes the amount. "It costs two-thousand," the woman says.

"Two-thousand? Oh."

"There's only fifteen-hundred here."

"Oh," Claire says, worried. "But the girl is only a child." The woman fingers her expensive pearls and adjusts her new hat. Her access to the paper and ink stamps, used for the official travel documents needed to travel from town to town, seems to be making her rich. "I was told fifteen-hundred covered the costs."

"You know what's at stake. You know what risks I'm taking."

"Prison. Or worse," Claire admits and thinks of her own precarious situation.

"I could be sent before a firing squad if someone reports me. It's two-thousand. Per person."

"Yes. I'll get it." But Claire doesn't know from where.

"I'll see what I can do. Be here tomorrow evening."

"Yes." Claire nods. "Thank you." But how will she get the money? *What to do? Go to Herr Schmid's? Or maybe to Herr Kaiser's?* She thinks of stealing the money from them. Herr Schmid might help her. The thoughts in her head turn like cogs in the wheels of a clock or a motor. Sometimes Herr Schmid has felt affection for her. She's sure of it. And he may have helped to move Alain. Maybe a baby will sway his instincts of kindness and preservation. Maybe he'll take pity and want to protect her.

First Claire goes to Herr Kaiser's hoping to search through his things for money. But he's home, soliciting sex from her. "I'm not a prostitute," she mutters. She drops off eggs and quickly escapes. The cathedral door stands open with the gilded statue of Mother Mary perched on top looking down with compassion. It's not usually her nature, but Claire makes a detour into the church. She collapses onto the pew first, then kneels at the feet of the gilded statue of Mother Mary surrounded with candles. The Mother cradles her baby with a gentle smile. Maybe it's because of the baby that Claire prays.

"Mother, please help me. Guide me. Only you will understand."

I sit close to Claire and pray too. I see the Mother's compassion extend down to us and bring comfort and soothing energy. Tears of gratitude fill me. Claire's worry makes it harder for her to feel the waves of softness, but her worry subsides a little.

"Please protect her, Mother," I pray. "And guide and protect me too."

The Mother is there right before me. Alive, vibrant. She fills the space with her gracious and loving presence. All we ever had to do was think of her and she is here among us. She's not just a myth. Not just a gilded statue. She's a very real, loving presence and my heart fills with warmth, reassurance, and gratitude. "Thank you," I say. Now I know why so many people turn to Her. In this moment, in her Divine and gentle presence, I kneel and my heart aches to ask her. I feel I shouldn't. But I must.

"Why, Mother? Why did I have to die like that?"

She smiles down at me, her eyes filled with loving-kindness. She extends her long elegant fingers and touches my hair. She says nothing. But I see in her eyes. And in that knowing, I know that all is simply as it is and that everything in all time is perfect. Incomprehensible. Paradoxical. Beautiful. Even my rape and death at his hands was beautiful, like an orchestrated scene on a stage at a theatre. And my grief about my loss begins to fade temporarily as I accept and love Her more. I place my hands together in prayer and bow my head. "Thank you, Mother. Thank you." I feel her loving presence surround me with such total acceptance and unconditional love that I feel unworthy and yet deeply grateful. She gives more love than my birth mother every could, even though I loved her too. "Forgive him," she says.

"I don't know how, Mother."

Claire's eyes fill with tears too and I hope she has experienced the grace.

"Do you feel her too Claire? Do you see her?" I whisper. "She's real. She's not just imagination!" I feel excited and hopeful. Claire sits back on the pew, head down. One hand lies on the wooden bench and I touch it. "I love you, Claire. Please don't feel guilty about what happened to me. I love you. Please stay safe." A ripple of goose bumps climbs Claire's arm from the place where I touch her, and she shivers and rises. As she heads to the large open doors at the back of the cathedral, Father Ansen emerges from the confessional. He moves toward her and Claire seems to want to escape his presence, but a sense of duty anchors her in place.

"My child," he says. Claire bows to him and he blesses her. "You look very tired."

"I'm fine, Father." But her voice cracks and the strain shows around her eyes.

"My child, I've thought about your questions about the girl and about your sister. It would be best to let it go."

Claire drops her head. "I don't want to let it go. I'd rather know. Sometimes the truth is a relief. It gives us what we need to know so we can act appropriately."

"Well, then…" He clears his throat and hooks a hand under her elbow, guiding her to the side aisle. "A German man came to see me. Nazi SS, I believe."

"What did he look like?"

"My dear, God protects," the priest says.

"Even killers?"

"He had remarkable blue eyes. I think he carried a brooch. A silver and pearl pin, and he kept rubbing it." Claire recalls that my coat was torn where I wore the pin.

"Thank you, Father." He turns to go, then stops.

"Her name…the other girl's name. It was Silvie. And there was one before your sister too. Same marks. Same…" His voice trails off as he avoids the difficult words. "Same defilement."

Claire takes in the words. "She was raped, you mean?"

The priest lowers his eyes with embarrassment. "I'm sorry."

His affirmation confirms Claire's suspicions about what happened to me as well.

"My child…" Father Ansen's eyes dart around the empty church as if he may be watched. "You must leave. There are ways…," he says. He scurries away behind the big thick wooden door at the back of the church, leaving Claire bewildered. She gazes at the door where he disappeared and ponders the options. Then the Mother attracts her attention again.

"Protect me Mother. I'm sorry, I don't know how to believe in you. But, if you're there, I humbly need your help."

38

EVEN THOUGH CLAIRE vowed never to return, her feet carry her straight to Hans Schmid's apartment to search for money and for proof of his hand in my death. She thinks of finding my brooch or something that indicates he's done dreadful things. Something that will give her a reason to shoot him. The night feels oppressive and gloomy as she climbs the dark stairwell to his apartment and checks the small pistol in the hidden compartment of her handbag. The cold metal waits patiently with the safety lock off.

She recovers the key, hidden by the concierge in a crack in the wall, and opens the door without ringing. She followed him quietly in the shadows before coming and watched him disappear behind the blacked-out doors of the German-run brothel, so she feels certain of a few moments of safety. The big black key turns in the lock. The thick door clicks open and squeaks on its old hinges. Claire flips on the electric lights and begins her frantic search. The drawers. The desk. Through his papers in the filing cabinet. In his bedroom. *Aurelie's brooch. Where is it?* she thinks. The rooms feel small and suffocating, as she opens the drawers in his bedroom. *God I'd hate to be a prisoner.* She thinks of Alain. "Be careful, you," she says and sends loving thoughts to him. I watch her thoughts fly out straight to him and comfort him in the cold, damp cell. "Mother Mary, please protect, Jean-Michel," she says. "Please play it smart, Jean-Michel. Don't be a hero. Don't die for this stupid war."

Claire opens Herr Schmid's closet and finds the flog hidden under the suitcase. In one of his pockets she finds the bracelet Ginny made for me and shudders.

"You will not have Ginny too." She stuffs the bracelet in her pocket.

Claire searches under the heavy mattress, squeezes the pillows, and runs a hand under the sheets. The floorboard creaks when she steps on it. She bends to find a lose piece of parquet. Lifts it. Instead of the brooch, she finds a list written in his beautiful cursive handwriting. A black list. Enemies of the Reich. She reads the names. "Jean-Michel…" "Alain…" "Claire Lançon." She sucks in her breath and knows she must escape now and take any money to pay the woman who forges the documents. Claire replaces the wooden slat of parquet. One of her square silk scarves peeks out from under the edge of the bed and she reclaims it.

"Here, Claire," I call out. "Here. Quick. Look on the mantel. It will help you to understand." She must sense my presence because she clasps her purse close and opens the small compartment to check for the pistol again. "Over here. Please!" I say, frantic, and nudge her with my energy.

On the mantel the silver charm with the "S" engraved on it remains there like a relic on an altar. I want to tell her that Herr Schmid kept a relic from each girl he murdered. She sees the lone lovebird earring. But Claire's too caught up in panic to notice or make the connection. With all of my force, focus, and concentration, I push the bracelet with the silver charm until it drops. Claire nearly jumps out of her skin when it hits the floor. All of her body tenses with adrenaline, ready to flee. She scrambles to pick it up and looks around. Nothing visible caused it to fall. The hairs stand on the back of her neck and she feels the chill of my presence.

"Look at the charm. Look, Claire. Please. Please pay attention."

I don't know if she hears me. Not consciously anyway. But she looks down at the silver charm in her palm. "S," she says. "S…S…S. Why S? S for Schmid?" She measures the size of the bracelet against her own wrist. "It's a young girl's. S…S..for…"

"Silvie," I say. "It's Silvie's. Listen to me, please!" When Silvie hears her name called, she appears beside me.

"What is it?" she says. When she sees Claire holding her bracelet, it brings back memories of the violence. Silvie cringes at the memory and nearly disappears again.

"Please stay and help me," I say.

Silvie moves in close to Claire's ear. "Herr Schmid killed me," Silvie says. At the same time she recreates the images of how he strangled her and sends them telepathically to Claire. "He murdered me, Silvie." Silvie creates an image of a sliver plaque with her name on it and sends it to Claire's mind. I watch Claire receive the images and her mind works to interpret.

"Silvie?" Claire's brow furrows and she seems to receive what Silvie communicates.

"I'm Silvie. Herr Schmid murdered me," Silvie repeats. "I'm Silvie, remember? The priest told you about me." She sends the image of her name again.

"Silvie?" Claire says aloud. Her heart stops. "Silvie! The gypsy girl Father Ansen spoke of. Oh *mon dieu*, no," she says.

But Claire knows with all of her being that our deaths are linked. It's a knowing of absolute certainty. Her desire to find my brooch intensifies. "I need proof," she says. "I won't believe it. He's not that evil. He always gave me food…like some part of him knew it was for the Jewish orphans." Anxiety rips through her every cell. Then she senses his presence and freezes. Herr Schmid leans against the doorframe, arms crossed casually, watching her with cool indifference. His steel blue eyes show no emotion. That frightens her the most. She knows instinctively that emotionless men can become dangerous killers.

"Aaaah, I see you've decided to come after all," he says, smoothly laying his black leather gloves on the bed.

Mother Mary, Claire prays in silence, and again Mother Mary appears near her. I'm there too with Silvie beside me. We form an ethereal shield to protect Claire from Herr Schmid's disparaging darkness. Claire's knees feel shaky, but a sense of calm strength descends and she feels she'll be safe. She steps back on one heel, like she does when she's normal and surly. "I forgot my scarf." She flicks it in his face. "It was under the bed. I was going to leave you in quiet, but you need punishment for your crimes, Schmid. So take your shirt off. Now." Claire reaches into the closet for the flog, temporarily turning her back on him in a show of confidence in her power. It's her bluff.

He hesitates, caught off guard by her readiness to take over.

"Obey, or you'll pay a high price," she insists. Her eyes flash with fire. Herr Schmid puffs up his chest and takes a threatening step toward her, still playing the role of the SS officer. But Claire laughs at him and stands in her power, shored up by our presence. "I'm the one in charge here," she says. "I'm your master, remember?" She clasps the flog in one hand and holds the purse with the pistol in the other. Armed with her knowledge of his aims to turn her into the Reich, her fury fuels her. Cool, anchored solidly in place, the power shifts. Overcome by the fatigue of always being in control and filled with an absolute desire for annihilation, Hans Schmid gives in.

"I said take off your shirt," Claire hisses through clenched teeth. He lifts his fingers to his buttons and feels the release of tension and anxiety in handing over control to her.

"Like this, *damen*?"

"No, you're doing it wrong." She holds the whip near his cheek and tells him to be more careful. When he pulls off his shirt, she sees the wide bandage around his chest and thinks it's for the lashes on his back. Her life is at stake now. She touches the tip of the flog to the bandage at the center of his chest and he winces in pain. Claire steels herself against caring. "Good. Very good. Pants now." He follows orders. "On your knees," Claire commands. He hesitates. A sense of resistance and suspicion momentarily ripple through Hans' mind again, but habit and desire win out. "Hands behind your back." He complies and Claire binds his hands with her scarf. Without forewarning, Claire lets loose and strikes his shoulders with all of her fury. He cries out, head bowed. "You deserve this," she says, lashing with all of her force. She loses herself in the fury and frustration of rape, wounds, my death, and suffering. The wounds reopen and blood laces Hans' back.

"Enough. It's enough," he says. When she comes to her senses, Claire stares at the whip in her hands and throws it away, shocked at her level of violence. She unbinds him and turns away.

Hans reaches for her limp hand and kisses it tenderly. "Thank you, dear one."

She stares back appalled at what she's done, and aware of his creeping influence on her heart. "No," she jerks away.

"It's only like this that I'm a man," he says. "I can feel again. You are my savior." He squeezes her hand with tenderness and affection. His blue eyes fill with light like a thousand doorways have just opened and let in the sun. He caresses her forearm with the back of his index finger and reaches under her skirt.

"Stop. Don't…" She pushes him away and moves to the doorway.

"I love you," he says. "I need you, Claire." He pleads and she knows that in this moment some part of him speaks truth. He lies on his back, his teeth gritting with pain. Water edges his eyes. "It's all I know, Claire. It's the only way I can love. I'm a broken man. Please, come back to me." He seems unusually weak and pale.

The nurturer in Claire wants to help. "Your bandage needs tending. It's disgusting. What did you do? Stab yourself from self-hate?" She recalls the stained shirts she took to the laundry and unhooks the safety pins that hold the gauze in place.

"No. Don't touch it." He pushes her away.

"It needs attention." It's only now that she recognizes how ill he is. "You have a fever," she says touching his forehead.

"I'm fine." But his face turns pale and his eyes roll back in his head.

"God, don't die! They'll think I killed you." She shakes him back to consciousness and unwinds the bandage. Under the final strips of stained gauze, she touches a hard knot in the center of his chest.

"What's this? What have you done to yourself?" She imagines a spear point or some jagged war object.

"No…" Hans Schmid feebly protests as Claire unfurls the bandage.

"It's infected. Let me see." She grabs a pair of nail scissors from the bedside table and cuts away the last strips of gauze stuck to his chest. The bandage closest to his skin is stained rust-colored from old blood and puss. Claire's brow creases as she cuts it away. She fights off the urge to gag.

Hans Schmid reaches up in a weak attempt to stop her again.

"You're sick. Let me help. The bandage is stuck to the wound. Breathe in. This may cause some pain," she warns. With a quick tug, the gauze rips away to reveal the infection. In the center of his chest my silver and pearl brooch lodges in his sternum, surrounded by an oozing, open wound. He turns on his side to hide it. Claire pales and works hard to maintain tight control of her feelings.

"Oh god," Claire says. "It's her brooch." It's an accusation.

"No, Claire, I didn't…" He fades into the in-between and I ask him to release my sister of the bond he's created to link her to him.

"Where did you get this?" Claire fights back tears. She already knows.

He whispers. "She made me, Claire." The infection eats deep into his flesh. He rouses slightly and watches Claire mechanically dress the wound. She takes a deep breath and rubs alcohol into the wound with force. He winces.

"I had no choice."

Claire stops tending to the bandage and slaps him hard across the face. She reaches for the silver charm.

"And this one?" Claire says holding it up.

"An accident. It was an accident. You must believe me. I didn't do anything, Claire." Clair turns her back to him.

She sees an opportunity. "You can make amends. You need medical help. We're going to get the good doctor off of the boat and Alain out of prison," she says. "Doc Norbert may even save you."

"Bring me paper and the ink stamp."

She carries the items from his desk to the bedroom.

"Stay with me for now," Herr Schmid says reaching for her hand. "You need to believe me. I'm not evil."

"I must go." Claire stands at the door staring into the other room.

"Claire," he calls behind her. "I left something for you on the table. Use it to go away from me. Save yourself," he whispers. A glimmer of tenderness slips from him and pierces her heart with the paradox of human nature.

"What made you this way?" She stares at him and shakes her head. "You're an angel of death."

She closes the bedroom door and exits into the living room, pulling on her coat. Gold pieces form the letter "C" on the table. With her index finger she counts. "One, two, three,…ten." She calculates quickly. "Three thousand francs a piece. Times ten. Thirty thousand." A weight lifts. "Enough to escape to Switzerland and go to America," she whispers.

"Go, Claire. Don't hesitate," I say. "Go!"

As she slides the pieces of gold off of the table and into her palm, she worries that they came from families looted during the war and a ripple of guilt courses through her veins. Mother Mary touches her forehead and relieves Claire's weighty thoughts. "Thank you," she says.

Claire touches her belly, aware of the new life stirring inside. A life that I can choose to *ensoul*, if I decide to, if I learn how. If I decide that it is worthwhile, I can go back into that thick stuff of life again. With all of its pain, struggle, anguish, and occasional pleasure. But watching the madness unfold on earth fills me with a strong desire to go Home to Mom, into that other world just beyond the in-between, where I'll be welcomed into a place of total peace and bliss by a crowd of friends and family. Why bother to go back there to the physical earth plane where they're all mad?!

39

SILVIE AND I accompany Claire on her bike ride home through the dusk and though dark forces descend closer, a calm determination fills her and I feel a renewed sense of hope and possibility. I want to thank Claire for her courage.

"When I was a little girl, Claire used to leave a penny on my pillow for luck. Can I do that for her?"

Silvie smiles broadly. "Some souls can. Want to try?"

"Naehelle says it's not possible, but I made your charm fall from the mantel."

"Naehelle says a lot of things to keep you from realizing your power."

Claire lights a candle in her room and I move in close to feel its heat. With a whish of movement I glide past the candle and it flickers in the airless room.

"Watch this," Silvie says. She rushes in close to the flame and blows it out.

"Oh, how did you do that?"

"Like you saw," Silvie says. "The easiest are electric lights. Watch!"

Claire slips into bed and flicks on the electric light on her night-stand. Silvie moves in close to the lamp and it flickers on and off. Claire looks startled.

"Ohh. Oh." I feel so excited. "I want to try." But when I move close to the lamp and touch the bulb with my fingers of energy, nothing happens.

"It takes practice," Silvie says.

"I want to send her a sign," I say.

"Here." Silvie indicates a lost penny fallen between the cracks of the old floorboards. "Help me lift this out."

"But how? My fingers are energy. And way too thick to get between the cracks."

"Focus," Silvie says. "And lift it. With your mind. You can add a hum to help you focus. Watch." Her focus narrows. And I focus too. The energy of our thoughts and the sound of her humming lift the coin until it lies flat on the floor beside Claire's bed.

"Ah." The excitement makes it almost impossible to concentrate. "You're a witch to know such things!" Silvie laughs.

With intent concentration, I slide the coin up the edge of the bed post near Claire's head. When the fire pops loudly, I drop the coin. "What was that?" Claire says. She gets up to check the door lock. By the time she's settled back in, I've managed to lift the coin and place it in the center of her white pillow.

Claire's eyes water and she holds her knuckles to her mouth. "Thank you, little sister," she says. "My heart is broken into a thousand pieces. I don't know how I will live without you."

For the first time I feel her love for me. It's like I was too self-centered to understand before. I mistook her attempts at protection and mothering as ways to stifle me. But it was all love. And she was trying to juggle it with protecting the Jewish kids too. I watch her in the dim light as she nears sleep and say what I should have said while I was alive. "Thank you, Claire. I love you so, so much."

◈

During the afternoon, the woman from the mayor's office waits behind the tree at the designated spot. Claire steps off her bike and holds the handle-bars. "Sorry I'm late," she says.

"I hope you didn't waste my time," the woman snaps.

"I've got the payment. You'll owe me some change, of course." The woman smirks at the sight of the gold pieces in Claire's palm. "Now show me what you've got."

The woman tries to snatch the coins. Claire closes her hand. "No. Once I see the papers are in order and satisfactory, you'll get your pay." The woman clears her throat and scans the area warily.

"Hurry. I believe we're being watched," she says. Claire unfolds the documents and sees Ginny's name on one and her own name on another. "They will give you passage to Annemasse, to the border. From there you're on your own to cross the barbed wire into Switzerland. You'll need 'passers' to help you."

"Humf. Four-thousand doesn't even get us out of the country and it's only forty-five kilometers away." Claire flips the documents shut and hides them in the top of her stockings. "If there's anything wrong with them, there'll be hell to pay," Claire warns.

"They'll do," the woman reassures her. Claire hands over the gold coins and steps back onto the bike with a sense of hope and freedom. She wants to take Ginny from school and leave now. I tell her to do it. "Don't hesitate, Claire." But she goes to the boat where some prisoners still wait for transfer. "Herr Schmid sent me for Dr. Norbert," Claire tells the guards and shows them the letter from Hans.

"He needs medical attention and he's ordered Dr. Norbert to come," Claire says. The guards debate darkly, then search the boat. They locate the doctor. Claire tries to get the two of the guards to go to the prison next, but they only agree to accompany Claire and the doctor back to Herr Schmid's. Claire walks quickly beside the doctor and tells him about the situation. The guards shoulder them, but don't understand French.

"I want to get rid of something," Claire says. "I need your help."

"You've brought me away to kill your employer?" Doc Norbert pushes his glasses up on his nose and walks ahead enjoying the moments off of the boat.

"Shhh. I may be pregnant. How do I stop it?" Claire says.

The doctor doesn't flinch. "Whose?"

She stares back in silence. He relents needing to know.

"No way now, outside of divine intervention. Of course, you could pray for a miscarriage. Or tough it out." The doctor scratches his head. "I don't even have a medical bag. I don't know what use I'll be to your, uh… employer." He faces Claire. "Does Jean-Michel know?"

"You sound like my father."

"No, just your family doctor who's known you since you were born."

"Yes. He knows."

"Good. He'll help you."

"If he can," Claire says. "He's gone to fight."

40

"HERE." RALPH, HERR Schmid's aide, shoves a medical bag into Doc Norbert's hands, eyeing him warily. "You'd be best advised to save his life," the young man threatens in German. "One of our own doctors will arrive from the battle field when he can be spared. He'll know if you've sabotaged Herr Schmid's life."

Doc Norbert looks above his glasses at the soldier and then at Claire. "Can you tell me what he said, Claire?" He reaches into the black bag and finds items that have been unavailable to the rest of the population for months. Alcohol for sterilizing. Scalpel. Opium-based painkillers. And the Nazis' favorite cure-all amphetamine, Pervitin.

"He's warning you that he'll be watching and that a German doctor will come eventually," Claire says. "I'm sorry, doctor. I thought this would be a way to free you."

"Well, I'll do the best I can," the doctor says to the German solider and Claire translates. "Where's the patient?"

Claire leads him to the bedroom. Even the doctor flinches and turns his head away momentarily from the stench when he opens the bandage covering Herr Schmid's chest. The skin shade varies from red, to brown to black. My brooch lodges in the center of the wound. The doctor presses on the skin and it crackles.

"What is that?" The doctor touches the pin. "A child's toy?"

"A brooch," Claire says. Herr Schmid remains semi-conscious.

"How did it get there?" The doctor says.

"I don't know," Claire says. "It may be self-inflicted."

"Your employer has a strange notion of penance. Gangrene has set in. Wet gangrene. Very high mortality rate. He needs emergency hospital treatment before sepsis sets in. Or he'll die soon." The doctor examines the brooch in the center of the wound and seems to recognize it. "Didn't that belong to…"

Claire flinches. "Aurelie. Yes."

"Why the lashes all over? The Germans beating him?"

"No…It's something else. Someone else." She feels guilty.

Doc Norbert narrows his eyes and returns to examine the mess of infected flesh. "I've been a doctor for forty years and I've never seen anything like this." The doctor touches the brooch with the tip of his scalpel and quickly dislodges it. He hands it to Claire on a white handkerchief. The doctor sighs and replaces the scalpel in the black leather medical bag. "How did he get that?"

"I have no proof." A chill fills the air between them.

"No one can make me believe that your sister died a natural death, Claire."

My heart stops. "Thank you, doctor. Thank you," I say.

A rising wave of emotion chokes in Claire's throat. A knowing passes between them, and unable to face the tide of emotions, Claire stuffs it all back down.

"He's dying." Doc Norbert studies Claire's face. "Can you tell the guards that this man needs to get to the hospital?" Claire translates into broken German and one of the men leaves to request permission from Gestapo headquarters.

"The infection's very deep and near the heart. The dead flesh needs to be surgically removed. Then they'll use maggots to clean up the rest." Claire nearly wretches at the thought. "Yes, I know. Disgusting, but it works," the doctor says. "They only consume the rotten skin."

Claire, thinks of her escape plan. But her attachment to Jean-Michel and the region tears her heart in two. Doc Norbert understands and lowers his voice.

"My advice to you, if you want any…get out of here while you can. In my long life, I've seen a lot of things. And I've wanted to help a lot of people. But some are beyond hope." He takes off his wire rim glasses and rubs them on a fresh handkerchief. "A lot of people gossip about your connections with the Germans. They think you're a collaborator. They're jealous of the ways you've had it easy. The food. The money…"

"Huh," Claire scoffs. "Great. So now I've had it easy. What a joke. The resistance thinks I'm collaborating with Germans. And the Germans think I'm working with the resistance." Her mouth holds a sarcastic smile, but a twinge of fear and sadness mark her face. "I'm just working for myself. To help who I can, when I can."

"I know you've been doing a lot. Maybe it's time to take a break"

Claire glances nervously at the German guards milling outside the door now, bored.

"Once he's gone, do you think you'll be protected? Word's out that they're going to be doing another raid on the town soon. And look out for Alain. You need to take him some food and blankets now that he's at the old prison," he says softly.

Claire stares out the window. I hear her thoughts. *You think I'm protected now?!* She wants to tell him that even she's on the German watch list now, but there's no time.

"I need to get Ginny. She'll be waiting for me in the schoolyard. Bye, doctor." She touches the doctor's shoulder.

"Well, be careful," he calls behind her, injecting a shot of morphine into Hans Schmid's arm.

"Yes, doc. I'll be careful. Thank you."

"The doctor's done all he can do," Claire says to the guards and they lead him away.

⚜

I move in close and sit at the foot of Herr Schmid's bed as he edges close to death and surround him with an energy of comfort to heal his soul. How can I want to help this man who murdered me? And yet at other times feel so much anger? I want him to suffer and yet I also want him to live.

So close to death, he sometimes steps beyond the veil and into the in-between. I create a protected secret garden around me and welcome him into the heart of my beautiful sanctuary. I hope, on this sacred ground, that I can let go of my anger and forgive him. But strange things happen when he crosses the threshold and steps foot here. My flowers, plants, and the grass that he steps on wither and die instantly. My garden turns black and I'm helpless to stop it. He was so seductive on the earth plane. But here in my secret, sacred garden, he can't hide the ugliness. Yet no human being is all black or white and I also catch glimpses of the diamond of his soul shimmering inside his ribcage. But it's thickly covered by dense, black muck. Hans doesn't like me seeing his flaws. In his view it makes me a threat. He approaches faster, and I fear he will annihilate me so that no one else will know the secret darkness he carries in his soul. With each step closer to me, I fear he will kill me again, even in this in-between. Does he have that kind of power?

I'd thought that death was only physical. That we could only die once. How has he gained power in this in-between world too? I wish Silvie's Gran were here. She'd know what to do. Then I hear her voice. "Love," she says. But panic nearly consumes me. I feel hypnotized and paralyzed by his presence, like I'm unable to be myself or use my own free will. He extends a hand to pull me into his darkness.

"Come, Aurelie." He steps closer. "Come," he whispers hypnotically. "Aurelie, my love, I know you want to be with me."

I try to scream for Naehelle or Silvie to help me, but I seem unable to open my mouth. Naehelle must sense I'm in danger because even as I think of her she appears instantaneously with Archangel Michael at her side. The light emanating from the angel burns so brightly that Herr Schmid turns his eyes away. Hans immediately exits the in-between and jerks back into his physical body. Herr Schmid's eyes open as he lies in the hospital bed and tries to recall the "dream."

Naehelle wraps her arms around me as I tremble.

"You are playing with dangerous forces," she says. "Your attachment to their world could have sucked you into the darkness of that creature. Into his hell." She towers over me. The angel, satisfied with his work nods and I feel ashamed at my mistake. Without any words, Michael conveys to me that I must be very careful around Herr Schmid. He communicates by sending me mental images of the SS skull on Herr Schmid's officer's cap and the two slashes of lightening sewn on the badge on his uniform. Then he shows me same symbols seared into Herr Schmid's soul too and I sense the dangerous occult powers they contain and how they've imprisoned him.

"Stay in the light," the angel says and disappears.

My beautiful inner garden is scorched and injured. The devastation hurts my soul. Naehelle sees my remorse. "It will grow back," she says. "Come home and rest now."

41

AT HOME, I sit under my thick duvet and stare out at my window to the world below trying to make sense of the dark and light. I know my mission to protect Ginny isn't complete yet. But I can feel the energy shifting in the in-between. My time to move on will arrive soon and I need to decide: Do I move on to Home, to see my Mother and step into her realm? Or do I go back and become a child *ensouled* in Claire's womb? What if she doesn't survive? I'll die to that life again too.

On one hand, I must say that I like this lightness of being with no body. I can think about a place and in an instant, I'm there. No need to move my body from one place to another. On the other hand, I terribly miss tasting strawberries, drinking hot chocolate, feeling the air breeze past my skin when I swing, and feeling every single cell in my body scream when I dive into the cold lake water in summer. Here, I feel only through imagination. It's not physical. It's not "real". And even though Claire and Herr Schmid's world is filled with suffering, death, and destruction, it's also filled with joy, physical love, and pleasure like nothing I could ever experience here.

But Mom's world, I know nothing about. Yet I feel drawn to the total peace and joy. It looks so light over there in her world. It seems like the people there play all of the time. And I love my mom. I will ask Naehelle about that world. As soon as I think of Naehelle, she appears in the doorway.

"Can you tell me about the other worlds? The ones I don't know. The one where my mom lives now?"

"Hummm." Naehelle's tries to keep her calm, soothing demeanor, but I can tell she feels agitated and upset with me.

"Don't lecture me, please. I know I made a mistake. I shouldn't have invited Herr Schmid into my soul garden."

"You don't know what danger you faced. It is possible to die in the in-between just as it's possible to die on earth." She's exasperated. "And you're naïve enough to think he wouldn't kill you again? People don't change when they pass over, Aurelie. They stay pretty much the same. That's why they have to come back. To try to do it better next time."

"I don't believe you. He once said he loved me." My eyes stare at the pillow and I hug a teddy bear and nervously rub its ears. A lightening rod of fear strikes through me about what could have happened.

"Well he has a pretty strange way of showing it. Is that what you consider love?!"

I trace my finger absentmindedly over the star patterns in the quilt. "I…I don't know."

"You would have gotten me into big trouble. I'm supposed to protect you, not lose you."

"I'm sorry."

Naehelle sits on my bed and I feel her loving energy embrace me. "It's okay," she says and I know she holds no grudges.

"Can you tell me about Mom's world?"

Naehelle conjures a cup of steaming chamomile tea for me and one for her. She sighs and hesitates. "It's like all worlds. It has its joys and its limitations. There are ways to learn and grow, if you decide to. What's your impression about it?"

"It feels like Home. Like total peace."

"Yes. It is." I feel the longing in her voice. "You miss it?"

"Mmmm. I'll be back there soon," she says. "I'm almost done here in the in-between."

"Oh." So my feeling was right that changes are coming. "What's the big difference between our world, Mom's world and theirs?" I point out my window in the direction of Claire and Herr Schmid.

She sips her tea and reflects. "In the physical world you have the opportunity to create in unprecedented ways. You can make love. Create babies. Create art. Build buildings. It's very physical and filled with struggle and frustration. There are many limitations, like time, and we forget our Divine origins. But we also have the opportunity to connect and remember and to Love in ways that you can't experience anywhere in the Universe. You can also step beyond the duality if you choose."

"So that's why people wait in line to become someone's baby?"

"How do you know that?"

"Silvie told me." Naehelle looks miffed, like I'm a teenager who's not supposed to know about metaphysical sex education. "Have you had a body before?"

"Oh yes, many times," she says wearily.

"So why are you here and not in some other world?" I want to understand this, but my head explodes from the magnitude of possibilities as I begin to see many worlds and many possibilities unfold before me. Like a million doors to choose from.

"I died too. Like you did." Naehelle coughs a little to get the words out. "At the hands of a man who I thought cared for me. I wanted to help. I wanted to stop him and make a difference to girls like you. Help you not to want revenge. Or feel attachment to the one who killed you. What you're feeling for Herr Schmid's not love. It's attachment."

"No. You're wrong." But I'm not so sure. When he fed me, I loved him. As I look inside my own radiant heart, I still feel love for him.

"We have this terrible human heart that, for some strange reason, can feel an attachment and even love for the one who has murdered us. At least some of us do. Some just want revenge and for our murderer to suffer like we did. Others, like us, want to heal the one who hurt us. It's another unhealthy form of connection. Another way of wanting to change and transform others, when we really need to learn the lesson about self-love and respect and move on. Just look at Claire," she says. "Claire, your sister, is risking a lot to help this man."

"She won't stay," I say. "She's smarter than that."

"No? Well, it's not about smarts. Just look at you inviting that demon into your secret garden. That was foolish."

"I'm sorry," I insist. Irritated. "You don't understand me." But she actually understands me better than I'd thought. Enraged, agitated, upset by all that's just happened, I collapse into the pile of pillows and give up.

"So what can I do to let him go?"

"I want you to be wise. Forgive him. It's the way to show love for yourself and for him. And stop wanting to heal him. He'll heal himself when he's ready."

"I detest him."

"See," she says. "As long as you hate him, you're not free. You're stuck in this in-between because you're attached to him. It happens to those of us who have sudden deaths sometimes."

"I'm stuck here because I want to help Ginny too." I feel restless and pace around my small room. It feels like an adolescent's room and I'm no longer an adolescent. I've out grown it. "My time's coming to an end here, isn't it?"

A look of sadness crosses Naehelle's face. "Yes. It is."

"Do we die to the in-between or do we simply transition naturally?"

"You'll see," she says. "For most people it's clear and easy. Like taking an elevator."

You're supposed to go Home, to your mom's world next. That's what's best for you. As your guide, I can tell you that."

"But you can't tell me why."

"No. I can't see the bigger picture."

"And you can't stop me if I make other choices?"

"I don't know. But I'll try."

"Thanks for being honest with me."

"Sure." She stands to go.

"And thanks for saving me from dying a second time."

42

CLAIRE RUSHES BACK home to talk to Ginny's mom to confirm their departure and then packs a few items of her own into a burlap backpack. She wants to buy train tickets for their travel, but the station's heavily guarded. The Gestapo check everyone's papers and then the French militia who collaborate with them check them a second time to harass people. Anyone going in the direction of Annemasse and the Swiss border undergoes extra questioning.

Ginny's mom packs some of Ginny's favorite things while Ginny watches. "I don't want to go," Ginny protests.

Her mom lovingly folds one of Ginny's blouses. "Would you like to take this?" Her mom holds up a photo of the two of us, tears edge her eyes. Ginny crosses her arms and stares out the window pouting. Her mom stands at her shoulder and touches her curls. "Honey, do you remember when we first came here?"

Ginny shakes her head no. "We've always been here," she says.

"No. We lived in the South of France and before that in Germany. We've moved many times because of the war and persecution. We thought we could stay here and we were safe for a while. But now it's time for you to go. With Claire. It's an opportunity you must take."

"Why did we move so much? I'm tired of changing places all of the time."

"We had to. It was the only way to protect you." Her mom glances at her worn shoes. "You remember the young Jewish children who were taken from your class earlier in the year?"

Ginny recalls that horrible moment, the fear and anxiety aroused in her. "Those boys disappeared. We think they were killed."

"Oh."

"Because they were Jewish, like you."

"But Mom, I don't want to go." Ginny pouts and thinks of me and Georges and Bernadette. I sit beside her and encourage her to leave.

Her mom sighs. "I don't want to frighten you, Ginny. But there's reason to fear the authorities. They're evil people. We wanted to send you to your aunt's house, but she's fled too."

"Sister Marie or Father Ansen might help us. Please don't make me go to Switzerland. I don't know anyone there," Ginny whines. "Aurelie thought Herr Schmid could help us, but she was wrong."

Ginny's mom blanches at the German name. "Who is this Herr Schmid?"

"An officer. SS, I think. Aurelie knew him. So does Claire." Ginny's mom closes her eyes tightly with concern.

"Darling. My darling girl, please put your favorite things into this small bag. You must be prepared to leave at any moment. I'll talk with Claire."

"Yes, mama." But as I watch her thoughts, all she can think about as she reluctantly packs, is Herr Schmid. On overwhelming intuition tells her that she must absolutely see him again.

⤙

Today instead of going to school, Ginny sneaks off to Herr Schmid's apartment. A neighbor exits as she knocks lightly on his door. "My dear, he's gone."

"Do you know when he'll return?"

The ancient lady with white hair eyes Ginny warily. "Not any time soon, I suspect. Doc Norbert sent him to the hospital. Says he's dying. Thank God."

"Oh. Thank you." A power stronger than Ginny pulls her to the hospital.

When she asks the nurses about his whereabouts, they eye her strangely. A nurse waggles a finger in the direction of some rooms. "He's in there. Alone."

He looks yellow against the pale green walls, eyes closed, asleep Ginny thinks, but not peaceful. Herr Schimd mumbles, groggy from the opiates. His fever sends him into the in-between where he battles the flesh-eating demons. The demons are winning and taking over his heart as he becomes smaller and weaker. A nurse comes in and changes the bandage. Ginny nearly gags when she sees the maggots eating away at the infected area. The nurse goes about her business and halts momentarily when she notices Ginny's discomfort.

"It's how they heal such a problem, you know. Strange isn't it?" the nurse says.

"He's dying." Ginny says.

"Unless a miracle occurs, yes." She seems to see death a lot.

"I watched a bird die earlier this year. I didn't know what death was. My friend, Aurelie's gone too. I don't want people I love to die…"

"Yes, that's the problem isn't it?" The nurse walks behind a metal trolley of water and medication. "No one wants their loved ones to die. You all right, love?"

Ginny nods. The nurse exits and pats Ginny on the shoulder. Ginny stares at Hans for a long time as if she wants to find answers or understand a deep mystery.

"Will you wake up?" she says standing by his bed. But he remains unconscious. "Herr Schmid," she whispers in his ear. "I'm here. It's Aurelie." I wonder why she pretends to be me. She's a bad liar and her cheeks flush with heat at the deception.

"Aurelie?" His eyes flutter.

"Yes, it's me." She hovers over him just out of reach and he looks up at her. His pale skin, offset by the black hair, gives him an other-worldly aura.

"You'll come to join me soon." I cannot read Ginny's thoughts or emotions. It's like her intentions are blocked to me for now.

"I'm sorry, dear one. So sorry it ended the way it did," Hans says. "You forced me."

"You hurt me," Ginny says. "Nothing can change that."

"You deserved better. You deserved love."

"Shhh," Ginny says. "I know."

43

CLAIRE STANDS IN the muck in Farmer Elli's barn. The farmer drives his old black truck to St. Julien every few days filled with goat cheese, fresh milk, and honey, if there is any. He sells at the market and also to some of the shops.

"How much to let me come along?" Claire stares intently at the farmer who rubs the horse's velvety muzzle. "The train's too risky."

"Now, Claire, I've known you since you were little," he says. "And I ain't in the business of transporting people," he says. "Not if I want to stay alive and out of jail anyways."

Claire opens her fist to reveal a gold coin. "Not even for that?"

He rubs his chin and reflects. "That's a lot of money."

"Yes it is. For only forty-five kilometers it's more than fair."

"Unless I get caught. Then they'll put me in with your brother." He lifts a bale of hay as he talks. "You got your travel papers in order?"

Claire nods. "All set." She knows that with his agricultural permit he can travel to the markets, with no questions asked.

"Let me sleep on it. I've got to go tomorrow. I'll let you know."

❦

Claire bites her nails and waits sleepless in bed. The worst is the wait. She thinks of Herr Schmid and wonders if he's dead yet.

"Not yet, Claire," I whisper.

Claire's hands touch her belly. Her throat constricts and her fat, wet tears plop onto the feather pillow as she imagines the baby growing inside of her. She feels helpless and alone. But you're not alone, Claire. I try to give her a sense of comfort and wrap soft energy around her. "I wish you were here, Aurelie," she whispers.

"I am here, Claire. I'm listening. We're protecting you. You're going to be all right," I say. And as she drifts into the in-between in her sleep, she stands before me. I take her hand and lift her up to the mountain peak, where Naehelle showed me the past, and I show Claire the future after the war, the lightness and joy, but I can't see individual destinies. "It's soon. The war will end soon. So just hang on." I touch her belly and think about going back to be with her. We hug and she goes on into deep sleep while I sit here and watch over her from the foot of her bed.

At three a.m. there's a knock on her window. The click of a rock falling against the side of the house. She starts awake. Another rock hits the porch. Fear grips her gut and she debates about hiding in the cellar or opening the front door to confront them. Another stone falls near her window. To look out she must peel away some of the blackened paper and edge her eyes up past the window sill. "My purse." She finds it and clasps the tiny pistol. "Here goes." She prefers to face the intruders rather than cower in fear. She peels back the edge of the black paper and sees nothing. Then a bird sound, like an owl or a nightingale in the night calls out, followed by a tap at the door.

"Claire." A whisper. A man's voice. "Claire, it's me, Jean-Michel." Joy shoots through her veins. Joy and sanity and the promise of peace now that he's back. She throws open the door and drags him in.

"Oh my god, it's so good to see you. What are you doing here?" She hugs him close, then steps back instinctively to check him for wounds or injuries.

"Hey babe." He smiles that quirky, crooked smile out of the corner of his mouth and she pushes the long strand of blond hair out of his eyes. "Guess I need a shave too." He rubs his stubble against her cheek.

"It's okay. I'll take you as you are." She pulls him close again and covers him in kisses.

"Hey, whoa, let me breathe there. You'd think I'd been gone for months."

"Well, you've been gone for a week at least," she says. He quickly fills her in on the resistance movement and the battles on the mountain plateau. Claire tells him about the increased repressions in the town and how there's more to come. "I got my papers," she says.

"Oh," he says and lights a cigarette.

"I know. Not much to be excited about," she says to soothe them both.

"How are you getting to Switzerland?" His face turns somber, his eyes darken.

"I can tell you're not happy about it."

"No. I'm not. I'd hoped we'd go together." He grabs her by the elbow. "But it's important for you to leave. We'll meet again when this stupid war's done."

"Yes," she says. But in her heart, I feel she has no idea about what the next days will bring, so she speaks without conviction or faith. "We're on the Black List. The *bosch* put us there. He was following me and must have found you that way."

"Bastard," Jean-Michel says. "You'll need to take the mountain route to Switzerland, you know. Over the Saleve. I know it's not the easiest road, and there's probably still a lot of snow in altitude."

"Oh? Farmer Elli was going to drive me to Annemasse."

"No good, woman. They've just set up roadblocks at Cruseilles, half way to the border, and you could be arrested."

Claire sighs. He offers her a cigarette. "So, what are our options?"

"Father Ansen might be able to help. He's got a network. Rumor has it that they're helping people cross the border."

"Are you sure? I don't trust anyone, Jean-Michel. I sent the kids who came to me with Sister Marie. She took care of them. I don't know her contacts. It's better that way."

"I think Father Ansen's a part of the network too," Jean-Michel says and shrugs. "But maybe Sister Marie'll help. Can you get to her?"

"No. Not now. Besides. She's on the list too." Claire's face tenses with worry. "Pretty soon there won't be anyone left in town. Thirteen prisons in town now. All full. They're using schools for prisons and basements for torture chambers."

"And a boat," Jean Michel says. "Then Father Ansen or Farmer Elli are all we've got at the moment. When you make it to the border near St. Julien. I know a passer there. He'll help you cross the barbed wire and get past the patrols. I'll join you when I can. Or else the war will end. One way or the other…we'll survive and I'll marry you."

Claire marvels at the solidity and sincerity in his eyes. Unlike Herr Schmid, Jean-Michel is transparent and clear. He's exactly who he seems to be, clear like the water of Lake Annecy. So clear you can see down to the brilliant light flaming in his heart. He has no hidden dreams or motives. No demons. He's pure. She reflects on the mountain to cross tomorrow and on what it would be like to live a life with him.

Claire stokes the fire and I sit nearby and caress the old cat who purrs in her sleep. "Look at that," Claire says. "She's purring like someone's petting her." Jean-Michel glances over his shoulder.

"It's another kind of pussy I'm interested in." She swats him. He lifts her up and carries her laughing into the bedroom.

44

THE GERMANS AND collaborators usually show up after dawn and catch the blacklisted people between six and eight as they prepare for work. But today the commandant orders them out in the middle of the night. I watch from the roof top as the Gestapo and French militia move across the land, break down doors, pull people from their beds, and arrest them. They take school teachers. Shop owners. Postmen. They use the black list and search for Claire and the others. But when they come, Claire's in the outhouse. She hears their voices as she cracks open the door and watches them enter her house. She escapes to Ginny's house and with her mom, they all slip into the hidden cellar under the apple trees in the backyard under cover of night. Jean-Michel's happy in a dream, dancing with Claire in his arms when the French militia men jerk off his covers and force him out of bed. They rap him in the face with a rifle butt and send him crashing to the ground, covered with blood.

Claire and Ginny watch through a crack in the old wood of the apple cellar as the militia men lead Jean-Michel away without a coat or shirt. A reflex sends Claire bolting upright. Her arms push at the heavy wooden door to go after him. But Ginny's mom pulls her back and they cower together in the damp, dark cellar that smells of earth and apple cider. When it looks like the soldiers have all gone, Claire leads Ginny to Farmer

Elli's through the thick underbrush. The farmer hides them under an old tarpaulin behind the wood he stacks to burn for the winter. They hear a truck motor. Claire and Ginny trade glances in the dark. They hear heavy boots on the ground and Claire clamps her hand over Ginny's mouth to keep her quiet. A single move could get them both shot.

Farmer Elli appeases the militia with his soothing voice. "Ain't nothin' around here. Just goats and cows," he says as he packs his truck for the market.

"Where are you going?" a man asks gruffly.

"The market. Annemasse. Been doin' it for thirty odd years now," Farmer Elli says casually.

"You seen that Lançon woman? The one who lives over there?" The solider points to our house. "We need to bring her in for questioning."

"Nope. Mind my own business here. Don't know much about the goings on of others."

The men poke around the barn and seem most interested in food. They help themselves to the goat cheeses and jars of honey.

"You won't mind, old man," the militia leader says.

Farmer Elli keeps his mouth shut and watches them take what they want from his truck and then go. Claire hears the truck of militia soldiers drive off and sees dark, muddy boots at the edge of the tarpaulin that she cowers under. The cover's lifted.

"They've gone, Claire. We need to go now. Hurry. We're taking the rough road, up that gravel path and around. It's the long way, but it's the safest way," Farmer Elli says.

"They're the ones who took Jean-Michel this morning." I see her shock and the emptiness of grief fills her as she recalls the scenes of Jean-Michel being led away. Farmer Elli leads her to the truck bed and she follows in a daze.

"No time to think about him now. Hide here, under these old feed sacks." Claire climbs beneath the coarse, woven sacks and curls up in a ball.

"What about Ginny?" She says.

"She'll ride up here with me." The farmer rubs mud on Ginny's cheeks and hands her a pair of muddy overalls used by his grandson. He puts her hair up under a dirty old cap so she looks like a farm hand. "Here." He rubs dirt on her hands and under her nails. "You work for me, if they ask. Got it?"

Ginny nods. For once, she begins to understand the severity of the situation. The farmer starts the truck.

"You have your papers?"

Ginny nods obedient and introspective. The truck rocks along a rough back road and the springs struggle to keep up with the shocks and bumps. After a few kilometers, Ginny breaks the silence.

"Will I get to come back home again?"

Farmer Elli keeps his eyes fixed on the gravel road to stay out of the ravine on his right. When they drive through a low creek that crosses the road, he glances at her.

"Don't know. War's a dirty, unpredictable business."

"I saw the faces of some of the kids who lost their parents. We saw them with my dad, at the market." She looks upset. "I don't want my parents to die."

"The Germans…they have strange ideas about who should live and die. Makes no sense to me. It's not natural."

Ginny stares ahead into the fog and rain. The farmer pats her knee with his calloused hand.

It takes an hour to travel the short distance to the old bridge at La Caille where they have to cross the gorge. The farmer stops his truck and hands over his papers along with some money lodged in the folds of the paper. The guard, used to seeing him pass every Friday, nods the truck on without any inspection. Above them, soldiers bearing machine guns stand guard in the turrets of the old bridge.

The farmer drives to the opposite side and stops a few kilometers away from the bridge to check in at the village café on the route and smoke a cigarette. Ginny waits in the truck. The farmer instructs her to sit on the floorboard and not move or attract attention. When he comes back smelling of smoke and barley coffee mixed with chicory, he peers under the tarp where Claire cowers and pretends to check his goods.

"The café owner says that Cruseilles is under lock down. May not even be able to cross myself today. I'd be a fool to think I could get you two across there too, Claire, even with your papers. But I'll have to go on alone, business as usual. There's a service station in the direction of the Saleve Mountain. I'll drop you both off and refuel there. Then you're on your own to cross over."

Claire's not free to lift her head and address him or protest. She must surrender to the circumstances. The truck slows farther on. Claire hears German voices and other trucks. Men. Guttural sounds. Harsh. Unforgiving. She feels the truck's motor labor as it begins to climb in altitude and then stop at a tiny service station run by a woman dairy farmer. The farmer pumps fuel and Claire hears a muffled conversation. A woman's voice this time.

"Here," Farmer Elli says lifting the tarp. "You'll stay here until nightfall. Then you'll be on your own to follow the path over the mountain. Straight down on the other side you're at Collognes. The border's right there. You'll surely find someone to help you there." Claire thinks of Jean-Michel's contact, "the passer", in St. Julien. "How far's St. Julien from Collognes?"

"Can't be more than a few kilometers," Farmer Elli says. "But go the direct route. Don't double back to St. Julien."

"You want me to get out now?" Claire stretches her cramped legs and looks out warily. Under the cover of fog and drizzle, the woman farmer who owns the service station, leads Claire and Ginny into the barn. She wants money to hide and feed them of course. Claire produces another gold coin.

"That'll do," the gnarly woman says. She's not one to offer warmth or much information. Farmer Elli turns the black truck around and drives away. Ginny tugs at Claire's coat and Claire puts a hand on her shoulder.

45

"CLAIRE, WHAT ARE we doing here?" Ginny says.

"We're waiting, Ginny. We have to wait for night to cross."

They shiver in a corner behind the straw in the barn lodged between two tan, Swiss milk cows who seem grumpy about the presence of visitors. As dusk falls, the farmer woman brings them bowls of hot onion soup and cheese with hard bread.

"Thank you," Claire says.

"Mmm. I don't like onions," Ginny says. The farmer frowns.

"Do you know the mountain road?" Claire says to the woman.

"Still snow there I imagine," she says, terse and tight-lipped.

"How long will it take to cross over?"

"Well, you're not the only one lately, you know. And a lot of 'em come back. Scared by the deep snow and the patrols, the barbed wire, and the German shepherd dogs. My guess is it'll take about nine hours to get over. Less you're a goat used to slogging through the snow melt." The woman tosses a pile of hay at the cows. "Course, a lot of 'em lose their way. Not easy to find it under the snow. But the road goes most of the way. Got to watch out for the German patrols up there. A guy got shot up there last week. Course I don't know the details. Just saw 'em carting down the bloody body in the back of an army truck. They stopped here for petrol."

Claire wants to stop the old lady from speaking, but simply looks away. Ginny looks frightened. "I'm sure we'll be fine," Claire says.

"I don't know. Women ain't faring well these days. Only reason they don't bother me's cause I've got old faithful here." She pats a rifle. A big white-haired herding dog stands beside her baring its fangs too. "I'd as soon shoot'em and bury 'em as let 'em touch my cows." The woman collects their empty soup bowls. "You'd best be gettin' on your way as soon as dusk falls."

"Yes," Claire says. "Thank you."

The old woman closes them in the barn and leaves them shivering beside the cows. "What are we going to do, Claire?" Ginny's worried eyes beg for answers.

"We'll wait," she says and rubs Ginny's shivering shoulders to heat her up. "It won't be long now."

I search the barn for anything to bring light and warmth to them. An old petrol lamp with a broken glass globe stands on a high shelf in a corner. "Here, Claire. I know it's not much, but it will probably work and the light will keep you cheerful and bring a little warmth." With intent focus, I light the area and send thoughts to Claire to show her. But she's too preoccupied. "Ginny, here's some light. Here."

Ginny looks up at the lamp. "Claire," she says excitedly. "Look. That will keep us warm."

I breathe a sigh of relief. I know how much Ginny and Claire both suffer from the cold and with this tiny mission accomplished, I head out to do reconnaissance for them and see how I can help guide their way. I slip out over the mountain and watch the light fade. The souls of those they've just shot in the field on the Route de Geneva at the edge of Annecy, go flying up through the dark astral plane and into the Light. Not a single one stays behind in the in-between. They're not like me. They all go Home and seem happy to be done with the war and the madness of the earth. These souls reunite with their loved ones and as they ascend, I feel their joy and the joy of their loved ones awaiting them in the stars.

I see many children who've been separated from their parents. Jewish children. Roma children. Children of people the Germans think are communists. Or children of parents who resist the German ideals. Their parents have disappeared into prisons. Or they've been placed on trains to Paris or

Germany. Or the militia who have personal vendettas against them simply beat them to death for the brutal pleasure of it. While the children remain abandoned. I don't understand this kind of madness. How some cruel people gain pleasure from a fist punching into soft flesh, hearing the sound of breaking cheek bones, watching the blood gush from broken noses. Kicking into kidneys and soft stomachs. Watching the beautiful mysterious blood of life flow out of bodies until the essence that inhabits them ascends into other planes. The madness of those violent men makes me feel dizzy, sick and crazy, until I turn away and don't want to know anymore.

The foxes and owls on the Saleve Mountain wait and watch in silence. They live in quiet harmony with all that passes. The sunrise. The rainfall. The fog. The ice freezing and thawing until the crocus push up from underneath. Only humans create such insanity. Total insanity. And I've seen more things now than I'd ever imagined or known. Things I wish never to see again. As I fly over the landscape, I scout out the safe path for Claire and Ginny. I want them to arrive safely and smoothly into the clean, clear, prosperous land of the Swiss. They're so, so close now. The mountain stands at the border, solid and quiet under the melting snow. As night falls, the dripping rivulets of water freeze again. A quiet tension reigns even here as German soldiers wait near the mountain peak at 1,250 meters in altitude before the road winds down to the Swiss border. It's like the whole land is covered with a weave of taut rubber bands ready to snap at the slightest provocation. At the same time, the soldiers act bored, stuck in fog and dreary rain. They dream of women, shooting, and committing heinous acts. It doesn't matter that they're high up near the invisible stars where the sheep and cows snore and dream of green pastures filled with edelweiss flowers.

The German soldiers sit around a worn table and drink and play cards in dim light.

"Your turn for the patrol," the colonel says. His nose glows red from the chill and too much alcohol. Gunter, the most vigilant guard who believes in the Reich and all its values of "family, country, and work", salutes and reaches for his coat and gun. He ponders a photo of Herr Hitler and remembers a meeting where the mesmerizing man shook his hand and inspired him to believe in his mission.

"You go too," the colonel nudges another young man who's about twenty. They both look like normal, kind people, but as I look closely, I see their recent past. The young man on top of a woman, a mother. Him laughing. Her crying. Gunter holding a gun at the woman's head to keep her quiet while his buddy did his dirty deed. The woman was not a human being to him, but more like a toy, a play thing without feelings. And him, he was like a little boy, when he's done playing with a toy and tosses it into the dirt without a second thought. This is what he did to that woman. This is how Herr Schmid treated me! That's not love.

How can they do that?! How can they be so cruel and unfeeling? I remember watching Joseph, a neighbor boy, pluck legs off of bugs and watch them squirm. He laughed and laughed gleefully at their pain and struggles. Then he'd toss the handicapped bugs aside. He was the same one who'd poke a stick into the cat's belly or yank at the dog's tail totally insensitive to the pain he caused. I couldn't understand then and I still don't. I know that Claire and Ginny need to steer clear of these dangerous, unfeeling men.

Despite the cold, Ginny dozes off. Claire checks her watch. "Wake up, Ginny. Time to go."

Ginny's used to the comforts of her featherbed and a warm fire. Me too. She immediately wakes up shivering, teeth chattering and starts to cry. Claire's exhale creates a long, slow cloud of steam, like when she smokes cigarettes. Ginny rubs her eyes and Claire brushes the straw from her hair. "Stand up," Claire urges. "You'll have to bear up. No time for tears."

"But I don't want to go. I don't understand," Ginny protests.

"If you stay, Herr Schmid will find you. If he does, then…" Claire looks down at the teenaged girl who refuses to understand. "Remember what happened to Aurelie." Claire says it in a way so that Ginny can feel what she knows. I'm standing right beside her sending Ginny images of my death at his hands.

"Yes, I know," Ginny says.

The silence rests between them and Ginny's mind races back to the day of my burial and the tear on my winter coat.

Sometime later, Claire cracks open the wooden door of the barn peers into the foggy night. "We'll follow the road as long as we can."

The road's cleared of heavy snow, but slick from ice and they'll need to walk beside it. Claire sees the snowshoes hanging on the barn wall and ties them on. "We'll borrow these." Ginny imitates her and laces on a pair.

"Very fashionable," Ginny says and poses. "Isn't this stealing?"

"She got a gold coin. She can make more. In the meantime, you must stay silent. Got it?"

Ginny nods.

"Good. Let's go."

46

HERR SCHMID'S TAKEN a turn for the worse. Fever and gibberish in his head. I sit by his bed even though Naehelle warns me against it. The nurses have stopped bringing him anything, because they expect him to die in the next hours. They're so used to being around death that some of them actually see me. In fact, there are many deceased people walking the corridors here, lost and not aware that they are dead. Some of them ask me if I've seen their family members or friends and I say, "No, I'm sorry."

"Honey, why are you hanging around that man?" one dead woman asks. "He's no good."

"I don't know," I say and shrug. She raises her eye brows and disappears. Now that Claire and Ginny are safe, I feel torn between wanting him to survive and feeling happy that he'll die.

One of the nurses comes to check his pulse and poke a thermometer in his mouth. He will need to make a decision, if he can, to live or leave. His fever spikes and his pulse races. The nurse knows the drill.

"Doctor Daudet," she calls, but the doctor's beyond feeling any urgency at this hour. "He's a German, so we need to be careful," the nurse warns.

"That one again." The doctor checks the wound again and administers an injection of opiates to kill pain. He thinks of his job and what the Germans will do if this man dies. "Keep an eye out."

"Yes, doctor." But I sense their hopelessness. "We need to send word to the commandant's headquarters."

The Nazis bring their highest ranking German doctor armed with potions and magic. They lock out the nurses and French doctors while the German doctor performs a ritual with a human skull and some electro-magnetic machine that he believes transmutes and heals the physical body. The doctor injects a high dose of amphetamines. I watch from the corner, near the ceiling while a monumental battle for Herr Schmid's soul ensues. The doctor and the SS invoke the dark astral forces and from the in-between. The tentacled Monstrous Force appears, offering an exchange to Herr Schmid. His life force for access to its eerie power. At first Hans cowers from the tentacled arm reaching out to him, but his fear and love for power resonate with the Monster Force and attract it closer. In a moment of weakness, Hans allows it to touch his back and the black tentacle of the Monster Force connects to him. The doctor commands Hans to return to his body and do his duty. A jolt of life bangs him back into his body. Herr Schmid revives.

"Get up and walk," the German doctor commands.

Even though weakness remains, Herr Schmid obeys, robot like.

"You have faith in the Reich," the doctor says.

"Yes, sir. Heil Hitler." Herr Schmid mutters and salutes automatically.

"Good man. You'll report to the commandant tomorrow at oh-eight-hundred. Heil Hitler," the doctor says and raises his right arm in a rigid salute. The other Nazis around them follow his example. By morning, the fever's broken and Herr Schmid walks out of the hospital. He's shaved and dressed before six. The German doctor arrives and injects him with more drugs. Together they drive to Gestapo headquarters.

47

"HAVE SOME COFFEE, Herr Schmid," the commandant orders. He sits behind his mahogany desk with an air of disdain. The commandant's military assistant pours a second cup of steaming coffee into a porcelain cup for the commandant. "Spoils of the war, Herr Schmid." He refers to the cup and the location. He gestures to the lake view behind him. "I could settle down here once the Russians are defeated. What do you think, Schmid? Will you stay or go once we're declared victorious in a few weeks?"

For some time the war effort has been dispersing German energies until it has stretched Germany to the breaking point. With fighting in Russia, the occupation of France, a front in Africa, and a whole world to conquer, the commandant's smooth comments belie his deep anxiety about a possible loss and what will happen if Hitler's war fails. His mask of smooth, glib energy covers the thick fog of fear welling up from inside him. The fear makes him very dangerous and unreasonable.

Herr Schmid feels taut with anxiety and strain, and far from healed. This cannot be a warm meeting. But the offer of coffee and the cordial tone sends Hans Schmid a cue to relax. He accepts the coffee in the thin cup, steadying his weak hand, and lifts the porcelain to his lips.

"Thank you, sir," he says. "I do not know the answer to that question, sir."

"I want to live and die right here, Schimd. With this beautiful view.

Right here. I will paint the light on the lake everyday as it changes. Look."
The commandant plucks a canvas from an easel near his desk. "This is one
of my efforts. It's not good yet. It's just a beginning. What do you think?"

Herr Schmid squints to focus his fatigued eyes. "Good, sir."

"Yes. It is," the commandant confirms. "The grays. All of the gray tones.
No black and white." He sighs, replaces the canvas on the easel. "Painting
helps me to concentrate." He sits back down and stares a moment out the
window. "I have warmed to the French girls."

Herr Schmid says nothing. His body tenses, in this uncomfortable
dance aimed to keep him off balance. The commandant allows the right
corner of his mouth to turn up as if beginning a smile. "They bring me
comfort." He rings a small bell on his desk. "I'm sure you understand,
Schmid. Bring them in," he says to the guard.

Two soldiers lead Claire and Ginny into the large open salon with the
lake view. "These two, for example. What do you think we should do with
them, Schimd? I've already violated that one." He points at Claire, but the
commandant's lying. In fact, he finds women disgusting. The commandant
studies Hans' every muscle for a twitch of emotion or betrayal. "So now,
they're yours to *take care of*. You will do your usual *work* in extracting information from them first. Our priorities are to learn more about the network,
the resistance, and where these two were headed. We caught them escaping
into Switzerland. The Swiss authorities wisely saw it in their best interest to
send them back to us. And well, *viola*." The commandant almost snickers,
but the dirty shadow of a beard and the cigar stains on his teeth make his
face resemble a snarling dog.

Claire searches for a flicker of recognition in Hans Schmid's eyes to
give her hope for clemency. Her leather shoes are stained from snow melt
and mud, her hair's uncombed, but a trace of lipstick still colors the cracks
in her lips. Ginny stands, head bowed, seeming faraway.

A truck awaits the three of them at the bottom of the steps of the
headquarters. Herr Schmid climbs into the truck cab in front and slams
the door. The guards force the girls into the back, hands bound, and sit
near them taunting and pinching their breasts and running their hands up
Claire's skirt. Ginny still wears the boy's muddy denim overall which makes
her less accessible.

"Do we have time?" One soldier says to the other.

"Try," he says. "Hurry."

He sets his rifle down at an angle and pushes Ginny into the straw in the corner of the covered, green army truck bed and jerks open his zipper. Her bound hands make it impossible to defend herself. The soldier struggles with the overall and yanks at the metal rivets.

"Claire!" Ginny screams. The man stuffs his wool scarf into Ginny's mouth to stifle her protests.

"Leave her alone," Claire snaps and receives a hard slap across the face.

"Silvie. Naehelle. Help me!" I call out.

Naehelle and Silive arrive, and the three of us watch helplessly. The men's rifles are right there. My hands are free. I try to reach out and jerk the man off of Ginny. With all of my force and will, I focus on him and put my energy into tearing him away. But to no avail. Frustrated, he rips the overall and one of the rivets snaps. The soldier growls with satisfaction and forces his whole weight on Ginny. I beat him with my fists. He looks over his shoulder absentmindedly, then goes back to Ginny. I scream. Rant. Tear up the energy in the truck and even make it rock. Then a miracle happens. The gun falls from the precarious angle where it leans against the side of the truck. A bullet discharges and hits him in the buttock. He screams and gropes his bloody backside. While the other soldier tries to help his buddy, Claire pushes Ginny into the street and jumps out behind her.

The army truck stops near the old town, and in the chaos that ensues, Claire and Ginny escape through the market stalls. They disappear into a narrow alleyway and through a low, open door. Claire slams the wooden door behind them and races through a winding maze of narrow passages that ultimately lead up narrow, dark stairs. The two reach the top floor and cower in a dark hallway.

An old woman opens the door and sets a pail of trash on the stoop. Her cataract-covered eyes make it hard for her to see the two girls clearly. "That's to take down later. What do you want?" she says.

"We're hiding," Claire says. "From the Gestapo."

"Fugitives, are you?! Damned Germans." She goes back inside and leaves her door open. "Well, come on in," she yells. "Don't just cower in the hallway. You'll get arthritis."

Her narrow windows look out onto the city. "We're in the tower," Claire says.

"Where'd you think you were? Paris?" The old woman heats up some strong-smelling chicory and hands them each a cup. Now that the immediate danger has passed, Ginny looks at her bruised legs and the marks on her face and arms.

"This is what happened to Aurelie. Isn't it?" she says, recalling my corpse. A horror fills her heart when she realizes it almost happened to her too. Claire pulls Ginny close.

"Do you have a place where she can wash up and rest?" Claire says to the old woman. "She's been through a lot in the past few days." The woman points to the bedroom and carries in a pitcher of water and a basin with a clean towel.

48

GINNY'S SLEEPING NOW. She doesn't want to come back to the physical world after the pain and humiliation and I don't blame her. I keep asking Naehelle why these kinds of horrors happen and she still has no answer.

"Experiences." She says we want to have experiences, even these hurtful, painful, humiliating kinds. She says something about the contrasts and paradoxes and how it's just a part of life that those who incarnate into human bodies desire to learn and to understand. That makes no sense to me and I simply want to shake her and scream as I stand over Ginny and watch her sleep. Ginny's soul rises out of her body to visit me in her dreams, in a quiet, gentle place by a beautiful turquoise river where alpine flowers grow and all the animals live in peace together. We sit on the grass with our arms around each other and watch the river flow by.

"I miss you, Aurelie," she says.

"I miss you, Ginny. I'm glad you're here now." But her soul guardian comes.

"Ginny, you can't stay. You can speak together for a few moments and then you must return. It's not your time to go yet." The guide radiates light and wisdom as if there can be no doubt and no choice.

Ginny casts her eyes down in sadness. "I don't want to go back there," she says. "It's too hard. It hurts too much."

"I wish you could stay with me, Ginny," I say. We hold hands, and she looks at me with such sadness. We can both feel she has to go and that it's like a journey she must make before she can come Home and we can be together. She glances at her guardian and guide.

"I guess I'll have to go, Aurelie," she says. We hug so tightly and we weep together. "Send me your love and energy, Aurelie. I really need it. I can't do this on my own," she says.

"I will. I love you, dear friend." And then I feel her slip away, pulled gently by her guides, back to her dreaming body, back into the physical plane of the earth and I can't stop weeping. I miss her so, so much.

⁖

I stay by the river and watch the water flow under an old arched bridge. It's so beautiful, this ethereal place and yet my tears won't stop. I feel Ginny's pain and I remember my own. I don't understand why life has to be such a struggle. Or why my heart aches to be with her. Or why we have to live in two separate worlds. Naehelle appears beside me. Her energy envelopes me in kindness and love.

"You saved her life," she says. "Your energy rocked the truck and knocked over the rifle. You allowed them to escape."

I wrap my arms around my knees and put my head down.

"Why the tears? We're not supposed to cry here," Naehelle says.

"Another one of your stupid rules?!"

She stays silent.

"Don't you feel the pain? Don't you feel anything anymore?" I accuse her. "I don't believe in God. I don't believe in you or anything anymore! Go away." My heart aches so much that I'm nothing but pain. I want to help Ginny. I want to cure Herr Schmid and extract the evil from his heart. I want to save Claire, Jean-Michel, Alain, and Dad.

"I've asked someone else to help you," Naehelle says and slips away. A very beautiful, golden-white presence takes her place. The energy of this being is so beautiful and divine. So totally loving and complete, that I lose my sense of anger and relax in the loving, gentle energy that flows around me like the river. This wise, loving presence opens up an awareness to me and I know It and It knows me. We are one. It gives me the experience of a love so vast and a plan so grand, that all is beautiful. All is love and joy. I remain in a cocoon of this golden, vibrant energy of love, merged and at peace. Total peace. I'm aware of my heartache, but this energy dissolves the pain. At the same time I'm aware of the pain and suffering all around me and in me, but I'm not that pain. And yet I am. This Energy, this Loving Presence, leads me up to the peak of a mountain and opens up the mystical and secret view of Time.

She opens Time and invites me to see the past first, and I see a time during the Renaissance where I fell in love with Hans, in another form and he murdered me. This is where this whole wicked chain of attachment began. Then she shows me my future, in Geneva, dotted with tall buildings and modern trams. In this future time, I see Hans Schmid, but he's no longer called Hans. And Claire, Ginny and Silvie. We all will meet again and join in another adventure soon. And Hans will try to murder me again. It's written in our destiny, the woman says. We have a *rendez vous*. All of us do.

This Loving Presence allows me to see and know that what is happening now is a necessary precursor to what will come. All of the darkness and division must come to light before the Golden Age of world peace descends. All of the manipulations of power must become manifest for all to know that this way of suffering and submission is not necessary and I'll not be alone. Claire, Ginny, Silvie, Nahelle, will come together with me to bring the evil out of darkness and into the light where everyone can see it. I feel a sense of mission and purpose, and for the first time in a very long time, peace fills my soul. I'm grateful to the Loving Presence for the vision.

"Thank you, Loving One," I say. If this is the outcome, it's like the dark storm before the brilliant sunshine. It can be no other way. So let it be.

49

HERR SCHMID STANDS rigid before the commandant once again.

"You allowed the enemies of the Reich to escape, Schmid!"

Hans Schmid's knees tremble. He's always been the perfect officer, yearning to make up for his brothers' failings. Perfect with detailing every surveillance mission. Perfectly keeping records on all of the suspected enemies, including Claire. He knows their weaknesses, their psychology. That has been the method of the Reich's secret service. Now, the commandant opens a file with a photo of Herr Schmid stapled to the front.

"We know your propensities, Schmid." The commandant smile-snarls through his sallow skin and the beard shadow that seems permanent. He folds his hands together and leans back in his leather seat. Hans Schmid stares out blank-eyed at the lake through the windows behind him. Thoughts of humiliation and suicide creep in. "You have a soft spot for that French girl?"

"No, sir." Hans stares straight ahead, unflinching.

"Good. We, of the Reich, are not allowed to be weak. Emotions must be eradicated."

"Yes, sir."

"So, Schmid, what shall we do now that your friends have escaped?"

"They're not my friends, sir."

"Oh, really?"

"Yes, sir."

"Well, then, you will have to prove it. When they are captured – and they will be captured. You will do everything necessary to extract the information needed to benefit the Reich. That one woman..." The commandant points his index finger at the file and searches for her name. "Claire. Her lover is a resistance fighter. And we know that she must have information about their sabotage units and his whereabouts."

Herr Schmid shows no emotion, but his eye twitches uncontrollably at the left corner.

"Your body is giving you away," the commandant says and points at his twitching eye. "You're dismissed."

In the old lady's flat in the tower, Ginny stands behind the threshold of the bedroom, peering vacantly into the kitchen. "You okay?" Claire says.

Ginny nods, but feels numb and empty. It's nighttime now and the old lady with the cataracts prepares a simple meal with rationed pasta and canned tomatoes. The woman uncorks a bottle of table wine and invites Claire and Ginny to sit at her tiny square table beside the narrow window that looks out over the town. She pulls the black curtains closed.

"We will have to go soon," Claire says. She despairs and has no idea of where.

"Oh missy, the Germans and the nasty French (this is what she calls the collaborators), blocked every street, set up check points, and knocked on every door in this building this afternoon before you arrived. At least for right now, you'll stay put," the old lady says. Her wool stockings sag around her ankles and her flower print dress hangs lose over her thick figure. The two girls eat while the old lady drinks wine.

I sit at the extra chair across from the old lady.

"I didn't set a plate for you," the old lady says to me. "Are you hungry too?" Claire and Ginny watch the old woman and trade glances. They think she's half crazy.

"Me?" I say.

"Yes, you." The old lady says as she stares right at me. Claire shakes her head at this and looks into the clouded eyes of the woman.

"No thank you." I'm stunned and excited. She sees me.

"You two look like twins," she says, pointing to Ginny.

"Ginny's my best friend, but lots of people think we're sisters. The older one, Claire's, my sister," I say. "I'm Aurelie. I've been trying to talk to Claire forever, but she never listens."

The old lady addresses Claire. "Why don't you listen to Aurelie. She says you ignore her."

Claire's face blanches. She places her fork on the side of the plate, no longer hungry. Goose bumps ripple up her arm and a chill creeps through to her core. The old woman stirs her hot chicory coffee laced with white sugar.

"What's wrong? Don't like the food?" the old woman says. She pours herself a glass of syrupy reddish liqueur from a glass bottle with no label and sips.

"No, I…" Claire stares in my direction, eyes wide. I can't tell if she sees me or not. "But…is Aurelie here?"

"Well, what's wrong with you, girl?" the lady says. "She's right beside you."

Claire and Ginny trade glances. Claire pushes back her wooden seat, crosses her arms and stands by the window covered with black curtains, her back to us.

"Aurelie?" Ginny whispers. "Claire, if she's here, I want to know."

I see an opportunity. This woman seems to see and hear me as clearly as she hears Claire and Ginny.

"Listen," I say to the lady. "Ginny has a hard time hearing, would you please repeat to her what I say. Maybe you can help her understand. I think she'll hear you better than she hears me."

"Go on," the old woman says still stirring her coffee and tapping the spoon against the side of the cup.

"Please tell Ginny, I love her. Tell her I remember the black stockings we stole from Claire's drawer when we played dress up together."

"Why don't you listen to Aurelie. She says, you're best friends," the old woman says. "And something about stealing Claire's black stockings."

Claire jerks around. "So that's where my stockings disappeared to."

Ginny's excitement grows. "Oh, Aurelie, I can almost see you." She reaches out and touches my hand. The energy warms me and I send her good energy too. Her eyes fill with tears. "Oh, Aurelie, awful things have happened. Your friend he did…terrible things."

"Thank you so, much," I say to the old woman. Please listen. Please interpret well. Ginny and Claire are in grave danger. Herr Schmid. He will torture and kill them when he finds them. They must disappear. Leave Annecy. I will see if I can help them to find a way out."

"Whoa," the old lady says to me. "You're talking too fast. I'm old. Speak slowly."

"Schmid. His name's Schmid." I repeat.

She points at Claire. "You're both in grave danger. From a German Smf…something."

"Can't you talk to your sister directly?" the woman says to me. "Or does she have a hearing problem too? This is wearing me out," the old lady says a bit annoyed at playing the intermediary.

"She never listens to me," I say. "But she will listen to you. His name is Schmid. Herr Schmid."

"Sss…mid. Shhh..mid," she says sounding it out.

Now I've got Claire's attention and I start to speak really fast. "He's afraid of the commandant. He needs to prove that he's not a coward. The only way he can prove it is if you're dead. He's going mad with fear. Don't trust him. Whatever happens. Don't trust him."

"Something about a commandant. And going mad. And dead. Don't trust him. Don't trust him. Don't trust him." The old lady sighs from exhaustion and empties the cordial liqueur. Her head droops to her chest and she dozes off. I feel exasperated. The woman snores lightly from the liqueur and the stupor of old age. Ginny shakes her.

"Please," Ginny insists, shaking the old woman.

A whole crowd of departed souls suddenly appear pushing and shoving to take my place at the table so they can talk to this old woman too. Not many people in physical form can actually see and hear us. A riot almost ensues among the dead. A mother in her thirties yells at me that she needs the woman to give a message to her young children. Many soldiers rush in too. They're all shoving me out of my seat and the chaotic energy feels like a big brawl will break out from the excitement and the urgency. I hold my hands over my head to protect from the blows. And when it seems a riot will start, I call out.

"Naehelle." She appears and drags me away.

"That was dangerous," she says. "You're in big trouble. You've been creating too many problems between the worlds."

"But I don't understand. What happened?" I shake my head and look back at the tower and my seat which is now occupied by a dead soldier in his twenties who desperately wants the old woman to give a message to his sweetheart. But now, half asleep, she seems confused and overwhelmed by the mass of energy produced from the rush of souls waiting to communicate with loved ones.

"But…" It was an opportunity. But I blew it. "Who was she?" I say.

"Just an old woman."

"Who can see us!" I say.

"It happens. She can't distinguish between the living and the dead. She'll be crossing over soon, so the veil's thinner for her." Naehelle maintains a tight hold on my arm as she guides me into an unfamiliar place. It's outside of a classroom. White light pours from the doorway and the sound of children laughing lilts out of the windows.

"What's this?"

"A sort of protection center. You'll not be allowed to leave until you learn some rules."

"You mean a detention center!" I protest.

"Then you'll be able to move on. When you pass the tests. People are not very happy with the ways you've been intervening in the different worlds, Aurelie. All of the worlds must remain completely separate. You can watch, but you cannot mix with them. That is the number one rule. I told you that from the start. But you don't obey. Otherwise it just causes fear and confusion."

"Wait. You can't do this. I have a mission. I need to protect Ginny and Claire. They need my help."

"No, that's an illusion. They have guardians and guides too. They'll be fine." I'm stunned and silenced. Even in the in-between, there's a place reserved for "bad" girls. For those of us who do things differently.

"No, I'm not going to go."

"What?!" Naehelle turns to me, horrified. "Only evil people don't go along with the rules."

"Look at them." I point to Herr Schmid's world. "He follows the rules strictly and so do his fellow soldiers. And what's the result? They're killing innocent people. That's evil."

"This is different here."

"Show me how," I say. "Prove it to me that this sort of confinement will make our world and theirs a better place." I stand at the doorway with my hands on my hips, defiant and rebellious. "Show me."

Naehelle storms off, exasperated. "I've never..." Then she turns back to face me. "I want him to die and be punished."

"Hans Schmid?"

Naehelles's usual, composed demeanor gives way to red-faced tears. She nods and brushes back her long hair from the sides of her face. I see a single dangling gold earring of birds on a love nest. It's identical to the one on Hans Schmid's mantel.

"He killed you too, didn't he?" I say and touch the earring.

"I'm not supposed to, but I hate him too. I want him dead."

"Oh." The shock halts me. She opens her kimono style blouse and I see stab wounds in her side. I want to vomit, but have no way of eliminating the emotions that overwhelm me like an earthquake. "Then help me," I plead. "Don't punish me and try to get me to be like the others here," I say. "I don't know if I want him dead. But I don't want him to kill my best friend or sister. And I think I can make a difference. Especially, if you help me."

"You think differently than I do. You follow your own path," Naehelle says. "I've always played by the rules and been a good girl. But I got murdered. I don't know where to start. As for me, right now, I want revenge."

50

A KNOCK WAKES Claire and Ginny. They huddle close in the tiny make-shift bed the old lady laid out for them on the floor by the fireplace. Claire blocks her breath and listens again. Boots on the wooden stairs. A rumble and pounding as they ascend and the noise in the stairwell grows louder.

"Ginny. Wake up, Ginny." Claire shakes her out of her fatigued sleep. The boots stop outside on the landing. There's no higher floor. No other apartment beyond this one. Claire feels the heat of the men's breath on the door, then the slam of a rifle butt against the wood.

"Open up!" a gruff voice commands.

The old lady sleeps in a back room and doesn't stir. More boots pound against the stairs until the glass in the windows rattles. "Open up!" The voices sound French. Not German. But it's hard to tell for sure. Claire glances around seeking out a place to hide in the tiny two-room apartment. An armoire holds old clothes. A narrow space opens under the bed where the old woman sleeps. She considers the window and weighs the choice between a fall to the street four stories below or a fall into enemy hands. With a hand on her stomach, the word "life" comes to Claire like a whisper. She thinks of the baby too and chooses a few more minutes of life rather than a certain end if she opens the window and dives out.

A harsh blow against the door handle sends the ceramic door knob

crashing onto the stone stairs as pieces shatter and fly down the steep stairwell. Claire cowers under the blanket and shelters Ginny. The old woman
continues to sleep. The men dressed in German uniforms jerk the girls to
their feet. One of the men pulls the covers off of the old woman, then with
a disgusted gasp pulls the sheet over her head.

"Dead," he says to the others.

"What are you taking us for? Why are you taking us?" Claire speaks in
a panic, not expecting an answer.

"Commandant's orders," the man in charge says. Claire still dressed in
a slip, and Ginny dressed in flannel pajamas that belonged to the old lady's
husband, are given only enough time to gather their shoes and put on their
coats before they're led out the door.

⤛

The soldiers push Claire and Ginny down the steep, narrow staircase and
drive them to the old prison. In the darkness of the early morning, they're
led down some worn stone steps and shoved through a thick wooden door
into a prison cell. Surrounded by damp, cold, darkness, Ginny whimpers
and Claire seeks to soothe her and try to figure out what to do next.

As dawn breaks through the heavy mass of clouds, the gray, dingy light
seeps into the cell and illuminates their grimy surroundings. Claire thinks
about this place, how this old prison has unjustly held people for centuries
– and now she stands enclosed inside this place she's always dreaded. Shivering. Damp. Cold. Some straw on the floor offers the only warmth and she
pushes some into a corner to create a make-shift cushion for Ginny to sit
on. Ginny seems out of her mind with grief and confusion. She whimpers
non-stop in a low, keening whine.

"I want to go home."

Claire holds her close. "There, there, *chérie*." She wants to say, 'it will
be all right.' I can feel the words form, but to actually say them would be a
lie. She hears the sounds of others whimpering from pain and fear in nearby
cells. As the day moves into early morning, screams cut through the air.
Screams of pain from some dreadful torture. The Germans and the French
militia resort to torture to get information from whoever they capture. The
thought fills me with dread and I want to help Claire and Ginny escape. A

key turns in the fat lock. The soldiers shove a bloodied figure through the door and relock it. The man lands on his face. At first Claire and Ginny cower against the wall, frightened. But when the man moans and barely moves, Claire approaches with a tender urge to help. She turns him over and wipes the bloody hair from his eyes with a handkerchief.

"Alain!" she cries out. The sight of our brother beaten nearly to death, burns what's left of her hope for survival to ash. She fights back her tears to keep Alain from knowing how upset and afraid she feels.

"Hey, sis," he says. He can barely open his swollen eyes.

"Hey Alain," she says gently wiping the blood from his face.

"Like my new look? Women will go wild for me now." His voice is weak, but not beaten. "Wha' you think? They love the tough guy look. No, sis?" He smiles revealing broken teeth. Claire turns her face away, but forces a tiny laugh to humor him.

I flinch and turn away momentarily too and feel a sudden affection for Alain. I suddenly understand my brother better. He has always been so quiet, distant, and shy. But he bears an inner strength and gentleness. A part of him thrives on the war. It has allowed him to discover his own mettle, courage, and ingenuity, and he feels proud of what he's done for the resistance.

Claire wants to ask him about Jean-Michel, but she fears the answer. "I'm happy to see you," she says, propping him up.

"Yeah. I meant to dress up for our little family reunion..." he snorts and wipes away blood from his nose with the back of his hand. "But they didn't give me time to shower." He forces a smile again, keeping a light tone even in the gravest moment. "Didn't take too kind to me bombing the train bridge."

"You're so brave," Claire says. Ginny cowers in the corner, unable to bear the sight of the blood that makes Alain look like a beaten monster.

"Yeah. Maybe they'll give me the *medaille d'honneur*, huh?" Alain says with his joking tone. Then his eyes roll back in his head and his neck goes limp. Claire's forced to let his weight fall back onto the straw. She shakes him, afraid he's dead. He rouses again. "I could use some water, Claire."

Claire stands and yells through the thick rusty bars of the prison door.

"Water. Help please. We need water." The sound of her voice echoes through the stone corridors of the prison.

"They've not brought anything. Not even food for days," a woman's voice calls out from a neighboring cell. But then she cries out too. "Water! Water!"

Claire adjusts Alain on a pile of straw on the floor and all I can think of is animals brought to slaughter. I turn in circles, mad, and then frenzied, trying to figure out how I can help. The window's solidly barred. Is there some way I can move the mechanism in the door to open the lock and allow them to escape? The stench in this dungeon smells so strong that even the guards don't want to come down here. The German soldiers at the entrance next to the canal are just boys. Sixteen and seventeen years old. They wear brown-green uniforms and would rather be drinking beer and flirting with German girls back home than standing in the cold chill. They don't love the Reich, the Savoy, or the cold damp prison they're guarding. They pace and chain smoke cigarettes to stay warm and occupied. One of them talks about eating his mom's pork chops back in Dusseldorf. They make fun of the SS and Gestapo with their rigid, cultish ways. This gives me an idea - Ginny. They're closest to Ginny's age and I see that one of them has a little sister who he misses very much.

"We need water," Claire repeats. At first the German boys ignore her, but I nudge Ginny to help. Ginny approaches the door and calls out in her girlish voice.

"Please help us. We need water."

The boy with the younger sister stirs and comes to the door. "We have none to give," he says in broken French.

"Please," Ginny says. "It would be awfully kind if you can you help us." She touches his hand which clenches the iron prison bar. We've done nothing wrong." Clarie steps back and lets Ginny talk. I stand close and support Ginny with encouraging energy and I urge the guard to unlock the door. Ginny's courage and boldness grow despite the recent violence she's known.

"Silvie," I call out. And in a split second she joins me. And to my surprise, Naehelle comes too.

"I want to help," Naehelle says. I reach out and embrace her.

"Thank you."

All three of us, Naehelle, Silvie, and I watch over Claire, Ginny, and Alain as Ginny seeks to get help from the young soldier.

"You can try to possess him," Naehelle says. I'm shocked. She's fully engaged now, ready to help us.

"But how?" I say. Silvie giggles for the first time ever, like she's amused that I don't know and pleased by the change in Naehelle.

But the SS soldiers arrive and drag Claire away.

51

CLAIRE HAS HEARD stories from some of the resistance fighters about the inhuman torture the Germans use on prisoners to extract information. But she decides from the start that she will not give in. That's her nature and she walks ahead of the SS soldiers with her head high. She has no fear or doubt, as if she knows that there's something beyond this physical world, and that even if this life doesn't pan out, something better awaits. There's a sort of fatality, a sense of fateful destiny that accompanies her. Not resignation, but certainty that what is meant to be will be. After seeing me at the old lady's house, she knows that even if her body dies, they can't kill her spirit. She'll go on living forever. But she wants to protect the baby, and she unconsciously calls on Mother Mary to accompany her. The Mother appears immediately and surrounds her with light and Claire feels the comfort.

She's heard the tortured screams and saw what they did to Alain. Dread pumps a high dose of adrenaline into her blood and creates a super human sense of endurance. The guards untie her hands and she jerks them free. She combs her fingers through her hair to tame it before the guards lead her into the interrogation room. Her eyes meet the commandant's and his steeliness freezes her heart. He's like a machine, she thinks. A cold, steely, heartless machine. Then Herr Schmid comes in wearing black leather gloves. He ignores Claire. Silvie, Naehelle, and I stand together, filled with concern.

"So, you know the procedure," the commandant says to Herr Schmid. Claire is no longer a person.

"Yes sir," Herr Schmid responds, dully. "*Heil* Hitler." He seems drugged, in a hypnotic trance, empty. He handcuffs Claire. Metal teeth inside the cuffs puncture the skin of her wrists. He does not look Claire in the eyes. When she looks at him, she sees no soul, as if no one's at home. He administers an injection of sodium pentothal, truth serum, into Claire's arm and the commandant begins.

"So tell us about the resistance fighters," the commandant orders. His tone remains casual. The atmosphere feels drained of life and energy, and Claire fears she will suffocate. A bathtub filled with water sits to one side of the room and she eyes it warily. Herr Schmid runs a rope through the chains of the handcuffs. The other end of rope hangs over a metal beam in the ceiling. With the force of a pulley, the commandant pulls the rope until only the tips of Claire's toes touch the stone floor and the handcuffs bite into her wrists. Claire looks at Hans Schmid with pleading eyes. As the drug kicks in, Claire struggles to focus. She continues to respond to questions about resistance with answers about knitting, stacking firewood, and how to sew a dress. Each question answered this way invites more tugs on the rope until she's lifted off her feet. Rivulets of blood trickle down her forearms.

"We're getting nowhere!" the commandant growls. He picks up a club and slams Claire across the buttocks. The sudden crack against her body makes her cry out in pain. She talks about her favorite cow, Nikita, at the farm. About the hedgehogs who slip out at night and nibble the flowers. About milking cows and how they must love Farmer Eli. The drug turns her conversation to drivel. She's able to focus enough to speak only of domestic matters. Herr Schmid slaps her cheek. He must perform convincingly for the commandant. In a glance, Claire catches his blue eyes and sees his own fear and struggle for survival. If he performs his role badly, he might die too. Herr Schmid's fear propels him to zealous beating with the club and Claire feels the irony of it, how he had invited her to beat him and now the situation has twisted upon her.

"Who is Jean-Michel?" the commandant demands.

Claire wills herself to talk gibberish. "Jean-Michel…a French singer. Nice records. *Ne me quitte pas….*," she says a line to demonstrate.

"Take her down." He commands. "Take off the cuffs." Herr Schmid obeys and as he does Claire whispers to him with perfect lucidity.

"I'm carrying a baby." She glimpses a pained ache in his face.

"Undress," the commandant orders Claire. She glares back with hot eyes. Somehow there will be justice and he will pay for this torture and humiliation, she thinks. "Step into the tub." She stands naked before the men and steps into the freezing water. Despite the drugs, a part of her remains proud, defiant. "Lie down." She glares at Herr Schmid and the commandant, then obeys. Her teeth chatter. "Good," the commandant says through narrow lips.

"We've got to help her," I say to Naehelle and Silvie. "What can we do?" I feel dread of what's to come. I don't want her to die. In this underground, desolate place I feel helpless and empty of ideas, like the very place has sapped me of energy. Naehelle and Silvie look at me, helpless as well.

Herr Schmid knows the routine. He gathers the rope and ties it around Claire's ankles. Each time the commandant asks a question, if he's dissatisfied with the answer, he nods at Herr Schmid. This means to pull Claire under the water. She comes up gasping, but still refuses to speak about the resistance or the Jewish children.

"*C'est dommage*," the commandant says with a mocking French accent. "But I admire your tenacity. It is too bad you are not a German woman. You could have been worth saving." He nods at Herr Schmid who pulls her under again. The commandant yanks Claire by the hair out of the cold water and she comes up sputtering and gasping.

"That's enough for now, I should think. We will let you reflect. Tomorrow, you will talk or else." The commandant jerks his head at Herr Schmid. "Get that out of here," he says. By "that" he means Claire. But she's not human in his eyes. Since he considers himself superior and superhuman, everyone and everything is beneath him.

I'm frantic and follow them back to the cell. When she and Herr Schmid walk alone through the corridor and no one can hear them, the drug begins to wear off and Claire breaks down. "How could you?" she accuses. He refuses to speak or acknowledge her.

"How many have you tortured? I'm just one of hundreds," she says shivering. Her own words freeze Claire's heart and any hope for freedom seems bleak. The thick prison door opens and Claire obediently walks in. Ginny hides in the back in the shadows.

"For a while, you saved me. You offered release from this work I do," he says.

"Help me," she cries out. He lifts his hands so as not to touch her. "Help us." She pleads. But he turns his back and walks away. Claire intends to devise a plan, but she can't think clearly. Not until the drugs wear off.

52

THERE'S NOTHING WORSE than feeling helpless. I try to shake the door open and finally cry out. "We've got to do something. He will kill them or send them to Drancy." It's the prison camp in Paris where they organize the trains to Dachau and Auschwitz. Night falls and the young soldiers from early morning return to duty again, exhausted and grumpy.

Then I remember Naehelle's idea of possession. "Hey, isn't that what Father Ansen talked about at mass? I thought that was evil," I say.

"It's not," Silvie says. "It's real. I've seen it happen."

"How can anyone highjack someone else's body?"

"Come here." Naehelle indicates for us to move close to the young man who has a sister like Ginny. It's very late now and the town lies still. I watch and feel the young soldier's energy and study him closely. He seems unformed. Ungrounded, and like he's half asleep and not fully in his body, but half back at home in Dusseldorf. He drifts between sleep and wakefulness, afraid of getting caught off guard by one of the Gestapo.

"Look," Naehelle says. "There's an opening. He's open to suggestion." I see a sort of hole or tear in his energy field so that it's not a smooth, even, oval egg around him, but more like a cracked shell with a hole punctured in the top near his head. "Now watch this," she orders us. "I believe I can influence his will. He's young and weak-minded and has no real aim or conviction about the war. He has a sister like Ginny. There's only one problem...sometimes it's hard for us to leave once we enter another body."

Naehelle enters him through the energy crack in the top of his head. The idea, to me is gross. She's sharing his body, his flesh, and I associate it with a sort of violation, not unlike what Herr Schmid did to me, but like an energetic rape. I would not like to do that to someone, but Naehelle may save Claire and Ginny's life. I watch carefully as Naehelle concentrates and creates a focal point to arouse an emotion of affection for Ginny in the young man. The emotion she creates resonates with the affection he feels for his sister. Then she begins the subtle suggestion.

"Let the girl go," Naehelle repeats. "Let the girl go. Release the girl. You'll be loved. She'll love you. Just open the door. Help her. Save the girl."

She repeats the phrases over and over with intent concentration and feeling until he's moved by her will.

"Help me," Ginny calls out in a meek voice and the young man appears.

"I don't know...," he says, while Naehelle repeats 'Open the door.'

"My friend's sick." Ginny looks up at him with pleading eyes.

"I can't...I'm not supposed to...," the young man says. But he opens the door with a heavy, black skeleton key as if he's in a hypnotic trance. He seems confused as he watches himself do this. The blonde boy-soldier's mouth hangs open when he sees what he's done. But it's too late. Claire's stolen a knife. She hid it in Ginny's clothes when they fled the old lady's house and no one searched Ginny. Claire grabs it and knifes the young soldier.

"I'm sorry," Claire says gently. She looks at her blood-stained hands with horror. "I hope it's not fatal."

Naehelle jumps out of the boy's body, stunned by the shock of physical pain from the stab and weakened by the blow. She clutches her side where the knife entered the boy's body. "I feel his pain. Like it's mine," she says.

I see blood drip from her side in the form of reddish energy. "Oh my god, are you okay?" I say. I rush to support her. "You're so brave." And I watch Ginny, Claire, and Alain escape up the unguarded stone steps and across the canal. "Will you be okay, Naehelle?" I don't know how these things work.

Naehelle groans. "It will take a little time. That drained my energy. I need to rest. I'll leave you two to it."

"Will you die again?" I panic.

"I don't know," she says. Tears in her eyes. "I'm new to this too."

"But you saved their lives," I gasp. "You made a sacrifice for them. Thank you."

❧

"Where are you going, Ginny?" Ginny darts off ahead and Alain limps along leaning on Claire's shoulder. Claire calls after her, still groggy from the drug.

"This way," Ginny calls. "To Herr Schmid's." She runs through the streets leaving them behind.

"No, Ginny. Stop!" Claire whispers with a strong, low voice. If she cries out, the patrols may stop them. Claire tries to stop Ginny, but the torture slowed her gait, and Alain limps beside her. "We've got to get out of here," Claire protests. "Don't waste time going back there." Weakened by the pain in her buttocks and her bloody wrists, Claire can't make a plan that makes sense. Her head fills with fog and confusion, similar to the thick, heavy fog that hides them and gives them safe passage through the guarded streets. The dense fog obscures soldiers and dangers that may lurk in passageways, but it also hides them from view.

"Believe me," Ginny says. "I need to see him."

"No, Ginny." Claire's desperate to escape. "We can't risk it. He will have us shot. Or kill us himself." A confusion of images rush through Claire's mind, one after the other. Herr Schmid demanding that she whip him. Him on his knees kissing and begging for her love and forgiveness. His tears. The light in those blue eyes. His physical power of attraction. Her heart rents in two. She mumbles to herself to try to sort it out. His beating her a few hours ago. "He's a Gestapo torturer," Claire says. She thinks of how he came to her for release and to relieve his guilt, how he couldn't bear to know of children starving. She shakes her head and sees the gentle, soul of the poet who loves the delicate scent of the dried rose petals. She recalls his mild manner as he read Baudelaire's poetry to her one night. "My heart is lost; the beasts have eaten it." At the time she scoffed and shrugged it off as silly, pedantic drivel. But he wanted her to understand, to make her flee. Now she realizes the truth. "He's a split soul. The beasts *have* eaten his heart…but sometimes he reclaims it. Can it grow back?" A glimmer of attachment to him shrouds her heart. Her soul trembles as she recalls the sound of his voice reading Baudelaire's words. "The Devil's hand directs our every move. The things we loathed become the things we love." Does she love him now? Did her heart trade away the pure-hearted Jean-Michel for a demon? No! I see it clearly, how she longs for Jean-Michel and only now fully appreciates this man who bears within him a heart of gold.

Knowing her thoughts, I rush out over the land and search for Jean-Michel. I think of his wry smile and his dark eyes and I'm immediately standing in front of him. He's on the mountain plateau in an old barn, scarred, but very much alive. He leans against a wooden stall and jokes with his buddies who sit around a meager fire rubbing their hands. I wonder how he escaped the Germans and if Father Ansen helped him. The Father visits prisoners and helps children escape to Switzerland. He has a big heart and doesn't fear the Gestapo. He feels it's his duty to help.

"Jean-Michel," I say. "Claire needs your help." In the silent mountain air, it seems my voice echoes out loud and clear.

"Did you hear that?" he says. His buddies look up at him. One of them throws a dried cow patty his way.

"You're losing it," the guy jokes. "You need a vacation."

"Yeah, you're right I guess," Jean-Michel says.

"But," another guy says. "I trust his sixth sense. He always knows in advance when the krauts are close by. Saved our hide a few times already with that ear of his."

"Claire needs your help!" I insist and send Jean-Michel images of Claire with emotions of panic and pain.

Jean-Michel draws aside one of the men. "Hey, I have this dreadful feeling that something awful has happened to my girl, Claire. Can I borrow your bike?"

"Man, you're crazy to go out now. The Germans are so damn tight on the roads that they shoot before they check your I.D." The scruffy guy shakes his head, but hands him the keys to his motorcycle with a sidecar.

"Thanks."

53

I RUSH BACK to Claire. "Claire! Don't go to Hans Schmid's."

But I know they all will. Ginny leads them there. She needs to see him, and Claire and Alain need to protect Ginny. They have no choice, like it's a necessary passage. He draws them to him with his magnetic, occult-like powers and personality. They can't escape, not without facing the demon. Claire and Alain follow slowly behind Ginny and aim to stop her. But she moves quickly and with determination.

Herr Schmid's apartment sits along the main street just a few blocks from the prison and the lake. The three escapees remain obscured by the fog and shadows. Ginny leads. Claire and Alain walk with their backs to the walls, and follow the outlines of the buildings. They dip into dark alleyways when they hear boots on the pavement or the sounds of voices echoing through the deserted streets. But Ginny steals through the night, fearlessly, driven by her need to see Herr Schmid.

The night, hangs over them like a heavy wool blanket. Not a single light shines through windows, and the silence in the streets gives Claire a sense of total vulnerability when the French militia or German patrols pass. The soldiers usually patrol in groups of four or five and present an intimidating wall of power, armed with rifles, machine guns, knives, and a hatred of the French resistance so keen and sharpened, that they will not hesitate to act swiftly when given an opportunity. The Gestapo has kept them all on strict alert and on tight leashes during these tense times. Human life means little to them. They shoot to kill. And hundreds of people have already died on these streets and before firing squads for no reason other than they displeased the Gestapo.

"Hurry," Ginny urges glancing back. Despite the pain and suffering, despite the bruises and sore muscles, she runs to Hans Schmid's door, certain that he will let them in. I help her open the door to quicken the pace. This is meant to be, and he's awaiting them, even though it's not conscious. I pull back the latch and it clicks open, ready, when Ginny pushes on the door. "Here, see," she says turning back to Claire. Claire slips Alain's arm over her shoulder and helps him up the steps. Neighbors hide behind the blacked-out windows and Ginny, rushes up the stairs. Claire and Alain arrive a few seconds behind her and make their way anxiously to the upper floors. My brother and sister hide on the landing below in the stairwell while Ginny, rings at his door. Claire's too stunned to react or protest. Alain's nearly comatose.

I'm inside. I've been watching him. Sitting in my red velour chair stroking the cat. I've been luring him to me. Trying to tempt him to pick up the small pistol of Claire's that lies on the mantel with his other souvenirs of death. "Come and join me," I whisper to him. "I surround him with my energy and lure him to death. "It's easy," I say. "It won't hurt. Just pick up the gun and pull the trigger." The notes of Shubert's piano concerto play through his wide apartment.

"I want to be free," he thinks, the infection continues to eat at his heart.

"Yes, come," I say and any forgiveness I'd felt falters, replaced by the old ambiguity.

Naehelle says I must let go of that attachment to him and my desire for revenge, but for the moment, my anger and rage return and overpower my softer senses. I want him to be hurt and entrapped like he hurt and trapped me and Silvie. I am willing to deceive, manipulate, and seduce, things I would not have done only a short time ago. Naehelle says this is "Old Testament" behavior. "An eye for an eye." I need to move into a permanent place of forgiveness and let him be, she says. It's the only way I'll be at peace. I think the only way I'll be at peace is if he's dead. I've been conniving about how to trap him in the in-between when he dies. Silvie's grandmother has shown me some ways. There must be a way to put him on trial, so that Silvie, Naehelle, and I gain a sense of justice for the life he stole from us. I think of the demons in the in-between, the flesh-eating ones that strip away his skin at night and how his skin grows back in his dreams. Then the demons start again, painfully stripping him of his flesh. When he dies, I want to chain him in that place on the path to Silvie's grandma's house and make him suffer there in the dark for a very long time. Maybe for eternity. That's the hell of the in-between. I want him to be sentenced by us to remain there and suffer. I want him to know the suffering he caused.

Hans Schmid lifts his eyes to me as he drinks whiskey. "I miss you, dear one," he says.

"Come and join me," I say. "Just pull the trigger." He reaches for the gun and caresses it with his index finger. "We can be together forever, like this," I say. I move close to him and surround him with my power. "Come," I urge him. He weighs the gun in his hand. "Come," I say. "It will be heaven." I lean in and kiss him with my energy and make myself seductive. But I'm lying to him. Deceiving him as he deceived me. I'm falling too. Falling into the place of souls who seek revenge and justice. Maybe I should let him be rather than drop down to his level of hatred and fear. Maybe there are things that have made him this way. The evil commandant who shot his brother, the wars, starving, fear, a hurtful stepmother? But other men who experienced the same things became heroes instead.

Does a soul grow? I wonder. Will he become a better man? Or will he forever be a hateful, heartless demon. Sometimes he appears cordial and kind. Ginny believed that side of him. She thought him worthy of love too. All smooth, beautiful, brilliant eyes, gentle attentions, perfectly shaved, clean, perfectly honed so that no one would perceive the evil inside. I hope Ginny has understood that she can't trust him, but I can't read her thoughts. When the doorbell rings, I watch him blanch and turn cold.

He puts down the gun. "Well, Aurelie, they are finally coming for me." His eyes widen and sparkle like dashes of sunlight falling on the blue sea. They fill with the same sensitivity that drew me to him the first times, and I lose my desire for revenge. Somewhere inside of me, I realize that if he suffers, I suffer, that we are all connected in this profound way. Maybe I'm split too, split between the confusion of love and hate.

When he opens the door, Ginny stands there, firmly planted on the landing. She looks up at him with wide, innocent eyes and reaches out to embrace him in her arms. Her soft, yielding figure floods him with a sense of humanity, and he begins to weep. She leads him inside by the hand, leaving the front door slightly ajar, just enough so that Claire and Alain can slip in.

I sit in my chair and watch. Ginny brushes his hand gently with her soft fingers. Her eyes study him with gentleness.

"Please don't give yourself to him, Ginny. Please," I say. "He will ruin you like he ruins every woman he touches."

She recalls the thrill of when he touched her in the broken temple behind the walled garden. That was when she knew. He pulls her to him, eyes closed.

"Come," he says and leads her into his bedroom. On the mantel above the fireplace near his bed, lies Silvie's charm and Naehelle's golden earring. Naehelle stands beside me, along with Silvie, and we all watch over Ginny.

Claire and Alain slip into the house. I hear the floorboards creak, but I'm riveted by Ginny's attentions to Herr Schmid and a part of me also feels jealous. He lies down, with his head in her lap and she strokes his hair tenderly. "Aurelie loved you so much," she says. "So, so much…," she says and slips into the other room an instant while he lies there, relaxed and trusting, just as I had trusted him.

Ginny walks to his desk. Claire's pistol lays there. The tiny silver pistol that they took from her when they were both captured. He kept it as a souvenir. Ginny lifts it, carries it back into the bedroom, and points it at Hans Schmid. He rises up on one elbow and smiles, thinking she's playing a game. Then she pulls the trigger. Clarie and Alain rush to the doorway as Herr Schmid falls back on the bed. Claire kneels beside him and watches his life slip away. She stares in shock at Ginny who still holds the gun.

"I know you killed Aurelie," Ginny says. "I've know it for a long time."

54

NAEHELLE, SILVIE, AND I wait patiently to collect his soul. We're not supposed to do this, but I don't care and neither do they now. He has to pay for the pain he caused. We trap his soul in an ethereal cage made of silver and gold threads of energy so high in frequency, that to touch the bars of his prison causes pain, like an electric shock. The three of us stand outside looking in at him. He looks different now. Not the tall, handsome, beautiful, blue-eyed man, armed with seduction. He's stooped, weak, fearful and withered.

"Don't hurt me," he begs. He believes in nothing beyond the earth and physical life. So nothing comes to rescue him. He's at our mercy. Naehelle wants to leave him in the cage and hold him as our prisoner, but she tells us she must call on the supreme council and asks for a special trial. She wants to hold him as our prisoner until we extract the time and energy from him that will pay for the pain. But the council wants to know how we caught his soul. How we stopped him from moving through the in-between. Only I don't know how. The three of us focused our energies so intently that he had no choice and his guilty thoughts brought him straight to us.

A being arrives and sets up a court with a hearing. Another being of light and energy, dressed in white carries a balance. I understand that this is an ancient court that has existed since the beginning of humanity. The head of the council places a feather on one end of a balance. The feather, he says represents purity and Truth.

"The innocent and good are light of heart," a woman in white says.

The council head, asks Herr Schmid to hand over his heart and places it on the balance. The balance falls heavily to the side of the weighty heart.

"You are guilty," the woman says. "These women will decide your fate for the next one-hundred astral years." She pounds her gavel and the court disappears. Naehelle, Silvie, and I are left with Hans Schmid suspended in his golden cage.

"I vote to leave him to the flesh-eating demons on the path of the in-between," Naehelle says.

"Me too," Silvie says. "What about you? It has to be unanimous."

"I…" I look at the man who deceived me. My hatred diminishes and only pity remains. My heart even aches for him and I want him to feel good, human, and light-hearted. I don't want to judge. Not even the harsh and hateful deeds he's done. "I need some time to reflect," I say. "I don't know." Near the scales, a fierce flesh-eating, heart-consuming demon guards the passages after death.

"Aurelie, we need to know now." Naehelle insists.

"He had a long and difficult life. The seeds for our deaths lie with his growing up, maybe even with the commandant." Both Silvie and Naehelle can now see the scenes from the past unfolding around Herr Schmid like a movie. "Haven't we all suffered enough already?" I say. "I'm tired of it. Do what you want, but I won't condemn him to suffer more."

⁓

Ginny, Claire, and Alain slip silently out of Herr Schmid's apartment. Claire kissed him tenderly on the mouth and covered his face with a white sheet before leaving.

"Where will we go, Alain?" she says. The whole of Annecy and the Haute Savoy teems with German Gestapo, SS officers and soldiers, and French militia collaborators.

"It ain't over till it's over," Alain says through swollen lips.

"We can try the border again," Ginny says. "I believe this time we'll make it. Aurelie will help us. She's been with us all along."

My heart's happy that she knows and I send her good energy and love. "Thank you, Ginny for thinking of me," I say. It doesn't matter if she hears me clearly or not.

"You're welcome, Aurelie," she says. The three of them go to Father Ansen to the church where Ginny lights a candle for me.

"Can you help us, Father?" Claire pleads. She tells him how they've escaped. He quickly makes contact with those in the network to come to their aid, even at the risk of his own life. Jean-Michel slips in through the back door. Claire nearly yelps with joy when she sees him.

"Shh," Father Ansen warns them. "You must remain quiet." He leads them into an underground passage that links to a building on the other side of town. "Here you will be safe. Just keep walking through the darkness. They'll meet you at the other side."

55

BY THE END of the next day, with the aid of the network, they've crossed the barbed wire fences between the Haute Savoy and Switzerland and moved deep into the Swiss Alps, avoiding the Swiss detention camps and the possibility of being deported back to France – or worse, to Germany. I've followed them this whole way to watch for their safety and now, I need to make some decisions. I'm sick of this somewhat impotent space of the in-between and I'm losing energy. I will "die" to this place and leave behind my memories of Herr Schmid and Ginny and all of the life I've lived up to now. So the decision remains. Claire's baby is growing inside. Will I go back or move on to higher realms to explore and grow?

I fly over the landscape, over the snow-capped Mont Blanc with its glaciers that shimmer in the night sky. The mountain rams sit regally on a rock shelf watching over their herd. They seem at peace despite the madness of men and the world war roaring to its final crescendo below them. I watch the souls leaving the world, drifting out of the prisons where they're dying in France. And they're leaving in droves from the camps in Germany, happily and lightly drifting up to better worlds. They don't care about what happened. They don't want to remember the pain. They seem to sense it all held some invisible purpose.

But I feel my affection for Claire, and Alain and Ginny draw me to them and without even making it so conscious, suddenly I enter Claire's belly and I'm once again embodied in a fetus. Silvie has told me that the memories of this life only last a short time. Sometimes they linger a little while even after we are born. We carry them with us, these stories of our lives as we come back again and again. We carry them in our energy bodies. But for now, I'm going to rest and sleep in the warmth. I drift off to the sound of Claire's heartbeat and her voice as she sings a lullaby song to me and rubs her belly. Ginny leans her head against Claire's belly. "I love you, Aurelie," she whispers.

"I love you too," I say and my soul's at peace as I return to them. I know our story will continue soon. And the war cannot continue forever. A golden era of peace and prosperity awaits. But I also know that my attachment to Hans Schmid, to Silvie, and Naehelle and even Claire and Ginny, will keep me coming back again and again. We have a rendezvous, Herr Schmid and I. We will meet on the earth again soon.

THE END

Author's Note

I was in the loft of an 1840's French farm house working on a book set in modern-day Charleston, South Carolina when the girl who became Aurelie came in. Writing, for me is a very expansive and visual experience and as I turned my vision inward and listened deeply, the WWII story began to unfold. I'd never felt drawn to write about WWII until that moment and I knew very little about what had happened locally.

While walking in Annecy, I had seen the WWII monuments and bronze plaques on buildings honoring those who had lost their lives during that harrowing time. One noted the demise of a young Catholic priest and another told of young Jewish school children who were removed from school by the Nazis. They all died. In such a beautiful city, so well-known for tourism, it's rare to think about that past where so many horrors occurred. But as I sat in the loft writing, I felt the presence not only of the young girl, but also of the many resistance fighters who wanted their story told. As they came in, I saw and experienced the conditions they faced. I wrote the scenes and images as they unfurled like a film, and I later verified with research in local historical reference books about the rationing, the black outs and the conditions. The accuracy of what I saw was astounding. It seemed the memory of the wartime lingered in the ethers around me and became available simply by tuning in.

At the time, I also participated in a spiritual circle in Geneva, together with some of the city's prominent people – bankers, business owners, investment advisors, social workers – people who you might not expect to find in this kind of an environment. They were very intuitive and many became gifted healers and lightworkers. Our circle leader was a psychic-medium who connected with departed souls. I attended the circle to focus on spiritual development and expand my intuition. When sessions touched on mediumship and connecting with departed souls, I felt a little intimidated and like it wasn't for me. But one still morning, while I sat in quiet meditation at 5 a.m., an energy moved in close. "Debra Moffitt!" an emphatic male voice said. Whoever he was, he knew that I could hear him – even though it was news to me.

This was the start to my awareness of how thin the veils are between the worlds of the living and departed. For the first time I truly realized how close our departed loved ones are to us. I asked the departed soul who spoke to me to please step back while I finished my meditation. And he did. A short time later, I awoke to a dream: *I watch as several 1940's black cars pull up in the drive outside my house. I know the people want to connect with me, but I'm hiding, and watching, unsure of what to do. I hope they won't find me.* Those in the cars were the young girl and members of the resistance who knew that I could hear and see them on the subtle level. They found me and I discovered the story of their courage as they struggled against a terrible, oppressive power. I have a strong sense that they felt the memory of what they had done was being forgotten and they wanted it brought back to life and shared.

The writing process was exciting as I watched the scenes unfold in my "mind's eye" and wrote at high speed. The first draft took only about five months to complete. Though I could sense the overall structure of the book, I discovered the scenes with excitement as they were revealed during the writing sessions in the loft with the wood stove burning downstairs. My psychic-medium teacher, perceived the departed souls around my writing space too and I have to wonder if some of them were once hidden in that very loft, waiting to escape the Nazis.

Most history books don't touch on the horrors and repression that took place here on the Franco-Swiss border during that time, and there is little written in the history books. If you'd like to read more, I'd suggest checking out the works by a local author, Michel Germain, who has devoted most of his lifetime to researching and writing about the conditions in this area during the war. He recorded interviews with some of the people who lived through that challenging time. One of my favorites of his is titled the *Les Sauveteurs dans les Ombres – Rescuers in the Shadows*.

Many of the historical incidents described in *The Girl on the Roof* are based on facts. There were about thirteen major internment locations throughout the Savoie (Savoy) and the Haute Savoie (High Savoy) areas during the state of siege by the Nazis from January to May, 1942. They were packed with hundreds and hundreds of prisoners during that time. The tour boat, La France, became a prison for the detainees when the Nazis ran out of space. That period in Annecy and the Haute Savoy marked the most deadly period of this region's history.

French men of military age had to choose between joining the resistance or being drafted and sent to Germany. Many different resistance groups existed and some worked together, while others didn't. There are many accounts of Catholic priests and nuns who worked with the resistance fighters or on their own to protect the Jewish children and families as well as others targeted by the Nazis. Many of the Catholic protectors lost their lives. The bombing on the Rue de Genève in Annecy, actually occurred in another area of the Savoy. I moved it to Annecy for the purpose of the story. And an ordinance required that all windows be blacked out. It aimed to prevent the city from being easily sighted by the Allies' planes at night.

The local ball-bearing factory that the Allies targeted, remains intact and continues production today. If you want to explore more, I encourage you to come to Annecy and the area and imagine that time of chill and fog while honoring the actions of some incredibly brave people. You may want to head up to the Glières Plateau where you'll find a memorial to the Resistance. And, don't forget to enjoy a glass of good French wine and a laze in the sun with a good book in the Old Town by the old prison or on the Paquier – the field by Lake Annecy. And finally, thank you, dear, dear readers, for buying and reading and sharing about *The Girl on the Roof!* I write for you. I love you. And I'm so grateful to you for reading this and supporting me in writing this book and many more to come! With Gratitude,

Debra Moffitt ♥

QUESTIONS FOR THE READERS

Thank you for reading, *The Girl on the Roof*! Debra says, "I hope you've enjoyed this as much as I enjoyed writing it for you." She loves to hear your feedback and appreciates your reviews on Amazon and on other social media. If you would like to connect with Debra for your book club to organize a Skype or video talk with the author, please contact Debra through her website: www.debramoffitt.com.

1. Aurelie feels compelled to discover what happened to her and also to protect her best friend, and she has to reach beyond the veil that separates her from her loved ones to do it. Have you ever had an experience where you felt a departed loved one tried to communicate with you? Share your experience.

2. As Aurelie discovers the new world she's in, do you feel she is religious or spiritual? What do you sense she might say about what's beyond the veil? What do you imagine is there?

3. The French Resistance was actually not in one united group as presented by many history books. It was split into factions with different motives, some noble, some not. The two factions here are based on research from French texts available about the events. What do you think of the way books and schools present war and the outcomes? Do you think it's always so black and white? Why does WWII seem to be a noble war in many minds?

4. Claire says women suffer the most during war. What's your opinion about this? Do you feel she will regret any of her choices and the consequences?

5. Herr Schmid and Claire have a complex relationship of power where Claire seeks to maintain her dignity and self-worth while

remaining committed to serving the resistance and saving children. How did she feel about Herr Schimd? How do you think he feels about her? Compare this with how Jean-Michel feels about Claire.

6. Aurelie sees Herr Schmid in two ways, - as Herr Schmid and also as Hans. How do you feel about this? Do you believe he should be excused because of his abusive childhood and the traumas of war?

7. What do you imagine will happen to Aurelie, Claire, Jenni and Jean-Michel?

8. Aurelie discovers she has an opportunity to return. How do you feel about her choice? Do you think she would return into the world at war? Why?

9. Do you believe in reincarnation? Say more about why or why not. If so, where do you feel you have lived before?

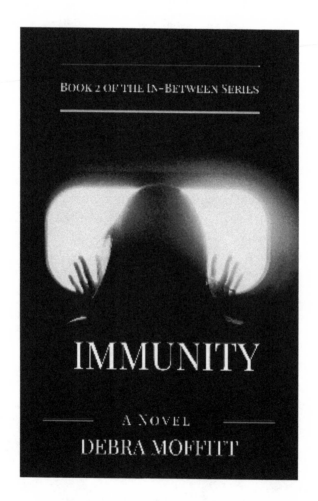

BOOK 2 OF THE IN-BETWEEN SERIES

IMMUNITY

A NOVEL

DEBRA MOFFITT

(PRELIMINARY COVER)

IMMUNITY
BOOK TWO OF THE IN-BETWEEN SERIES

Set in Geneva, Switzerland in 2020, Jon Smyth, a high-ranking diplomat involved in profiting from human trafficking, loves power and status. Publicly he portrays himself as a humanitarian and he's nominated for a humanitarian award, but when Aurelia, a private language tutor, discovers the secrets he's hiding in his personal life, she threatens to reveal them to the public and the police. But Smythe's a protected man with diplomatic status who may literally get away with murder.

Naïve Aurelia is drawn into a world of corruption and power. Unaware of the influential and sometimes violent forces opposing her, she will stop at nothing to help the child victims of the crimes she unwittingly uncovers, but it may be at the cost of her own life.

As the story unfolds, Aurelia's nightmares plague her with scenes of being murdered by a WWII Nazi officer. She suspects that Smyth was that officer, and she fears he will attempt to murder her again. But she has a choice and can step into her power if she dares. Will she break the pattern of victim and save herself and many other girls from a terrible fate? Or will she and Jon Smythe repeat this terrible loss of life once again?

Immunity is another suspenseful novel about the journey of a group of souls where anything can happen.

Available for preorder at divinelyinspiredbooks.com
and on Amazon.com.

STEP INTO THE LUXURY AND BEAUTY OF THE
FRENCH RIVIERA THROUGH FICTION

RIVIERA STORIES
JUST BELOW THE SURFACE

A famous musician who's lost the music in his soul in Monaco and becomes a nobody to get it back; an American expat on the Cap d'Antibes who lost her husband and goes looking for love in the wrong places; a Moroccan waiter at the Hôtel du Cap with big dreams and desires for one of the hotel's guests; some Riviera commuters who are stopped by a roadside stripper, a camel, and a crash; and an islander whose lover is the sea. Mysteries open up as these French Riviera residents seek something that makes sense beyond the crazy, materialistic world around them. Riviera Stories spotlights Monaco's playground of the rich and famous, Antibes' beaches and restaurants, and the lush mountains and perched villages beyond the coast and brings them to life. The author's love of the Riviera and her experiences living on the Cote d'Azur invite you to see the Riviera in a new light.

108 Practices to Live a Divinely Inspired Life

"This book is a vital resource that can help you find your place in the stream of life"
— Mark Nepo, NYT Bestselling Author of *The Book of Awakening*

Awake
in the
World

DEBRA
MOFFITT

PRAISE FOR *AWAKE IN THE WORLD* – NEW EDITION

Awake in the World offers 108 practices to help you reconnect with your inner wisdom and find balance and harmony in a complex world. It offers keys that, if practiced, lead to self-mastery and spiritual self-confidence.

What others say:

> "With *Awake in the World*, Debra Moffitt offers an abundance of inner practices that are immediate and accessible, as well as being rooted in the world's spiritual traditions. This book is a vital resource that can help you find your place in the stream of life. Debra is a gentle teacher who offers water for the spiritually thirsty."
>
> **—Mark Nepo**,
> author of *Inside the Miracle* and *The Book of Awakening*

> "Debra Moffitt has gleaned the essence of what truly matters in life and has given you simple, yet profound pearls of wisdom. These practices transform your life!"
>
> **—Denise Linn**,
> author of *Sacred Space* and
> *Feng Shui for the Soul*

> "Debra Moffitt brings the noble and universal yearnings of the human soul down earth, down to the ins and outs of daily life, down to practice."
>
> **—David Kundtz**,
> author of *Quiet Mind:*
> *One-minute Retreats from a Busy World*

Garden
of
Bliss

Cultivating the Inner Landscape
for Self-Discovery

DEBRA MOFFITT

GARDEN OF BLISS
LOOK FOR THE NEW EDITION
WITH A NEW COVER

Garden of Bliss begins on the French Riviera, where Moffitt, despite her glamorous European lifestyle, feels empty. Realizing that financial success doesn't necessarily equate to happiness, she looks inside herself and decides to make some changes.

The message of her journey is simple: bliss is a destination that exists within all of us. Using the metaphor of a secret garden, Moffitt encourages readers to manifest this space in the physical world and connect with the divine feminine through nature. *Garden of Bliss can be read as a stand-alone book or as a companion text to Moffitt's award-winning debut, Awake in the World.*

"*Like Eat, Pray, Love without the whine!*"

—Janna McMahan,
best-selling author of Anonymity and The Ocean Inside

"Everyone has a secret garden, but few of us are aware of it. That's why it's secret. By inviting you into her garden Debra Moffitt uncovers and unlocks the gate to your own. This is a book for the spiritual gardener eager to till the soil of self and harvest the wisdom of Self."

—Rabbi Rami Shapiro,
author of Writing, The Sacred Art and columnist for Spirituality &
Health Magazine

"If you are feeling depleted and spent, Debra Moffitt gently guides you to your inner space to refresh and inspire a serene state of joy, awakening, and creativity. *Garden of Bliss* is a must-read in today's harried world. I keep it on my bedside table to read again and again."

—**Mary Alice Monroe**,
New York Times bestselling author of Beach House Memories